"For God's sa... ...e are you?"

Jackson stood and paced the length of the room and back.

"Well, gee, thanks a lot." Maggie rose and walked stiffly to the doorway.

"Wait a minute." Jackson hurried after her. She turned to face him, unable to disguise the pain that showed in her eyes. It was hard to believe that after everything Jackson Hawk had put her through, she still thought him handsome—the handsomest man she'd ever seen. His smooth skin stretched over a blade of a nose, sharply defined cheekbones and firm jaw and chin. His long black braids did nothing to detract from his masculinity; he was so tall, his shoulders so broad, his voice so deep and rough, she doubted anything would be able to do that.

Jackson reached out and touched her arm. "I didn't mean that the way it sounded. I'm just afraid you're too trusting."

"Well, it's obvious that you don't trust me, either...."

Myrna Temte

grew up in Montana and attended college in Wyoming. She currently resides with her husband in Washington State. Known for her highly emotional, compelling stories, Myrna has developed a loyal reader following. This bestselling author is also a Romance Writers of America RITA award finalist, in the Long Contemporary category, for her books *Silent Sam's Salvation* (1993) and *The Forever Night* (1994).

This book is dedicated to Kathie Hays, who keeps my head on straight (most of the time), my plots on track and my morale up. Thanks, Kemo sabe!

My sincere thanks for help with research go to Mr. Moses Spear Chief at the American Indian Center, and Mrs. Saundra Pathweaver of Pathweaver's Book and Trading Co. of Spokane, Washington. Any mistakes I have made in portraying the lives of Native Americans are strictly my own.

Myrna Temte

SLEEPING
WITH THE ENEMY

Silhouette Books

Published by Silhouette Books
America's Publisher of Contemporary Romance

Special thanks and acknowledgment to
Myrna Temte for her contribution to the
Montana Mavericks series.

Text and artwork on page 8 is reprinted with permission from
NEVER ASK A MAN THE SIZE OF HIS SPREAD:
A Cowgirl's Guide to Life, by Gladiola Montana.
Copyright © 1993 Gibbs Smith Publisher. All rights reserved.

 SILHOUETTE BOOKS

ISBN 0-373-50167-6

SLEEPING WITH THE ENEMY

MONTANA Mavericks

*Welcome to Whitehorn, Montana—
the home of bold men and daring women.
A place where twelve rich tales of passion and
adventure are about to unfold under the Big Sky.
Seems that this charming little town has some mighty
big secrets. And everybody's talking about...*

George Sweetwater: Out for a relaxing day of hiking and hunting, he discovered human bones. Maybe he'll just leave that mystery to...

Jeremiah Kincaid: This tough old cowboy and ranch magnate was after land that rightfully belonged to the Northern Cheyenne. To get it, he'd wheedle, cajole or even blackmail...

Congressman William C. Baldwin: Good sense went out the door when he let Jeremiah tell him how to run his district. Now he was in too deep—but he might still be able to save his own hide with a little help from...

Sara Lewis: Didn't like bureaucrats from Washington, especially when they came 'round the Laughing Horse Reservation. They never treated her people fairly before, but even leopards could change their spots like...

Mary Jo Kincaid: Pretty as a picture and sweet as pie, this happy-go-lucky newlywed was cheerfully helping out at the reservation. It was the least she could do—while keeping up with rumors of an unidentified body....

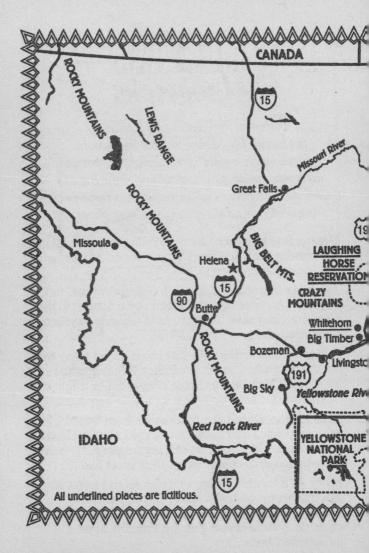

CANADA

[15]

ROCKY MOUNTAINS

LEWIS RANGE

Missouri River

ROCKY MOUNTAINS

Great Falls

19

Missoula

BIG BELT MTS.

LAUGHING HORSE RESERVATION

Helena

CRAZY MOUNTAINS

[90] [15]

Butte

Whitehorn

Big Timber

ROCKY MOUNTAINS

Bozeman

Livingsto

[191]

Big Sky

Yellowstone Riv

Red Rock River

IDAHO

YELLOWSTONE NATIONAL PARK

[15]

All underlined places are fictitious.

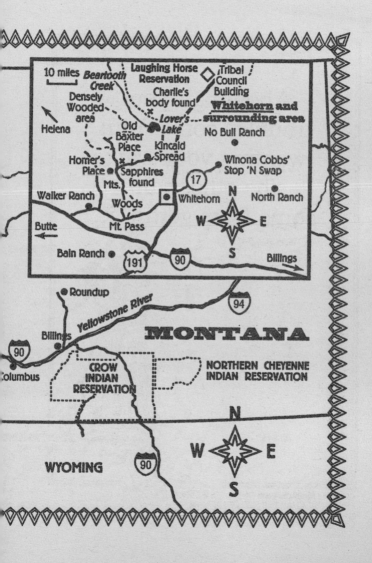

10 miles

Beartooth Creek

Laughing Horse Reservation

Tribal Council Building

Charlie's body found ✕

Whitehorn and surrounding area

Densely Wooded area

Lover's Lake

No Bull Ranch

Helena

Old Baxter Place

Kincaid Spread

Winona Cobbs' Stop 'N Swap

Homer's Place

✕ Sapphires found

17

N

Mts.

Whitehorn

North Ranch

Walker Ranch

Woods

W E

Butte

Mt. Pass

S

Bain Ranch ●

191

90

Billings

● Roundup

Yellowstone River

94

Billings

90

MONTANA

Columbus

CROW INDIAN RESERVATION

NORTHERN CHEYENNE INDIAN RESERVATION

N

W E

WYOMING

90

S

About half your
troubles come from
wanting your way;
the other half
come from gettin' it.

Prologue

Glaring at the man seated on the other side of his desk, Congressman William C. Baldwin of Montana silently cursed the day he'd let his fear of losing an election run away with his good sense. At first meeting, Jeremiah Kincaid came across as just another big, friendly rancher, a real salt-of-the-earth kind of a guy, who wore cowboy boots and a Stetson whether he was in Montana or in the nation's capital. Surprisingly handsome for a man pushing seventy, he also had a well-earned reputation for being quite a charmer with the ladies.

But underneath that affable good-old-country-boy exterior, lurked a greedy, bullying, unscrupulous son of a bitch who had the disposition of a rattler with a sore tooth. Baldwin loathed and feared Kincaid, but he was doing his damnedest not to let it show. What a lousy way to start the New Year.

"Come on now, be reasonable, Jeremiah."

Kincaid sat back in the maroon leather wing chair and let out a derisive snort of laughter. "Reasonable? I don't have to be reasonable, Billy boy. That's why the Whitehorn Ranchers' Association decided to buy a congressman."

"You and your associates made some contributions to my campaign, but you don't own me," Baldwin said.

"The hell we don't! I could be wrong, but I don't think all of those contributions were exactly legal."

"And might I remind you, Mr. Kincaid," Baldwin retorted, "that it was just as illegal for you to give them to me as it was for me to accept them."

Jeremiah laughed. "Yeah, but we'll never get more than a slap on the wrist." He gazed around Baldwin's office, as if he were taking in the plush furnishings for the first time. Then he chuckled and shook his head. "This setup ain't bad for a poor miner's kid. Be a shame if you lost it all and had to go back to a half-assed law practice in Butte. Mighty slim pickin's in Butte these days, from what I hear."

"It won't do any good to threaten me," Baldwin said. "I'd help you if I could, but what you're asking is impossible."

Kincaid raised an eyebrow at him. "Nothing is impossible in Washington."

Exasperated, Baldwin picked up the letter Jeremiah had tossed in front of him half an hour ago and shook it. "This *is*. The Northern Cheyennes *own* that land. They have every legal right to refuse to renew your grazing leases."

Kincaid propped his elbows on the arms of his chair and laced his fingers together. "I don't give a damn about their legal rights. My friends and I have held those leases for over forty years. We've put up fences and built irrigation systems and made all kinds of other improvements, and we're *not* gonna hand it all over to a bunch of lazy, good-for-nothin' Indian drunks. Hell, we should've exterminated all of 'em when we had the chance."

Some people might agree with those sentiments, Baldwin thought grimly. But only a man as rich and powerful as Jeremiah Kincaid would have the gall to say them out loud, in such a calm, implacable tone of voice.

"Times have changed," Baldwin said. "Every president since Nixon has endorsed the self-determination policy for Indian tribes. If the Bureau of Indian Affairs doesn't even have the power to renew those leases, why do you expect me to have it?"

"You're on that subcommittee on Native American affairs, and on the appropriations committee. One of them oughta give you an opportunity to clear up this mess, if you really want to." Kincaid tipped his head to one side and studied Baldwin for a moment, a speculative gleam entering his cold gray eyes. "But then, maybe you don't really want to."

"Of course I do, Jeremiah. Why the hell wouldn't I?"

"I met a real pretty little Indian gal while I was out there waitin' for you to let me in. Told me she works for you.

Maybe you've got somethin' extra goin' on the side with her, and you don't wanna tick her off."

"You mean Maggie Schaeffer?" It was Baldwin's turn to laugh and shake his head. He wouldn't have minded doing exactly what Kincaid was implying, but this time, at least, he was innocent. "Don't be ridiculous. I'm old enough to be her father."

Kincaid let out another one of his derisive snorts. "So? I'm old enough to be her grandpa, but if I wanted her, Billy boy, I'd *have* her."

Just the thought of a nice young gal like Maggie Schaeffer with this randy old coot turned Baldwin's stomach. "Maggie's one of my best research aides, Jeremiah. Our relationship is strictly professional."

"I don't care whether it is or not," Kincaid said. "Pretty as she is, it wouldn't take much to start a few rumors flyin' around. I don't think your new little wife would like that. Ya know, I really like Georgina, but she doesn't strike me as the kind of gal who'd stand by her man if he was involved in a dirty ol' sex scandal. Do you read me?"

"Yeah. I read you, Jeremiah." Baldwin stood then, forcing an end to the conversation. He didn't offer to shake Kincaid's hand. "I'll do what I can."

Kincaid got up and set his black Stetson on his head. "A smart fella like you shouldn't have any problem gettin' a bunch of Indians under control, especially that sorry bunch up at Laughing Horse. It's just February now, so you've got four months before the June deadline, Congressman. We'll be expecting some results."

The second the door snapped shut behind Kincaid, Baldwin collapsed into his chair, leaned back and closed his eyes. Damn that old man to hell and back, he knew exactly which buttons to push, which fears to exploit.

Bill Baldwin had put in twenty years of honest government service—honest by Washington standards, anyway. He'd golfed with presidents. He'd been a hero in Vietnam. And now he'd made one lousy decision in a moment of panic, and Jeremiah Kincaid would destroy him without turning a hair if he didn't deliver the goods.

For a moment, Baldwin considered going public with the truth about his campaign finances. That would take some of the wind out of that old blowhard's sails, now wouldn't it? He wished he still had that much nerve.

Baldwin picked up the letter and glanced at the signature again. Well, Jackson Hawk, Tribal Attorney, whoever the hell he was, must have plenty of nerve. Jeremiah Kincaid controlled the Whitehorn Ranchers' Association, the town of Whitehorn, and the county, too. To take the old coot on like this, Mr. Hawk had to be crazy. Either that, or he had balls like a Hereford bull.

Unfortunately, Baldwin knew his own balls weren't that big anymore. He was almost fifty years old, and he'd grown accustomed to the perks and privileges of his office. He liked having money and a glamorous young wife who made other men drool. And the only way he ever wanted to go back to Butte on a permanent basis was in a coffin.

Damn it, he'd worked too hard for too long to give everything up for the sake of a few Indians who never voted. Hell, they probably wouldn't know what to do with that land if they ever *did* manage to get it back from Jeremiah and the Whitehorn Ranchers' Association. Possession *was* nine-tenths of the law. Of course, it wouldn't do his image much good if the press found out he was hassling an Indian tribe.

There had to be a way to get Jeremiah off his back without bringing the wrath of every bleeding-heart liberal in the whole damned country down on his head. If he could find an Indian to do most of the dirty work for him . . . maybe somebody from the Bureau of Indian Affairs who needed money. No, that wouldn't work. The folks at the BIA had gotten way too concerned about their own image lately. What about the Bureau of Land Management? No, they wouldn't have jurisdiction.

When the solution finally hit him, he smacked his forehead with the heel of his palm and laughed at his own stupidity. He'd send Maggie out to Laughing Horse on a fact-finding mission, and use her research to close down that miserable place for good. The Northern Cheyenne didn't need two reservations. Since most of them were on welfare, it wouldn't hurt a thing if the Western Band got moved over to Lame Deer to live with the others.

Hell, he should have thought of this before. He'd have to take his time and plan it carefully, of course. Maggie wouldn't like it one bit when she found out what he was really doing with her work. But hey, this was politics. Rule number one in this game was, you did whatever you had to do to cover your ass. If he played his cards just right, Maggie Schaeffer would cover his nicely.

One

"Yes, Aunt Sally, I'm still listening," Jackson Hawk said into the telephone receiver, rolling his eyes in fond exasperation. "Of course I'll be polite. I'm always polite. Tell Uncle Frank he can stop nagging me any time now."

While Aunt Sally rattled on with a seemingly endless stream of advice, all of which he didn't need, Jackson propped his feet on the corner of his desk and rubbed the back of his neck with his free hand.

"Whoa! *Ne-xohose-neheseha!* Say it again in English, Aunt Sally. Yes, I've been studying Cheyenne again, but I can't follow you when you talk so fast. Uh-huh. Uh-huh. Oh, yeah? Tell him I said he's been lying around like an old woman for too long. If he doesn't like the way I'm doing his job, he'd better hurry up and get well so he can do it himself."

Aunt Sally dutifully relayed the message. Jackson chuckled when he heard his uncle's outraged howl in the background. "Yeah, I thought that'd get a rise out of him."

A knocking sound drew Jackson's gaze to the doorway. A pretty young woman he'd never seen before stood there, clutching a black leather briefcase. The color of her hair, skin and eyes told him she had a substantial amount of Indian blood, but the gray wool coat draped over her arm, her conservative navy blue business suit, her sensible pumps and her short, chic hairstyle made her look out of place. And there was an obvious air of tension about her that made him wonder if she'd ever set foot on a reservation before. He held up one finger to indicate that he'd just be a moment.

"Aunt Sally, I have a visitor," he said when his garrulous aunt paused to take a breath. "I don't know. I don't know that, either. I'll call if anything important comes up. All right. Take good care of yourself, too."

Jackson hung up the phone, swung his feet to the floor and swiveled his chair to face the desk again. The woman still stood in the doorway, looking as if she'd rather be someplace—no, make that *any*place—else. Must be from the government. He'd guess she was a Fed, although she certainly had better-looking legs than the last one he'd had to deal with. The rest of her wasn't too shabby, either. But a Fed was still a Fed, and it never hurt to be cautious.

"May I help you?" he asked.

She gave him a tentative smile. "I'm sorry I interrupted your phone call." When Jackson merely shrugged at her apology, she continued. "I'm looking for Mr. Frank Many Horses. I believe he's the tribal chairman?"

"He's on a medical leave," Jackson said. "I'm filling in for him at the moment. And you are?"

He'd never seen a Fed blush before, but this one did. Quite prettily, too. Then she uttered a soft, husky laugh that charmed him right down to the scuffed toes of his cowboy boots. He decided she was more cute than pretty. But on her, cute looked damn good.

"Excuse me," she said, stepping into the room. "I guess I've spent so much time alone in the Library of Congress lately, I've forgotten my manners. I'm Maggie Schaeffer. From Congressman Baldwin's office in Washington."

Baldwin? Jackson thought, barely managing to keep a grimace of disgust off his face. What was that snake up to now? He'd never met the man personally, but he'd heard enough about him from Uncle Frank to be suspicious.

"What can I do for you, Ms. Schaeffer?"

"Oh, dear." She walked closer to the desk. "You weren't expecting me, were you, Mr., uh... I'm sorry, I didn't catch your name."

Jackson stood and briefly shook the hand she offered. It was small and soft and delicate, and he felt oddly reluctant to let go of it. "Hawk. Jackson Hawk. I'm the tribal attorney here at Laughing Horse. And, no, I wasn't expecting you."

She shot him a startled glance, as if she couldn't believe he was really an attorney. Of course, she probably hadn't met many male lawyers who wore their hair in braids. His jeans and faded blue sweatshirt weren't exactly standard office attire, either. Well, tough. He didn't live or dress by the white man's rules anymore.

A worried little wrinkle appeared between her eyebrows. Then she squared her shoulders and gave him a rueful, lop-sided grin. Damn, but she really *was* cute. And young. Probably only in her mid-twenties, which made her at least ten years younger than he was. Maybe that was why she worked for an S.O.B. like Baldwin—she was too young to know any better.

"Well, I apologize again, Mr. Hawk," she said. "Some-one from the congressman's office in Whitehorn was sup-posed to call and set up an appointment for me for the first of March. Obviously, there's been a mix-up. I can come back tomorrow, if this isn't a convenient time."

Jackson gestured toward the straight-backed wooden chair on the other side of his desk. "It's as convenient as it's ever going to get. Have a seat." When they were both set-tled, he asked, "What brings you to Laughing Horse, Ms. Schaeffer?"

"I'm sure you're aware Congressman Baldwin serves on the House Subcommittee on Native American Affairs."

When he nodded, she smiled at him like a teacher re-warding a student for a correct answer. Then she went on in a brisk, businesslike tone that reminded Jackson of the years he'd spent working for a Wall Street law firm, pretending he wasn't an Indian. Her cuteness faded; when the gist of her mission became clear, it vanished completely.

"At the last meeting of the subcommittee, it came to the congressman's attention that conditions here at the Laugh-ing Horse Reservation have not improved as much as they have on Montana's other reservations," she said. "He's quite concerned that we find a way to rectify the situa-tion."

"Yeah, I'll bet," Jackson muttered.

"Excuse me?" She looked him straight in the eye, with-out the slightest hesitation.

It was a small thing, really, just one of those funny little differences between the Indian and white cultures that had caused tons of misunderstanding. It had taken him years to learn to look whites directly in the eye when he talked to them. That she did it so well told him a lot about how thoroughly she'd been assimilated into white society. He wondered if she even knew that most traditional Indians would consider such an action rude. Well, it wasn't his job to teach her.

"It's nothing. Go on, Ms. Schaeffer."

She shot him a doubtful look, but continued in that same irritating, businesslike tone after a moment. "My assignment is to interview some of the people here, make a list of the specific problems you're facing and formulate recommendations for legislation. If you could call a special meeting of the tribal council—"

"No."

Both of her eyebrows shot up beneath her wispy bangs. "I'm afraid I don't understand."

"That's obvious, Ms. Schaeffer. You don't have a clue about what life is like on this or any other reservation, and neither does your boss."

Jackson saw sparks of anger flash in her eyes, and she opened her mouth, as if she were going to say something. But then she inhaled a deep breath and pursed her lips, obviously struggling to rein in her emotions and come up with an appropriate response. He could hardly wait to hear it.

She spoke slowly and distinctly, as if she were choosing each word with great care. "You're absolutely right, Mr. Hawk. Which is precisely why Congressman Baldwin has sent me here to collect data. I'll do everything possible to avoid taking too much of your time. One or two meetings should be enough."

"No."

He saw more sparks, and heard a huffy little note of indignation in her voice when she replied. "May I ask why not?"

Jackson leaned back in his battered swivel chair and smothered a grin as best he could. He probably should be ashamed of himself, but he wasn't. If he was honest, he'd have to admit he was enjoying this immensely.

Since taking over for Uncle Frank two months ago, he'd been forced to deal with representatives from the federal, state and county governments on a daily basis. All of them wanted something from him or his tribe, but they didn't want to give anything in return. And they didn't care whether or not they understood the people they were supposed to be serving.

Well, he'd finally had enough of trying to accommodate these idiots. He felt stupid for ever having thought this one was cute. Hell, she was just another insensitive bureaucrat. The fact that she was Indian herself only made it all the more inexcusable, as far as he was concerned. Damn it, she should know better, and by the time he was done with her, she *would*.

Lacing his fingers together over his belt buckle, Jackson stared at her until the tension nearly crackled between them. "Why not? Because we're sick and tired of being studied like bugs under a microscope. And because I don't think you really want to understand our problems, Ms. Schaeffer."

"I beg your pardon?" She drew herself up as tall as she could and still remain seated. It didn't help a whole lot, because she was only about five foot four when she was standing. "I didn't come all the way to Montana from Washington for the fun of it, Mr. Hawk."

"I'm sure you didn't," Jackson said. "You came here looking for easy answers, so you can write your little report and make points with Baldwin. Well, here's a news flash, Ms. Schaeffer. There aren't any easy answers. If you really want to understand the problems of this reservation, you come out here and live with us for a year."

"Don't be ridiculous. I couldn't possibly stay for a year."

"Then don't waste the taxpayers' money writing another useless report about Indians."

"Why are you being so obnoxious about this with *me?*" she demanded, poking the center of her chest with her index finger. "I certainly don't have any prejudice against Indians. I was chosen for this assignment because I *am* one."

Jackson had to chuckle at that. "You may have the blood, honey, but you don't have the soul."

Red patches bloomed over her cheekbones. She jumped out of her chair as if the seat had suddenly caught fire and propped her fists on her hips. "If you're implying—"

"I'm not *implying* anything," Jackson said, rising from his own chair. Bracing both hands on the top of his desk, he leaned forward until his nose nearly brushed hers. "I'll call you an apple right to your face, if you want. You know what that means, don't you? Red on the outside, white on the inside?"

"I've heard the term."

"I'm sure you have. You're trading on a heritage you know nothing about to further your career, and I'll be damned if you'll do it at my tribe's expense. Go on back to Washington and find somebody else to write about."

Her chin rose another notch. She slowly lowered her fists to her sides, her movements stiff and jerky enough to make Jackson suspect she was having a hard time fighting off an urge to punch him in the face. "I'm afraid I can't do that, Mr. Hawk. And might I remind you that I'm a *federal* employee?"

"So was Custer, lady. He didn't belong here, either."

She gave him a glare that should have singed his eyelashes off. Then she put on her coat, picked up her briefcase and rested the bottom of it on the seat of the chair. "You really think you know everything about me, don't you?"

"I know enough."

"Perhaps. But then again, perhaps not."

He didn't like the grim smile that slowly curved the corners of her mouth. He straightened to his full height. "What's that supposed to mean?"

"It's not important. But get one thing straight. With or without your help, I *will* write my report. Congressman Baldwin will be using it to draft legislation that will directly affect the people on this reservation. Since you have refused an opportunity to offer input, you'll have only yourself to blame if you don't like the results. Have a nice day, Mr. Hawk."

Jackson remained standing behind his desk, listening to the angry clicks her heels made on the tile floor as she marched down the hallway. When he heard the exit door open and close, he swore under his breath, plunked his butt into the chair and reached for the phone.

Not only was the woman an apple, he'd bet his law degree she was an apple with some kind of an ax to grind. One of his old friends from Georgetown University's law school worked on Capitol Hill. Bennie Gonzales had a network of contacts among congressional staffers that a gossip columnist would kill for. If there was anything worth knowing about Maggie Schaeffer, Bennie already knew it, or he could get it within an hour. The call went through, and when he'd chitchatted enough to be polite, Jackson made his request.

"Maggie Schaeffer," Bennie said. "That name's familiar. Let me think a second. Maggie Schaeffer, Maggie Schaeffer... Yeah, I've got her now. Research aide for Baldwin. Native American. Kinda short. Cute. Hair like Katie Couric's?"

"That's the one," Jackson said, grinning to himself as he imagined Bennie sitting behind a desk piled high with papers, tapping his forehead, as if that would help him spit out pertinent facts faster. "What do you know about her?"

"I've met her once. She's got a good rep. Supposed to be one of the best researchers on the Hill. Has a master's in public administration from Harvard."

"Do you know if she's ever worked with Native American issues?" Jackson asked.

"Not that I remember. She's done a lot of work on labor and transportation issues, though. Did a report on the timber industry a few months ago that was really excellent."

"That's all you know about her?"

"Professionally," Bennie said. "I heard a rumor about her last week, but I doubt there's any truth in it."

"What?"

"You know Washington gossip. Everybody's always supposed to be sleeping with their boss. I can't imagine Maggie with ol' horse-faced Baldwin, though."

Jackson couldn't imagine that, either, and it was surprising how distasteful he found the idea. "Are you sure this rumor was about the same Maggie?"

"Oh, yeah. The word was, Baldwin was shipping her out of town because his wife was jealous. The source really wasn't all that reliable, Jackson. I wouldn't jump to any conclusions."

"All right, Bennie. Thanks. I owe you one."

Jackson hung up the phone, then leaned back and propped his heels on the desk again. Should he call his uncle about Maggie Schaeffer or not? Kane Hunter, the doctor who served the reservation, had said they weren't supposed to upset Uncle Frank, but it had been two months since his heart attack. At this point, Jackson figured discovering he'd been kept in the dark about a potential problem with a congressman would upset his uncle more than hearing about it now.

Bracing for a scolding he probably deserved, Jackson grabbed the phone again and punched in his uncle's number. Sure enough, when he finished describing his encounter with Baldwin's aide, Uncle Frank cut loose with a list of insults, spoken in rapid-fire Cheyenne. Jackson caught one that sounded like "turnip brain" and considered himself lucky he couldn't understand the rest.

"All right, I get the message," he said, when his uncle started to slow down. "I don't know how you stand dealing with these people all the time, Uncle Frank. They drive me nuts. It made me feel better to finally tell one of them off."

"The job isn't about making *you* feel better, Jackson," Frank said, his voice deeper and gruffer than usual. "It's about doing what is best for the *tribe*. And what is best for the tribe is to stay on polite terms with our congressional delegation."

"I know, I know. But why should we waste our time like that? I'm telling you, this lady knows nothing. What good will it do for her to write a stupid report about us?"

"There's probably a warehouse in Washington as big as the Pentagon that's full of stupid reports about Indians," Frank countered with a chuckle. "One more won't hurt anything, nephew. Besides, what right have you to judge anyone for being an apple?"

Jackson winced as his uncle's pointed question struck home. What right, indeed? Maggie Schaeffer wasn't doing a blessed thing he hadn't done himself—for almost half his life. He'd been back on the res for four years now, but he still didn't like to be reminded of the man he'd once been. Maybe that was why he'd reacted so strongly to Ms.

Schaeffer—he couldn't look at her or listen to her without remembering his own folly.

"You know what you have to do, Jackson," Frank said, after a moment's silence.

"Yeah. Don't worry, I'll take care of it." Jackson swung his feet to the floor. "Answer one more question, Uncle Frank. How do you always manage to say the one thing that will make me squirm the most?"

Frank let out one of his deep, rumbling laughs. Jackson treasured that sound, especially since he'd come so close to never hearing it again. "Haven't you figured that out yet, kid? I'm a wise old Indian. Just like in the movies."

Breathing deeply in an attempt to bring her chaotic emotions under control, Maggie Schaeffer tossed her briefcase onto the passenger seat of her rental car and slammed the door. It didn't help much. She marched around the front end, unlocked the driver's door, climbed in behind the wheel and slammed that door, too. She poked the key at the ignition, but her hand was trembling too much for her to fit it into the narrow slot.

She dropped the keys into her lap and pounded the steering wheel with the side of her fist. "Damn that arrogant jerk!"

There were better words to describe Jackson Hawk, but she refused to lower herself that far. Her chest was so full of rage it ached, and she blinked back the tears of frustration stinging the backs of her eyes. She would *not* let him get to her. He wasn't worth it. It wasn't the first time she'd been called an apple, and she doubted it would be the last.

"So why does it still hurt?"

Maggie sniffed, then sighed and shook her head. She'd grown up surrounded by white people. Her mother had been the only other Indian she knew until she left home. Beverly Schaeffer hadn't seemed very different from the other kids' mothers, though, and since Maggie had worn the same kind of clothes, played with the same toys and taken the same lessons after school as the other kids, she hadn't felt all that different, either.

Oh, once in a while somebody would make a remark about her being an Indian, but she hadn't thought much about it then. Her mother and father had kept her too busy being an adored only child for her to worry about being inferior to anyone. She'd certainly never felt that way about herself.

Still, she'd always known she wasn't exactly like the other kids. She wasn't white, and she never would be. Her mother's refusal to talk about her own childhood, her relatives and Maggie's biological father had raised more than a few questions in Maggie's mind about her Indian heritage. One of her secret goals when she went off to college had been to meet other Indian students and find out if she would feel more at home with them than she did with her white friends.

"Hah!" she muttered, rolling her eyes in disgust at the painful memories flitting through her mind. She'd been rejected by white people over the years, but they had usually been so obviously ignorant, she was able to ignore them. It had hurt a thousand times more when her fellow Indian students took one look at her and despised her on sight.

It wasn't *her* fault she hadn't been raised on a reservation. It wasn't *her* fault she'd been raised with plenty of money, or that she'd received a better education in an upper-class white suburb of Denver. It wasn't *her* fault she had a white stepfather, or that he'd been allowed to adopt her. And yet she'd been rejected by her fellow Indian students for all of those reasons.

Sighing again, Maggie gazed through the windshield, silently reading the black letters painted on the door of the huge complex that housed the tribal offices, a restaurant, and heaven only knew what else. "Welcome to the Laughing Horse Tribal Center. Home of the Northern Cheyenne, Western Band."

Well, if this was really the home of the Northern Cheyenne, then Maggie Schaeffer had as much right to be here as Mr. High-and-Mighty Hawk did. Her mother had been born and raised here. Maggie herself had been born here.

If she had received a warmer welcome, she might have found the nerve to look up a few of her relatives. She wouldn't dream of doing that now, though. Any relatives she had living here might well be as mean and nasty as Jackson Hawk.

Just thinking the wretched man's name was enough to raise gooseflesh on her arms. The meeting had started out so well. And then, in the space of a heartbeat, his attitude had changed from cautiously welcoming to downright hostile. What on earth had she done wrong?

It was hard to believe she'd thought he was so handsome at first—the handsomest man she'd ever seen. In a primitive sort of way. She closed her eyes for a moment, imagining his face.

He had smooth, coppery skin stretched over a bold blade of a nose, sharply defined cheekbones, and a firm jaw and chin. His long black braids did nothing to detract from his masculinity; he was so tall, his shoulders were so broad, his voice was so deep and rough, she doubted anything would be able to do that.

But it was his eyes she remembered best. Black, black eyes, shining with intelligence, glittering with anger, eyes that had looked into the darkest corners of her soul. And found her wanting.

A shiver zipped up her spine, and she felt a hollow, aching sensation in the center of her chest. Sighing, she opened her eyes and shook her head. It didn't matter whether or not he liked her. There was no point in feeling sorry for herself. She had a job to do. Perhaps someone at the BIA office would help.

She looked up at the sprawling building again, searching for a sign to tell her which way to go. Her stomach fluttered, her heart contracted, and a strangled gasp escaped her lips. There, at the top of the steps, stood a man wearing jeans, a denim jacket, and a black Stetson with a white feather sticking out of the hatband. It was Jackson Hawk. Though he also wore a pair of aviator sunglasses, she just knew he was staring straight at her.

Two

Jackson stepped outside, slid on his sunglasses to soften the sun's reflection off the snow and felt a sharp tug at his heartstrings that was part guilt, part relief. So, she hadn't left yet. Though her powder-blue rental car was only a compact, Ms. Schaeffer looked awfully small and fragile behind the wheel. And why was she just sitting there with her head back and her eyes shut? Maybe he'd given her a headache.

That was only fair, he thought with a wry grin. She'd sure as hell given him one. Then she sat up and looked right at him. His stomach lurched as if he were in an elevator that had suddenly plunged twenty stories. Her shoulders went rigid. Her chin came up. Even from this distance, her eyes looked as huge as a doe's during hunting season.

Damn. He hadn't thought he'd been mean enough to send her into a fight-or-flight response. She climbed out and stood behind the car door, facing him, her expression clearly indicating she'd give him one hell of a fight long before she would ever run from him. Well, good. He would have really felt bad if he'd scared all the spunk out of her.

Shoving his hands into his jeans pockets, he ambled down the steps and crossed the sidewalk. She braced one arm across the top of the car door and propped her other hand on her hip. Her face betrayed no emotion now, but he could see her chest rising and falling with rapid, choppy little breaths.

When she spoke, her voice was so carefully controlled it was a challenge, whether or not she intended it to be one. "Is there a problem, Mr. Hawk?"

Yeah, there was a problem. He'd never been any good at making apologies. He hoped he could figure out a way to do this without having to swallow a whole crow, feathers and all.

"Not exactly."

The top of her head barely reached his shoulders. She looked up at him expectantly, and for an insane instant, he wanted to touch the graceful curve of her neck. He cleared his throat, shoved his hands deeper into his pockets and inclined his head toward the vehicle.

"Havin' trouble with your car?"

"No."

"Good. The road between here and Whitehorn's not the best."

Her eyebrows shot up beneath her bangs again, and the corners of her mouth tightened. "Is that supposed to be a subtle way of telling me to leave?"

Feeling like an idiot, Jackson shook his head. "That's not what I meant."

"What exactly *did* you mean?"

No one could ever accuse her of having less-than-perfect diction.

"Nothing, really. I was just, uh, tryin' to make a little conversation."

Her eyes widened slightly at that. Jackson felt even more foolish when he saw the light of understanding turn on in her big, dark eyes and heard a trace of amusement slide into her voice. "Why?"

"It's no big deal," he said, raising one shoulder in a half shrug. "I just realized I may have been a little...abrupt when you were in my office."

Oh, damn. She was on to him, all right. He hadn't given her any reason to make this easy for him, but she was enjoying his discomfort entirely too much. Her voice took on a sweetness that made him grind his back teeth together.

"Abrupt? Don't be so modest, Mr. Hawk. I would have called your behavior insulting, at the very least."

"You don't have to be sarcastic," he grumbled.

She tipped her head to one side and gave him a wide-eyed look. "I don't? You certainly were."

"Yeah, I know. And I'm sorry, all right?"

Straightening away from the car door, she crossed her arms over her breasts. "Funny. You don't sound very sorry to me."

"Well, I am."

She grinned openly at that. What he wouldn't give to kiss that sassy little smile right off her face. She'd probably deck him, but he figured the pain just might be worth it.

"Be honest, Mr. Hawk," she said. "You're not the least bit sorry about the way you treated me. You're just afraid I'll make trouble for you with Mr. Baldwin."

Jackson stiffened. Man, she could really be a snot when she put her mind to it. "I'm not afraid of you, or of Baldwin."

"Not personally, maybe," she agreed. "But I think you're afraid of anything that might threaten your tribe. If I were in your position, I know I would be."

Jackson shrugged again. She was right, of course. But he'd be damned if he'd admit it out loud. "Are you gonna accept my apology or not?"

She rolled her eyes in disgust, then leaned inside the car and grabbed her briefcase. "Don't worry, Mr. Hawk," she said, straightening to face him again. "I'm not in the habit of blaming a whole group of innocent people for the actions of one rude jerk. Now, if you'll excuse me, I'm going to find the BIA office."

Punching the lock button, she stepped out from behind the door, shut it, and would have brushed right past him if he hadn't reached out and grabbed her arm. She stiffened, but didn't try to pull away. Oh, no, she had too much dignity for that. She simply glanced down at his hand, then looked up at him again, her expression one of bored patience.

Jackson couldn't hold back a chuckle of admiration. She was small, all right, but every inch of her was packed with feisty determination. Releasing her, he held both hands up beside his head in a classic gesture of surrender.

"All right, all right. I really am sorry, Ms. Schaeffer. My behavior was inexcusable. Please accept my apology."

"Why should I?"

"Because Frank Many Horses is my uncle, and he's gonna kick my butt up between my ears if you don't," Jackson admitted with a sheepish grin. Encouraged by her startled laugh, he rushed on. "And because, honest to God, that's the best apology I know how to make. Besides, the BIA can't help you as much as I can."

She smiled back at him, naturally this time, as if she finally believed in his sincerity. Damned if she wasn't cute after all. "And just how do you intend to help me?"

"We could start with a tour of our social agencies. That'll give you an idea of what we're trying to accomplish."

"Thank you, Mr. Hawk," she said. "I would appreciate that very much."

He eyed her pumps doubtfully. "Do you have any boots with you? We'll have to walk, and it's pretty muddy in places."

She shook her head. "Don't worry, I'll manage."

Jackson held out his hand in an after-you gesture. She rewarded him with a gracious nod and set off in the direction he'd indicated. Oh, brother, he thought, falling in step with her businesslike stride. This was gonna be a *long* afternoon.

To his surprise, however, it didn't turn out that way. Though she didn't loosen up much with him, Maggie radiated a genuine warmth toward everyone else she met that excused her occasional lapses in Indian manners. She did more listening than talking, and she asked intelligent, probing questions that made people eager to tell her more. Even crusty old Earnest Running Bull at the alcohol rehabilitation center invited her to come back when she had more time.

They arrived at the day-care center fifteen minutes before the start of the story hour. To Jackson's surprise, after checking out the facility, Maggie sat right down on the floor with the kids and listened to Annie Little Deer's rendition of the Cheyenne creation story as raptly as any of the three- and four-year-olds. When little Emma Weasel Tail crawled onto her lap without an invitation, Maggie smiled and cuddled her close, as if she honestly enjoyed holding the child in her arms.

At that point, even Jackson, with his well-developed cynicism toward government employees in general and Feds in particular, couldn't deny he might have been a tad hasty in judging her. In fact, he could almost believe he'd finally met a Fed with a heart. Unbelievable as it seemed, he was actually starting to like Maggie Schaeffer.

The thought made him nervous. It was okay to give her a grudging sort of respect. It was even okay to think she was cute and lust after her curvy little body. But it wasn't okay to feel well...drawn to her. And it definitely wasn't okay to want her to smile at him the way she'd smiled at Earnest Running Bull—not as much as he wanted her to, anyway.

Something about her assignment smelled fishy. For one thing, Jackson just couldn't buy the story about the House Subcommittee on Native American Affairs suddenly noticing the problems at Laughing Horse. For another, Congressman Baldwin had never been interested in helping the Northern Cheyennes, or any of the other tribes in Montana. Why was he interested now?

Though he was intrigued by and attracted to Maggie Schaeffer, Jackson couldn't afford to forget she worked for Baldwin. Hell, according to Bennie, she might even be sleeping with the bastard. Whether or not that was true, Jackson sincerely doubted she would ever choose the tribe's interests over those of her boss. She seemed too ambitious for that.

He also couldn't afford to like her enough to let down his guard just because she'd let a little girl climb into her lap. Well, he'd finish giving her this damn tour, and then he'd go back to work and mind his own business. He didn't have time for Feds. Not even cute ones.

Entranced with the story and the child who had unabashedly climbed into her lap, Maggie gently brushed her cheek against the little girl's glossy black hair. Her mother must have heard this story when she lived here. Why had she never shared such a beautiful tale with her own daughter?

The children were as bright, sweet and eager to learn as any of the kids Maggie had baby-sat when she was in high school. But after brief conversations with the people at the employment office, the welfare office, the Indian Health Service clinic and the drug and alcohol rehab center, she knew the chances for long, happy lives were slim at best for too many of them.

Hearing about the poverty and despair so many of the adults on this reservation lived with had been disturbing enough. Realizing these adorable little ones were destined to face the same problems made her fighting mad. If there was any way she could help these people, she intended to find it.

She felt a tingly, almost itchy sensation at the back of her neck. Great. Jackson Hawk was staring at her again. What *was* the man's problem? Was he this suspicious of everyone who visited the reservation? Or the res, as most of the people called it, she reminded herself.

But back to Mr. Hawk. What did he think she was going to do to these people, anyway? What did he think she *could* do? Maybe the real question was, what did he have to hide? Everyone she'd met had greeted him with friendliness and respect, but had there been a subtle attitude of reserve toward him? Or had she simply imagined that?

Well, if there was some kind of skulduggery going on, she would find out what it was, and she'd best be getting on with the process. Releasing the little girl, Maggie climbed to her feet and tiptoed across the room, so as not to distract the children's attention. Then she thanked the center's director for the tour and followed Jackson outside.

There was still quite a bit of snow on the ground, but surely, with all this sunshine, spring couldn't be too far off. Hundreds of questions formed in her mind as she walked beside Jackson, but she kept them to herself. He definitely was not the chatty type.

The last stop on the tour turned out to be what Jackson called the "Indian school," which was housed in a barnlike prefabricated structure northeast of the tribal center.

"It's pretty quiet around here right now," he said, flipping on the lights in the entryway. "But it'll really be busy when the school buses from Whitehorn show up at four o'clock. This program's my favorite."

Maggie followed him down a hallway, occasionally pausing beside him and peeking into the rooms. "Why is that, Mr. Hawk?"

"This is where our children learn how to be Indians. It meets a lot of other needs in the community, too. The kids have a place to go after school and get help with homework their parents may not be able to provide. We try to have at least two volunteer tutors available every day."

They moved on to the next room, and he continued. "This is the crafts room. The older women come in a couple of times a week and teach the girls how to sew and do beading. There's also a room where the boys can learn to make bows and arrows and drums, and we have a peer counseling center for the teenagers."

There was also a dining hall, and, finally, a gymnasium. Jackson raised one hand and gestured toward the vast open space. "The elders teach our traditional dances in here. We also hold community meetings here, and when it's not in use for some other purpose, the boys play basketball."

He led her back to the entrance then, extinguished the lights and turned to her when he'd locked the door. "If you want to meet a good cross section of folks from the res, this is the place to come. You'd probably learn more here than you would from a tribal council meeting."

Maggie looked up at him and wished he'd take off those sunglasses. Darn it, he really *was* a handsome man, one she would like to know better. While he hadn't exactly gone out of his way to charm her this afternoon, he had at least been civil, and she sensed that he cared deeply about his community.

"Is there some reason you don't want me to attend a tribal council meeting?" she asked.

He raised one shoulder in a half shrug, a characteristic gesture she had noticed from the beginning. "Not really. You'll have to attend one if you want to learn about our economic development plans. I just wanted you to know there are real people here, not just a bunch of statistics."

Maggie chuckled, and felt rewarded when he flashed her a broad grin. "I do realize that, Mr. Hawk. Thank you for giving me a wonderful tour."

They set off for the tribal center again. "How long will you be in the area?" Jackson asked.

"I had only planned on a week, but I'm beginning to see what you meant about needing a year to understand the problems."

Her remark earned her another grin, which prompted her to consider the possibility of extending her visit. She really couldn't stay for an entire year but if there were other things she could accomplish in the congressman's Whitehorn office, in addition to her research at Laughing Horse, a few months might not be out of the question. She glanced at her watch and figured out the time difference between Montana and Washington. If she called in the next fifteen minutes, she could probably catch the congressman at his office.

"Tell me, Mr. Hawk," she said, halting at the foot of the steps leading up to the tribal office, "is there a pay phone nearby I could use? I need to make a long-distance call."

"If you've got a credit card, you can use the phone in my office."

Jackson escorted her inside and left her alone to make her call in private, with a gruff "Help yourself." Perplexed by his sudden mood shift, Maggie stared at the closed door through which he had disappeared for a moment. Then she shook her head and reached for the phone. First things first. If she had any luck with the congressman, she would have time later to figure out what made Jackson Hawk tick.

The temptation to eavesdrop on Maggie's conversation was great, but Jackson forced himself to move away from the door and start a pot of coffee. Since he'd spent the afternoon playing tour guide, he'd have to stay late to finish the paperwork he'd neglected. He didn't regret the loss of his work time, however.

As his uncle had said, staying on polite terms with Montana's congressional delegation was important to the tribe. Jackson figured an afternoon was a small price to pay to repair the lousy impression he'd made earlier. Maggie had obviously enjoyed herself and, he hoped, learned something about the Laughing Horse Reservation.

Now she would spend a few days visiting with people, and then she would go back to Washington. Her report would be filed and forgotten, and he could forget he'd ever met her. At least he hoped he'd be able to forget her.

Shoving his hands into his pockets, he ambled over to the window and gazed out at the parking area in front of the building. The sight of Maggie's rental car brought up a vivid mental picture of her holding little Emma Weasel Tail in her lap. Jackson shook his head in disgust at the warm, fuzzy feeling the vision produced in his chest.

"You've just been alone too long," he muttered, turning back to the coffeemaker.

That was true enough. His marriage had ended four years ago, and he hadn't been seriously interested in a woman since. What he couldn't understand was why Maggie Schaeffer, of all people, was the one who had made him realize how much he'd missed spending time with a woman.

Oh, sure, she was cute. Even sexy, in an understated sort of way. It didn't hurt that she was well educated and intelligent, either. But she wasn't any more right for him than his wife, Nancy, had been.

If he really wanted to have a woman in his life, he should pursue Sara Lewis, the curator of the Native American Museum in Whitehorn. Sara was every bit as educated and intelligent as Maggie, but she understood and embraced traditional Indian values, and she was as committed to the tribe as he was. Unfortunately, though he liked and respected Sara, he was no more attracted to her than he was to his sisters.

Well, if *Maheo,* the Creator, intended for him to marry again, Jackson figured, a suitable woman would eventually come along. Meeting Maggie Schaeffer had only served as a reminder that he still had a libido. Maybe he should start paying more attention to Aunt Sally's attempts to find him a "nice Indi'n gal."

Hearing the office door open behind him, Jackson turned and felt his heart slide clear down to the toes of his boots. Wearing an infectious grin almost as wide as her face, her dark eyes sparkling with excitement, Maggie stood in the doorway. How was he supposed to resist her when she wrinkled her impish little nose at him? Didn't she know bureaucrats weren't supposed to do things like that?

"Well, I've done it," she announced, holding her hands out like an actor preparing to take a bow.

"Done what, Ms. Schaeffer?" Jackson asked.

She wrinkled her nose at him again, hurried across the room and stopped in front of him. He caught a whiff of the light floral fragrance she wore. He'd noticed it a time or two during their tour. It reminded him of wildflowers. Oh, jeez, *wildflowers?* What the hell was the matter with him?

Her eyes taking on an earnest, hopeful expression, she laid one hand on his forearm. "We didn't get off to a very promising start, but I thought we'd made some progress this afternoon. Would you mind very much if we called each other by our first names... Jackson?"

A shiver of pleasure rippled down his spine when she said his name, her voice soft and a little husky. Somehow, at the moment, it didn't seem to matter that she was all wrong for him. He liked feeling her touch him. Though he knew she only intended it to be a conciliatory gesture, he liked it too damned much.

He pulled back enough to dislodge her fingers from his arm, then, irrationally, wished he hadn't done that. Man, he was gonna be in big trouble if she didn't go back to Washington soon. "Well, yeah. I guess we could. If you want, uh... Maggie."

There went her nose again. "It didn't hurt *that* much, did it?" Her eyes glinted with a gentle, teasing light that made it impossible to do anything but smile at her. "Anyway, I'm sure it will make working together more pleasant for both of us."

"Working together?" Jackson shook his head in confusion. "Have I missed something?"

"Well, we won't exactly be working together, but I'm sure I'll be seeing you fairly often during the next two months."

"Two *months?*"

"Oh, didn't I tell you? No, I guess I didn't." She laughed and dodged around him when the coffeemaker started to spit and hiss, a sure sign that the brew was ready. "Ah, plasma..." she said, reaching for the pot. Then she stopped, as if she'd suddenly remembered she was a visitor. "Sorry. I'm such a coffee hound. Do you mind if I have a cup?"

"Help yourself," Jackson said, feeling more confused with each passing second. She poured him a cup first and handed it to him before filling one for herself. "What didn't you tell me?"

"I took your advice, Jackson."

She sipped, then closed her eyes and sighed with obvious pleasure. If a little swallow of coffee made her sigh like that, what did she do in bed when she— Refusing to allow himself to finish the thought, Jackson shook his head again.

"What advice?" he asked.

"Your advice about living here for a year so I can understand the people's problems. I knew Congressman Baldwin would never agree to a year, but I did talk him into two months. Actually, I can stay until the middle of May, if I need to."

"You can?"

"Uh-huh. It was surprisingly easy to convince him. I'll have to work in the Whitehorn office once in a while, but for the most part, I'll be right here on the res. Isn't that great?"

Jackson gulped, then stared at her, wondering where this bubbly little elf had come from. This couldn't be the same woman he'd disliked so intensely a few short hours ago. He'd found her to be more likable as the afternoon wore on, but he never would have dreamed she could be so... vivacious. Yeah. That was the right word—*vivacious*. And she was smiling at him. Really giving him her killer-diller smile, and damned if it didn't make his heart beat a little faster.

"I said, isn't that great, Jackson?"

With a start, he realized he hadn't answered her question. "Uh, yeah. It's, uh, great, Maggie."

She shot him a puzzled look. "Is something wrong? I know it's not a whole year, but I thought you'd be pleased I'd be working on this for more than a week."

"I am, Maggie. Pleased, I mean. It's more than anyone else from the government has ever done."

"I really want to do a fair and honest study, Jackson. I know it won't solve all of your problems, but it could be the start of some good things for everyone here."

"I hope it will be."

"Me too." She gazed deep into his eyes for a moment, then glanced away, as if she'd somehow embarrassed herself. "Well, I guess I'd better go back to town and develop an action plan."

Jackson took the cup she held out to him, set it on the counter by the coffeemaker and waited for Maggie to retrieve her briefcase from his office. She returned carrying it, and she suddenly looked like a bureaucrat again. Before he could stop to consider the wisdom of offering her advice, the words popped out of his mouth. ·

"We're not usually too formal around here, Maggie. If you really want people to talk to you, you should ditch the briefcase and the suits."

She glanced down at her clothes, then looked up and grinned. "I'm so used to these things, I never would have thought of that. I'll stop at the trading post and see what I can find. Thanks, Jackson. Thanks for everything. I'll see you tomorrow."

A moment later, she was gone. Jackson poured himself another cup of coffee and walked into his office. Though it didn't have much in the way of comforts, compared to the cushy office he'd had in New York, he'd never minded working here. But now the whole building seemed too quiet. Too empty. Too lonely.

The phone rang then. Jackson wasn't surprised to hear his uncle's voice on the other end of the line. The moccasin telegraph had always been active on the Laughing Horse Res.

"Everything's fine, Uncle Frank. Oh, you talked to Earnest Running Bull, did you? Annie Little Deer, too? That's quite a network of spies you've got."

While his uncle fired one question after another, Jackson propped his feet up on the desk and rubbed the back of his neck.

"Yeah, she turned out to be okay. Was she cute?" Jackson rolled his eyes, crossed his fingers and lied. His irrational attraction to Maggie was the last thing he wanted to have blabbed all over the res. It didn't mean anything, anyway. Just a few hormones acting up.

"Hell, I didn't notice. She's gonna stay for two months, Uncle Frank. No, I didn't charm her. I didn't have to. She figured out she didn't know anything all by herself. I still don't trust her, though."

Now the advice started. "Yes, Uncle Frank. I know. I know. Hey, have a little faith in me, will ya? I'll keep an eye on her. Yes, I promise."

Hanging up the phone, Jackson assured himself he'd keep an eye on Maggie Schaeffer, all right. But, for his own peace of mind, he'd do it from a distance. Uncle Frank wasn't the only one on the res who had a network of spies.

Three

For the next two weeks, Maggie immersed herself in becoming more acquainted with the people who ran the social agencies at Laughing Horse, and with their clients. Following Jackson's advice, she bought jeans, sneakers, and beautifully decorated shirts and sweaters made by a co-op of Northern Cheyenne women at the trading post. Her new clothes were comfortable and practical, and she believed they did help her to blend in with the reservation residents.

She also exchanged her briefcase for a large purse, in which she carried a small notebook. She didn't take many notes, however. Before long, she found herself so involved with whatever was going on at the day-care center or the clinic or the employment office or the Indian school, she simply didn't have time. She didn't need notes to remember the conversations she had during the day, anyway.

These people were absolutely fascinating, and one of the things she liked best about being around them was their humor. They teased and harassed each other without mercy, but there was usually an underlying tone of affection that went along with it. Given the problems they often dealt with—unemployment, alcohol and drug abuse, domestic violence and so on—Maggie realized they probably needed a strong sense of humor to survive.

Though people treated her with courtesy and respect, Maggie also realized she was only seeing the surface of their lives. It would take time, probably a lot more time, for them to learn to trust her enough to really open up with their concerns. While it was frustrating, she tried to understand, and told herself she would know she'd finally been accepted when they started to tease her as they did each other.

She visited with the tribal police, the elderly people who told stories at the day-care center, the waitresses at the tribal center's restaurant. She interviewed the postmistress, the salesclerks at the trading post and the members of the women's sewing society. She talked to the Catholic and Protestant clergy who served the reservation, and the tribal priests and medicine men.

Every night she returned to her motel room in Whitehorn, feeling physically and emotionally drained, but eager to write up her impressions and insights on her laptop computer. Every morning she went back for more, always asking, "Why do you think that happens?" and "What should be done to change things?"

At first she regularly dropped by the tribal offices and tried to talk with Jackson Hawk, hoping to verify her perceptions of the things she was learning. Unfortunately, he rarely had time to see her, and when he did, his manner was cool and distant. She was puzzled, disappointed and a little hurt by his attitude, but she finally decided to leave the man alone and get on with her business.

If she occasionally felt lonely and depressed from observing the grinding poverty of the res, Maggie reminded herself there were more bright spots in her days than dark ones. One of the brightest was Sara Lewis, the curator of the Native American Museum, who was one of the volunteer tutors at the Indian school. Sara had welcomed Maggie and befriended her from the moment they met. Maggie admired her tremendously.

Tall and statuesque, Sara was cheerful, organized and dedicated. Her thick, shiny black hair fell to her waist when she wore it down, and her beautiful dark eyes carried a serenity that seldom wavered. Proud of her Northern Cheyenne heritage, Sara knew who she was and where she belonged, in a way Maggie envied.

Eager to spend time with her new friend, Maggie signed up to help tutor the junior and senior high students in the after-school program. The kids were as cautious about accepting her as their parents and grandparents, but on March 15, Maggie still caught a disturbing glimpse of what life was like for them at the public schools in Whitehorn.

A group of high school girls came into the study room and spread their books and papers out on a big round table. Their mood was unusually glum, and Maggie was just about to go ask Sara for advice on how to handle them when a girl named Wanda Weasel Tail broke the silence.

"You went to college, didn't you, Ms. Schaeffer?"

Another girl—Nina, if Maggie remembered her name correctly—rolled her eyes in disgust and slammed her chemistry book shut. Maggie nodded at Wanda. "Yes."

"Did you like it?" Wanda asked.

Maggie nodded again. "It was a lot of hard work, but I enjoyed most of it."

"Was it worth it?" the girl persisted. "I mean, all that hard work, you know? Did it make white people treat you better?"

"I'm not sure I can answer that," Maggie said slowly, choosing her words with care. "I guess in some ways it did, but I didn't grow up in an Indian community. I've always been so used to white people, I've never had many problems in dealing with them."

"But college helped you get a good job, didn't it?"

"Of course it did. I wouldn't be working for a congressman if I hadn't gone to college."

"Aw, Wanda, give it a rest," Nina muttered. "You're not gonna go to any college. None of us are."

"Why do you say that, Nina?" Maggie asked. "You're all doing very well in your classes, and there are scholarships available for Indian students."

"It's not the money." Nina's eyes flashed with anger for a moment, then suddenly took on a dull, defeated expression that wrenched Maggie's heart. "We're not even gonna graduate from high school, because we're all flunking English."

"Now, I know that's not necessary," Maggie said firmly. "I can help you with almost anything that's giving you trouble. And if I can't, I'm sure Miss Lewis can. That's why we're here."

"It's not that we don't know how to do the assignment," Wanda said. "We just can't do it."

Maggie pulled out a chair and sat down with the kids. "I'm afraid I still don't understand. What's the assignment?"

"It's our senior research paper," Nina said. "You know, one of those ones with footnotes and all that garbage?"

"Why can't you do it?"

"Because they have to be typed, and we don't have any typewriters or word processors," one of the other girls said.

"And because we don't have time to do the research at school, and the librarians won't let us check out any books," Wanda added. "They say they never get 'em back when Indian kids check 'em out, so they won't let us take 'em home."

"But that's ridiculous!" Maggie squawked.

Nina shrugged. "That's the rules, Ms. Schaeffer."

"Rules can be changed," Maggie said.

"Not these rules," Wanda said. "You don't know those librarians."

So furious she could hardly see straight, Maggie shoved back her chair and stood. "Well, those librarians don't know me, either. I want a list of your research topics, girls. And I promise you, one way or another, you're going to write your papers."

"Oh, yeah?" Nina scoffed. "So what're you gonna do, Ms. Schaeffer? Beat up the librarians?"

Maggie gave her a grim smile. "If I have to. But I don't think it'll come to that."

"What about the typing?" Wanda asked. "None of us have taken it, because we can't do the homework. 'Cause we don't have equipment, you know? The papers are due next month."

Fearing she would explode with some inappropriate remarks if she didn't get out of this room fast, Maggie collected the papers with the girls' research topics. "You just do the writing, and let me worry about the rest. Get busy on your other homework for now. I have to go talk to someone."

Unable to concentrate on his work, Jackson tossed his pen onto the desk, swiveled his chair around and gazed out the window at the Indian school. He told himself he really wasn't hoping for a glimpse of Maggie Schaeffer, but he didn't believe it for a second. Though he hadn't seen her for three days, she was seldom far from his thoughts.

How could she be, when everyone he ran into asked him what he knew about her? Hell, he hadn't needed a spy network to keep up with her movements; she was the talk of the entire reservation. She'd even earned herself a nickname. She was now known as Maggie the Little Fed Who Actually Listens, which was high praise indeed for an outsider who'd been here such a short time.

Sighing, Jackson started to turn back to his work, then caught a flash of movement that drew him to the window again. Uh-oh. The Little Fed was headed this way, in one heck of a hurry, and she looked mad enough to spit nails. Jackson whipped around and picked up one of the court documents he'd been reading, so that he'd look busy if she was coming to see him.

Sure enough, she stormed into his office a moment later, bristling with righteous indignation. Without so much as a greeting, she waved a fistful of crumpled papers at him. "Do you have any idea what's going on at Whitehorn High School?"

"Lots of things are going on at the high school," Jackson said, hiding a grin. Man, the lady was *steamed*. "Could you be more specific?"

"The discrimination, Jackson! Outright, blatant, illegal discrimination. Why are you letting them get away with it?"

Jackson climbed to his feet and stepped out from behind his desk, approaching her with one hand held up like a traffic cop. "Whoa! Calm down, and tell me what this is all about."

She took a deep breath and blew it out, ruffling her bangs with the breeze she created. "You're right. I'm sorry I barged in here like this. But it just makes me so furious, I want to hit somebody!"

"I can see that." Jackson gestured toward the straight-backed chair. "Sit down. I'll get you a cup of coffee, and we'll talk about it, okay?"

She obediently sat for a moment, then bounced out of the chair, as if she couldn't contain all the energy generated by her fury. She followed him to the coffeemaker, yapping at him like an enraged pup while he filled two cups.

"I'm telling you, Jackson, this situation is absolutely intolerable. No one deserves the kind of treatment the kids are getting. Those librarians should be drawn and quartered, tarred and feathered, ridden out of town on a rail."

Jackson handed her one of the mugs. Grasping her shoulder with his free hand, he gently herded her back into his office and pushed her into the chair again, then parked his butt on the edge of his desk. The aroma of the coffee finally got to her, and when she stopped to take a sip, he asked, "What's this about librarians?"

Maggie shot him an impatient look, but proceeded to explain the high school students' dilemma. By the time she finished, he felt ready to spit a few nails himself.

"We've got to do *something*, Jackson," she said. "For heaven's sake, the dropout rate for Indian kids is high enough, without those idiots making it impossible for them to succeed. You should take the librarians and the principal and the whole lousy school district to court and sue them for damages."

"I wish I could, Maggie," he said, shaking his head in disgust. "But I can't do it right now."

"Why not?" she demanded. "Those kids don't have a minute to lose. You're the tribal attorney—"

"Yes, I'm the tribal attorney, and at the moment, this tribe has more important legal matters to contend with."

"Such as? What on earth could be more important than helping those kids graduate from high school?"

"The tribe's economic survival. We're in a fight for our lives, and I can't take on any more than I already have."

That shut her up for an instant. But only for an instant. When she spoke again, however, her voice had softened. "What's going on, Jackson?"

Taking a moment to consider the wisdom of telling her, Jackson studied her face. She cared deeply about the kids, he was certain of that. But could he trust her with information as sensitive as this? Well, shoot, he'd already spilled half of it, and if she kept poking around on her own, she'd probably hear the rest, anyway.

"Have you ever heard of Jeremiah Kincaid?" he asked.

She nodded. "I've met him, once. In the office in Washington. As I recall, he's the president of the Whitehorn Ranchers' Association."

"That's right. He's pretty much run the whole county for the last thirty years. His father ran it before that."

"What's he got to do with the tribe?" Maggie asked.

"I'll get to that in a minute. But first, I want you to tell me something."

"I will if I can."

"You've been talking to all kinds of people here for two weeks now," he said. "What's the most common problem you've heard about?"

She didn't even pause to think about it. "Unemployment. Some decent jobs would probably solve a lot of the other problems I've heard about, too."

"Exactly. And why do you think we have so much unemployment?"

"A lack of education is one reason."

"Yeah, it sure is," Jackson agreed. "And racial discrimination's another. But a lot of other tribes have even less education per capita than we do, and their unemployment figures are about half of what ours are. How do you suppose they manage that?"

She tossed her head impatiently. "I don't know. Why don't you just *tell* me?"

"All right," Jackson said, smiling at her impatience. "They have a better land base, Maggie. And they've managed to keep the whites out and employ their people themselves. We haven't been able to do that."

"Now you've *really* lost me," she complained. "Are you saying Jeremiah Kincaid and the Whitehorn Ranchers' Association are trying to steal your land?"

"In a way. See, until the Indian Self-determination Act was passed in 1975, the government treated Indian tribes as wards, with the Bureau of Indian Affairs acting as a legal guardian. Anything the tribal governments wanted to do had to be cleared through the BIA, and the BIA had the power to lease out lands that weren't being used. Mr. Kincaid and his pals got in pretty thick with our local BIA superintendent, and were granted long-term leases at rock-bottom prices on almost half our land."

"Can't the leases be revoked?" Maggie asked.

"They don't need to be. They're due to expire on the first of June. When I informed Mr. Kincaid the tribe would not be renewing those leases, the ranchers' association filed a lawsuit against us."

"On what grounds?"

"Guys like Kincaid don't need solid grounds, Maggie. They buy judges and congressmen, and even U.S. senators."

Her eyebrows swooped into a scowling *V.* "Now, wait a minute—are you implying my boss takes bribes?"

She was quick, all right, Jackson thought with a grin. And so damned earnest. "I don't know. Does he?"

"I hardly think so, Jackson."

"What was Jeremiah Kincaid doing in his office?"

"I don't know, and I wouldn't tell you if I did. I have *some* integrity, you know." She shot him a huffy glare that dared him to challenge her last statement. "But constituents visit him every day. That doesn't mean he takes bribes."

Jackson shrugged. "You're right. But I have to tell you, it makes me damn nervous to find out Kincaid's been to see him. I'll bet he's one of Baldwin's biggest campaign contributors."

"So what if he is?" Maggie demanded. "Congressman Baldwin doesn't have any control over the courts."

"No, but he has a certain amount of control over legislation concerning Indians. And when it comes to Indians, Congress has the power to do any damn thing they want. Frankly, I'm worried about Baldwin's sudden interest in us. It was clever of him to send you out here."

"You think he's using me somehow? To harm the tribe?"

"It's a possibility."

She gaped at him for a second, then firmly shook her head. "No. He wouldn't do that. I *know* he wouldn't."

"For God's sake, Maggie, how naive *are* you?" Jackson stood and paced the length of the room and back. "If you really believe that, you need to go to the library and read the history of federal policy toward Indian tribes. Look up the

Allotment Act, the relocation program and the termination policy.''

"Oh, come on, Jackson. That's all in the past.''

"Are you willing to stake the tribe's survival on it? I'm not. Any time whites have wanted our land, ninety-nine times out of a hundred, we've lost it. Kincaid wants our land, and believe me, he's got plenty of powerful friends to back him up.''

"But he can't possibly win in court. Can he?''

"Haven't you ever heard that possession is nine-tenths of the law? The leases were supposed to expire in January, but he's already managed to get a six-month extension. And damn it, we *need* those acres. If we can ever get them back, we've got plans that will put one hell of a dent in our unemployment problem.''

"But I still don't see how anyone could use me or my work to help Kincaid. Mr. Baldwin asked me to report the truth about conditions here. That should help you, not hurt you.''

Jackson shrugged. "Maybe it doesn't have anything to do with your report. For all I know, he might already be drafting legislation to force us to renew the leases or sell the land, and he wanted you out of the office so you wouldn't be around to protest if you found out about it.''

"That's a pretty paranoid—''

"I'd rather be paranoid than stupid.''

"Well, gee, thanks a lot.'' Maggie got up and walked stiffly to the doorway.

"Wait a minute.'' Jackson hurried after her. She turned to face him, hurt showing in her eyes. "I didn't mean that the way it sounded. I'm just afraid you're too trusting.''

"Well, it's obvious you don't trust me, either,'' she said, thumping her chest with one finger. "After all, I *do* work for the evil congressman.''

She was so damn cute when she was furious, Jackson had to grin. "Actually, I kind of admire your loyalty to your boss. I only wish I knew how much loyalty you feel toward the people here. You don't have any real connection to us.''

She raised her chin to a proud, almost haughty angle. "I'm as Northern Cheyenne as you are, Jackson Hawk.

And I happen to have a very direct connection to the Laughing Horse Reservation."

"What are you talking about?"

"Take a look at your tribal rolls. I'm listed as Margaret Speaks Softly. My mother was listed as Beverly Speaks Softly."

Jackson frowned. He'd heard that name before—recently, in fact. When the memory surfaced, he had even less reason to trust Maggie. "I've heard of her. She left over twenty years ago and never came back. Married some bigshot white man, didn't she? The guy who owns all those motels?"

"That's right. My father's name is Calvin Schaeffer."

"Then you're half-white? You don't look—"

"No. My biological father was Northern Cheyenne, too. He abandoned Mama before I was born. When he died, Cal adopted me. He's been a wonderful father, Jackson. I love him very much."

Well, that explained a lot of things about Maggie Schaeffer, Jackson thought. "You never even said you were Cheyenne. Why the hell didn't you tell me this before?"

"You were so busy judging me and telling me I didn't belong here, I didn't think it was any of your business. I'd appreciate it if you wouldn't spread this around. It's no one else's business, either."

"You have family here, Maggie."

"I know, but I'm not too sure I want to meet them. My mother must have had her reasons for staying away. Until I find out what they were, I'd rather not have any contact."

It was too late for that, Jackson thought, grimly shaking his head. She'd already met her grandmother, Annie Little Deer. Annie's husband of fifty years had died a month ago, and Jackson remembered her mentioning her long-lost daughter. He believed Annie would love to know Maggie was her granddaughter. But it was Maggie's decision to make.

"All right," he said. "I won't tell anyone."

"Thank you. Since you're not going to be able to help the kids, do you mind if I take a shot at it?"

"What are you going to do?"

"You *still* don't trust me. . . ." she said, shaking her head as if in amazement.

"Should I?"

"Yes, damn it. What have I done to make you believe I would ever willingly hurt anyone?"

"Nothing," he said. "But I told you, I can't afford to deal with any other legal hassles right now."

"I won't create any. All I plan to do is visit the superintendent of schools tomorrow morning. There's got to be Federal funding for Indian children in this school district. I think I can rattle his cage enough to make him take some action."

Jackson smiled at the thought of her doing that. She'd go after the guy like a mama grizzly protecting her cubs. It would serve the son of a bitch right.

"All right," he said. "The superintendent's name is Edward Reese. We've got BIA records of all the funding allocated for our kids during the past five years. Would you like to see them?"

Her mouth curved into a wicked grin. "Would I ever!"

He led her into Frank's office and dug the appropriate file out of the cabinet. She scanned the contents and tucked the folder under her arm. Promising to let him know how the meeting went, she left with a cheery wave. Jackson shook his head in bemusement.

Maggie Schaeffer had a healthy temper, and she wasn't afraid to show it. But when an argument ended, she didn't seem to hold a grudge. He liked that about her. That, and a lot of other things.

In fact, the only thing he didn't like about her was her boss. Damn it, an Indian woman as intelligent and educated as Maggie had no business working for a jerk like Baldwin. She should be working for her people in some capacity. So why the hell wasn't she? They could use her talents right here at Laughing Horse.

"Forget it," Jackson muttered. "Calvin Schaeffer's daughter would never live on a reservation. Not in a billion years."

* * *

Eager to study the file Jackson had given her, Maggie drove to Whitehorn, stopped at a fast-food restaurant for dinner and hurried back to her motel room. Two hours later, she set the folder aside, confident she was prepared to tackle Mr. Reese. If the man proved difficult, Jackson had given her plenty of ammunition to handle him with.

She got up and wandered over to the window, telling herself she shouldn't be thinking about Jackson. He was suspicious and irascible, and sometimes he could be an absolute stinker. He was also intelligent; though he invariably infuriated her, she had to admit she enjoyed the challenge of arguing with him.

And she still thought he was the most attractive man she'd ever seen. Lord, those eyes of his made her feel all shivery and jittery inside. However, unless he was yelling at her, Jackson masked his emotions so well she usually found it difficult to guess what he was feeling or thinking.

It had seemed as if they'd reached some level of understanding this afternoon. His giving her the file had been a demonstration of trust. Hadn't it? Surely he didn't think she would betray her own people, even if she hadn't ever lived with them.

"You probably don't want to know what he really thinks of you, Schaeffer," Maggie muttered to herself.

Sighing, she turned away from the window, crossed the room and flopped down on the bed. Linking her hands behind her head, she stared up at the water-spotted ceiling. Every time she talked with Jackson Hawk, she ended up feeling confused about something. Her attraction to him, her background, her career—after today, especially her career.

Darn him, anyway, she'd worked long and hard to get a job on Capitol Hill. Congressman Baldwin was a good boss and a kind, decent human being. He had an impeccable record; she'd checked it out before accepting a position with him. He couldn't be involved in the sleazy kinds of things Jackson had implied. He just couldn't.

She wasn't nearly as naive as Jackson obviously thought she was, either; if Mr. Baldwin was involved in corruption, she would have seen or heard something about it by now. So why was she suddenly doubting him? And her own judgment?

The phone on the bedside table rang before she could find a suitable answer. She picked up the receiver and smiled when she heard her father's voice.

"I haven't heard from you in ages, Maggie," he scolded. "How are you?"

"I'm fine, Dad. I've just been awfully busy."

"Busy doing what?"

Touched by his interest, she launched into a description of her activities during the past two weeks, finishing with the story about the kids. She wasn't ready to talk about Jackson yet. As always, her father listened intently. And, as always, he picked up on her turbulent emotions without her having to tell him directly.

"You sound like you could use a hug," he said. "I wish I could be there to give you one."

Imagining her big, burly father, with his unruly red hair and his hazel eyes that usually sparkled with laughter, Maggie felt a lump form in her throat. He gave the world's best hugs, and she suddenly missed him desperately. "Me too, Daddy."

"Oh, it's *Daddy*, huh?" he said with a soft chuckle. "That sounds pretty serious. What's wrong, honey?"

Maggie shrugged, then remembered he couldn't see her. "It's nothing, really. I mean, nothing's happened that I can't handle. I'm just feeling a little..."

"Confused and overwhelmed?" he asked.

"Yeah. That about covers it. The reservation is exactly what I expected in some ways, but not in others."

"What did you expect?"

"I knew I'd see a lot of problems, of course. And I've certainly seen them. I just didn't realize I'd feel so personally affected. When those girls told me what was happening to them, I felt like it was happening to *me*."

"Aw, Maggs, it's natural for you to identify with those people. They're Indians, and so are you."

"Am I?" Shaking her head, she choked out a bitter little laugh. "I look like them on the outside, but I don't have all that anger and despair on the inside. I guess I really am an apple.''

"You're not an apple. You're just Maggie. And Maggie's one heck of a special lady.''

"You've always made me feel that way,'' Maggie said. "But here, I feel so ignorant. I don't know anything about being a Northern Cheyenne. I don't know their stories or their customs or their history. Why didn't Mama ever teach me those things?''

Her father was silent for a long time. Fearing she'd upset him, Maggie tried to smooth things over. "I'm sorry, Dad. I shouldn't have said that.''

"It's okay. I'm just not sure how to answer your questions, that's all,'' he said. "But go ahead and ask them.''

"Are you sure you don't mind?''

"Of course, not. Honey, you know I loved your mother, but she wasn't a saint. I always thought you should know about your Indian heritage, but she'd get so angry when I'd try to talk about it, I finally stopped bringing it up.''

"Was she ashamed of being an Indian?''

"No, I really don't believe she was. I think she faced an awful lot of discrimination, though, and she would have done anything to protect you from it.''

"Even give up her own family?''

"That's what she did, all right. She never would tell me why, either. She didn't seem to be angry with them, but...well, who knows what really goes on in someone else's family? All I can say for sure is, I never understood her attitude. Have you met any of her relatives?''

"I don't think so. There's one older lady who tells stories at the day-care center who gives me funny looks sometimes, but she's never said anything.''

"I know your mother had at least one sister and a brother. And I'm pretty sure her parents were still alive when she left. Maybe you should look them up.''

"I don't know, Daddy. Mama would be furious if she knew what I was doing. I feel like I'm betraying her memory, just being here.''

"You couldn't do that if you tried." Her father sighed. "Maggie, your mother chose the way she wanted to live. But she's gone now, and you need to make your own choices."

"I know, but—"

"But nothing. Her family is your family, too. When I'm gone, you won't have anyone from my side. And besides that, I hate to think of you living the rest of your life with so many unanswered questions. It's not fair to you."

"I'll, uh..." Her voice cracked, and her eyes suddenly filled with tears. "I'll have to think about it."

"You do that. And trust your instincts, honey. They've always been pretty darn good ones."

"I will. Thanks, Daddy. I love you."

"I love you, too—and remember, I'm so damn proud of you I can hardly stand it."

Maggie hung up the phone and wiped her streaming eyes with the back of one hand. Then she crawled off the bed and went into the bathroom to splash cold water on her face. Honestly, she rarely cried, and she didn't know why she'd started to now.

"It's just stress," she muttered, turning away from the mirror. "You've been under too much stress."

She suspected the reasons were a lot more complicated than stress, however. Her father was right in at least one respect. She *did* have a lot of unanswered questions about her mother. Maybe it was time she found some answers. But first, she was going to help those kids—or die trying.

Four

Deciding the occasion called for a professional appearance, Maggie dressed in her gray pinstripe suit the next morning. Then she slid the file Jackson had given her into her briefcase and drove to the school-district administration building. She introduced herself at the front desk, asked to see Mr. Reese and followed his secretary down a carpeted hallway to an office at the end. The secretary, Mrs. Adams, knocked on the door and opened it.

Before she could say anything, Maggie brushed past her into the large office. Flashing what she hoped was a brilliant smile, she crossed the room to the massive teak desk and extended a business card to the scowling man sitting behind it.

Edward Reese appeared to be in his mid-to-late fifties. He wore his gray hair in a bristly crew cut. A pair of black horn-rimmed glasses perched precariously in the middle of his sharp nose. His navy wool suit, white shirt and subdued tie fairly shrieked, "Conservative."

He accepted the card without speaking, glanced at it and did a double take—when he caught Congressman Baldwin's name, no doubt, Maggie thought cynically. Suddenly all smiles and cordiality, he heaved his considerable bulk out of his high-backed leather chair and shook the hand Maggie offered him.

"This is quite a surprise, Miss Schaeffer," he said. "Welcome to Whitehorn."

"Thank you, Mr. Reese." She glanced apologetically at his pristine desktop, then smiled at him again. "I'm sorry to interrupt your busy schedule."

"I'm never too busy for a member of Bill's staff." Reese waved toward a chair to Maggie's right. "Have a seat."

So it was *Bill*, was it? Maggie thought, mentally raising an eyebrow. Mr. Reese had obviously had years of practice at power games. Well, he would soon learn she was no amateur. She settled herself in the chair he had indicated and smoothed the hem of her skirt over her knees. Then she opened her briefcase and took out a legal pad and a pen.

"This shouldn't take long," she assured him, closing her briefcase and setting it on the floor. "I'm here on a fact-finding trip for the congressman. I need to ask you a few questions about the students from the Laughing Horse Reservation who attend your schools."

His eyes narrowing slightly, Reese leaned back in his chair. "Ask whatever you want."

"Thank you. How many Native American children are you presently serving, Mr. Reese?"

"That varies from week to week," he said. "The Indian families are frequently unstable. I'm afraid their children's attendance records tend to be rather hit-and-miss."

Ignoring the condescension in his smile, Maggie continued. "Could you give me an average number?"

"It's usually somewhere between four and five hundred."

"I see." Maggie dutifully wrote down the man's answer. "What percentage of your budget comes from federal funds for these children?"

"Approximately twenty percent."

Though Maggie knew the figure was closer to forty percent, she noted the answer without commenting. "Would you say the funds you receive for Native American children are adequate?"

Reese pushed his glasses up against his face and studied her for a moment. Maintaining a neutral expression, Maggie calmly returned his scrutiny.

"Frankly, Miss Schaeffer, they're not," he said. "Students who come from a deprived background, such as most of our Indian students have, need extra help and attention. We could do much more if our funding were increased, of course, but we do the best we can under the circumstances."

"I'm sure you do, Mr. Reese." Maggie made a show of consulting her legal pad. That should be about enough rope to let this pompous ass hang himself, she thought, giving him a disarming smile. "I just have a few more questions. Could you tell me what percentage of the Indian high school students actually graduate?"

Reese sighed and sadly shook his head. "I'm afraid only about twenty percent of them graduate."

"Eighty percent of them drop out?" Maggie widened her eyes in feigned astonishment. "My goodness, isn't that an awfully high rate? Even for a minority group?"

He raised his hands in a what-can-you-do? gesture. "As I said, we do our best for all of our students, but the Indian kids simply don't have the discipline they need to succeed academically. They start drinking and taking drugs. Some of them commit suicide. Many of the girls get pregnant. You, of all people, must know what it's like on a reservation, Miss Schaeffer."

"I'm learning, Mr. Reese," Maggie said, struggling to maintain a calm, professional tone after his obvious dig regarding her background. Perhaps she should inform this twit of her master's degree from Harvard. "In fact, I've spent quite a bit of time tutoring some of your high school students lately."

"Oh, really?"

"Yes, they have a marvelous after-school program out at Laughing Horse. The students have mentioned some of the problems they've been having in school." She leaned back and crossed her legs, settling more comfortably in order to enjoy wiping that smug smile off Reese's chubby face. "I'd be happy to share them, if you're interested."

Leaning forward, he rested his forearms on the desk. "Of course. We're always looking for ways to improve communication with our Indian students."

"Well, the first one is something I'm afraid I just don't understand." Opening her briefcase, Maggie pulled out the file Jackson had given her and studied the top sheet inside. "The kids told me they couldn't take typing because they didn't have access to equipment to do their homework. According to my figures, however, during the past five years, federal funds were allocated for fifty computers for White-horn High School. Is there some reason—"

"Excuse me," Reese said sharply, interrupting her. "Where did you get those figures?"

"From the Bureau of Indian Affairs," Maggie replied, trying for an innocent expression. "They keep very complete records, Mr. Reese. Would you like to compare them with yours?"

He pursed his lips and studied her, giving her the impression he was trying to calculate the wisdom of disputing the figures. She seriously doubted he wanted to open his own records for her inspection. Sure enough, he gave his head one decisive shake. "That won't be necessary."

"Well, as I was about to say, I don't understand why the Indian students aren't aware those computers are available for their use. Don't you have a computer lab at Whitehorn High?"

"Of course we do. The Indian kids just don't use it."

Maggie shot him a doubtful look. "The students I spoke with are all very concerned about getting their senior English research papers typed. As I understand it, that's a graduation requirement?"

Reese nodded.

"Well, I'm sure you understand that, because of their *deprived* backgrounds, none of those kids have computers at home," Maggie said. "Frankly, Mr. Reese, I would think that if you really wanted to increase the number of Indian graduates, your staff would make sure those students have plenty of opportunity and encouragement to use the equipment the taxpayers have provided for them."

Her thinly veiled sarcasm was not wasted on the superintendent. A dull red flush climbed up his face and disappeared into his crew cut. "Are you implying we *don't* want our Indian students to graduate?"

Maggie smiled. "Heavens, no, Mr. Reese. I'm sure a dedicated educator like yourself must be terribly embarrassed by this school district's abysmal performance in serving your Indian students."

"Now, see here," Reese said, thumping his index finger on the desk. "It's not the school district's fault. Those kids are lazy. They don't show up half the time, and when they do, they're not prepared for class."

Dropping all pretense of pleasantness, Maggie glared right back at him and brought out her second round of ammunition. "Perhaps they would *be* prepared for class, if they were allowed to check out library books, like the white students."

Beads of sweat popped out on Reese's forehead. "They never bring the books back—"

"*Never?* I doubt that's true. Tell me, do your white students *always* return library books?"

"Of course they don't." He shifted around in his chair, as if the plush seat had suddenly become uncomfortable. "However, we have a reasonable chance of collecting fines to pay for the books the white students don't return. That's not the case with our Indian students. Surely you can understand that we can't afford to give books away."

"Certainly. And I believe you've just given me an idea for solving these problems." Maggie pulled her briefcase back onto her lap and put away her things. Then she stood. "Thank you, Mr. Reese. You've been very helpful. I won't take up any more of your time."

He heaved himself to his feet again and braced his knuckles on the desk. "Wait a minute. What are you planning to do?"

"The federal government gives this school district twenty thousand dollars a year for new library books, specifically intended for Native American students," Maggie said, drawing herself up to her full height. "I'm going to recommend to the agencies involved that those funds go directly to the Northern Cheyenne tribal council. The same will be true of the equipment funds, and any other funds I find are being misappropriated."

"Misappropriated!"

"If you were a Native American parent, what would you call it?" Maggie demanded. "The children need books and computers. If you can't allow them access, we'll have to find another way to get it for them. The after-school program at the reservation has plenty of room for a library and a computer center."

"You can't do this!"

"Oh, but I *can,* and what I'm proposing is only the beginning," she said, digging the knife in a little deeper. "It's obvious your schools are not capable of meeting the Indian students' needs. There *are* other communities within busing distance. If this discrimination continues, the tribal council may well decide to make new arrangements for the children's education. Have a nice day, Mr. Reese."

With that, Maggie strolled out of the room, mentally dusting her hands every time she heard another outraged sputter coming from the superintendent's office. She nodded politely at the secretary, then continued unhurriedly out to her rental car.

The first fit of giggles erupted when she was safely inside the vehicle. Another followed, and then another and another, until she gave up trying to control them and whooped with laughter. Finally regaining enough composure to start the car and back out of the parking space, she headed for the res.

"Hey, Jackson, wait until you hear about this!"

Jackson looked up at the sound of Maggie's voice in the hallway outside his office, as did his Uncle Frank. She charged into the room a moment later, wearing one of her power suits and an exuberant smile that was bright enough to compete with the spring sunshine streaming through the window. Dropping her briefcase on the floor, she raised one fist in triumph and wrinkled her nose at him.

"Jackson, you should have been there!" she crowed. "It was great! The look on his face was absolutely priceless!"

Jackson exchanged an amused glance with his uncle. Maggie followed the direction of his gaze and blushed when she saw the older man.

"Oh, I'm sorry. I didn't realize you had company."

Frank Many Horses chuckled and muttered to Jackson, "You didn't notice she was cute, huh? You need glasses, nephew."

Ignoring the remark, Jackson introduced Maggie to his uncle.

"I've been wanting to meet you, Mr. Many Horses," she said, offering her hand, along with a sincere smile. "I've heard so many nice things about you."

While Frank shook her hand, Jackson cleared a stack of folders off another chair and pulled it over for Maggie. She shook her head when she saw it.

"I didn't mean to interrupt you. I'll come back later."

"It's all right, Maggie," Jackson said. "I told my uncle about your visit with Reese this morning. He's as interested in hearing what happened as I am."

Giving him a delightfully wicked grin, Maggie waggled her eyebrows at him. Then she was off, enthusiastically acting out her part and Reese's part until Jackson and Frank were laughing so hard they had to wipe tears from their eyes. She ended with a flourish, cheerfully bowing in response to their applause.

Jackson studied her glowing face and shining eyes and thought she was absolutely beautiful. That she had achieved such beauty by accomplishing something good for the tribe enhanced his attraction to her. He wished he could pull her into his arms and kiss her sensible pumps right off her feet.

"Can you really do all that?" Frank asked a moment later.

A sober expression came over Maggie's face, and Jackson appreciated her reluctance to promise something she might not be able to deliver.

"I'd need some authorization from the tribal council, but I'd be happy to try, Mr. Many Horses."

Chuckling, Frank slapped his knee and grinned at Jackson. "There will not be a problem with the council."

Jackson nodded in agreement. "I don't think we should rush into anything, though. Maggie's performance this morning is bound to shake things up. Why don't we wait and see what happens?"

"That won't help the seniors, if they don't finish their papers on time," Maggie said quietly. "And some of those kids have real college potential, Jackson."

She was right, of course. Which meant they needed a quick solution. Before he could come up with one, however, the telephone rang.

He answered it, listened for a moment, then covered the mouthpiece with one hand. "It's Congressman Baldwin, Maggie. You can take it in Frank's office, if you want."

"Thanks. I'll do that."

Frank shot him a worried look when she left. "What would you bet ol' Reese has already been on the phone to Washington?"

Jackson nodded grimly. The possibility of Maggie getting into trouble with her boss over this had occurred to him. He knew it also must have occurred to her, and he'd admired her willingness to get involved anyway. Still, he had to admit he was curious to see how she would handle it. He eyed the phone with longing, then sighed and hung it up.

Uncle Frank had fewer scruples about eavesdropping than he did, however. Jackson watched in amazement as his big, barrel-chested uncle tiptoed to the open door and stood to the left, his head cocked to one side. Since Jackson couldn't see his face, he had no idea what, if anything, his uncle could hear. The temptation to join him was too strong to resist. Taking a position on the right side of the doorway, he listened intently.

"*I* didn't create the problem, Congressman. Mr. Reese and his staff did. They're systematically discriminating against those students—and misappropriating federal funds."

Jackson grinned. Maggie's voice sounded cool and professional, but he'd tangled with her enough to recognize the note of steel that meant she was prepared to dig in her heels but good.

"I disagree, sir," she said. "As a federal employee, I believe it was my duty to intervene. I couldn't possibly have ignored the situation."

She was silent for a long moment. Jackson held his breath in anticipation of her next response.

"I know you have to stand for reelection next fall. Yes, I'm aware I'll be unemployed if you lose. But under the circumstances, I did the only ethical thing I could do." There was another pause. Then she said, "Do you want my resignation?"

Frank shot Jackson an appalled look. Jackson shrugged and shook his head. Maggie had gone into this willingly, and there was nothing they could do to help her.

"No, I don't want to resign, but I will *not* apologize to Mr. Reese. And I *will* resign if we don't take appropriate action here. The Northern Cheyenne are also your constituents, Congressman. They're only asking for justice."

The next pause was even longer. "All right. I appreciate your understanding. Thank you, sir. Yes, I'll be in touch. Goodbye, sir."

Racing back to their chairs like a couple of naughty schoolboys in danger of being caught, Jackson and Frank barely got themselves settled before Maggie walked back into the room. Her expression was thoughtful, but not fearful, Jackson decided after studying her face for a moment. Damn, but he was proud of her. The look in his uncle's eyes indicated he felt the same way.

Uncle Frank cleared his throat. "Is everything all right, Ms. Schaeffer?"

Smiling slightly at him, she nodded. "Everything's just fine, Mr. Many Horses."

"My friends call me Frank," he said gravely. "I would like it very much if you would also call me that."

Her smile brightened. "Thank you. Please call me Maggie." She picked up her briefcase. "Well, I'd better get back to work and leave you gentlemen to your meeting."

"We appreciate what you did for the kids this morning, Maggie," Jackson said.

She gave him another one of those wicked grins. "Believe me, it was *my* pleasure. And one way or another, I'm going to get the kids what they need."

Frank and Jackson eyed each other until they heard the outer door shut. Then Frank leaned back, laced his fingers together behind his head and stretched his long legs out in front of him.

"The Little Fed has a big heart, nephew," he said.

Jackson nodded. "So it would seem."

"Courage, too." Frank added. "And strong convictions."

"Yeah," Jackson said. "She sure didn't take any bull from Baldwin, did she?"

Frank chuckled. "Didn't sound like it. Why do you suppose he backed down?"

"From what Bennie Gonzales told me, I'd guess Baldwin knows she could get another job on Capitol Hill without breaking a sweat. Or maybe he was afraid she'd expose him if she quit."

Or maybe, Jackson silently reminded himself, Maggie and Baldwin were lovers. He didn't want to believe it, especially not now. But this whole assignment of hers still had a funny smell to it.

"Could be," Frank agreed. "She say anything about what she's gonna put in her report?"

"I haven't talked to her that much," Jackson said.

Frank shot him a knowing grin. "Yeah, I heard you've been hidin' out in the office a lot lately. You haven't been avoidin' that little gal, have ya?"

"I've been *busy,* Uncle."

"Uh-huh. Maybe *too* busy. I think she's got you runnin' scared."

"You're way off base," Jackson insisted, though he didn't expect his uncle to believe him. Hell, he wasn't too sure he believed himself. When it came to Maggie Schaeffer, he wasn't too sure about anything. "I'm not interested in her that way."

A touch of impatience entered Frank's voice. "It's time you took an interest in women again. Maggie looks like a pretty good one to start with, if you ask me."

"I didn't ask you, uncle."

"That's a fact. But women like her don't come along every day. She had lunch with the good doctor the other day. Kane looked plenty interested."

"Well, good for Kane," Jackson muttered, suddenly wanting to track down his old friend at the clinic and punch his face in. Aw, damn, he was really losing it.

Frank's eyes danced with amusement. "She didn't look all that interested in him, though. Not like she looked at you."

"Uncle, I know you mean well—"

Frank cut him off with an impatient snort. "That's right, I do. I want what's best for you and what's best for the tribe. A woman like Maggie could be one hell of an asset for us."

"I'd do a lot of things for the sake of the tribe," Jackson said. "But I wouldn't marry that woman just to—"

Frank interrupted him again. "Who said anything about marriage?"

"You did. You implied it, anyway."

"No, I didn't." Frank laughed and pointed a finger at Jackson. "You thought up that word all by yourself. And you were thinkin' it about Maggie, too."

Jackson pinched the bridge of his nose with his thumb and forefinger. "You're giving me a headache, uncle. Knock it off, will ya?"

Frank climbed to his feet and smiled down at Jackson. "All I meant was, it would be a good idea if you got to know her better. For the sake of the tribe, of course."

"I don't have time," Jackson grumbled. "I'm still doing your job, too, remember?"

"What if I came back to work?"

"Did Kane say you could?"

"Oh, sure. The doc told me that a week ago."

Delighted with the news, Jackson grinned. "You sly old wolf, why didn't you tell me?"

"Because you're getting good experience," Frank said, his tone completely serious. "And I'd like to know the tribe is in experienced hands if I drop over dead someday."

"You're not gonna do that, uncle."

"How do you know? How do any of us know when that time will come? I want you to be ready just in case."

"What makes you think the people would elect me to chair the tribal council? Most of them despised me for years."

"You've changed since you came back, Jackson. Their opinions have changed with you. The council would never have let you fill in for me if you hadn't won their respect."

"I don't know if I really want your job," Jackson said. "It's a real pain in the butt sometimes."

"That's for sure. But it makes you feel good to do things for the tribe, doesn't it?"

"Yeah," Jackson admitted. "It does."

"The Little Fed felt the same way this morning. I could see it in her eyes. We need somebody with her knowledge and enthusiasm."

"All right, uncle. When you come back to work, I'll spend more time with her. Just don't expect any big romance, okay?"

"Whatever you say, nephew." Chuckling, Frank headed for the doorway. "Whatever you say. I'll be in tomorrow."

Jackson tried to get back to work when his uncle left, but the effort was futile. After ten minutes of zero concentration, he threw down his pen in disgust, leaned back and propped his feet on the corner of the desk. It was time to do some serious thinking.

He was interested in Maggie Schaeffer, all right. And it was a hell of a lot more than a professional interest. The Little Fed just plain turned him on. With her smiles and her laughter. With her temper and stubbornness. With her intelligence and courage and convictions.

Realizing he hadn't even gotten around to thinking about her body yet made his chest feel tight. He took a deep breath to calm himself, but a sick sensation invaded his stomach. Damn it, he shouldn't *like* her so much.

His relationship with Nancy had started out the same way. The liking had grown into love, of course, but not even love had been enough to hold their marriage together. He'd been so hurt and humiliated when she left him, he'd wanted to crawl into a hole and never come back out. Only his anger at learning she'd never really loved him at all had kept him going. Not the real him, anyway. The Indian him.

The sick feeling in his gut came from realizing that Maggie fascinated him more than any woman he'd ever met, including his ex-wife. He might be able to fall in love with her, but she would never be able to love the real him, any more than Nancy had. Damn it, he wouldn't go through that again. He couldn't.

At the same time, he knew himself well enough to know that his attraction to her was not going to go away on its own. Avoiding her hadn't helped a bit. So, maybe Uncle Frank had the right idea. If he spent more time with Maggie, he might discover things about her that would turn him off.

If that didn't happen, well, he still didn't have to get romantically involved with her. He was thirty-six, not sixteen. He could control his libido, and he'd outgrown having affairs years ago. Since an affair was all he'd ever be able to have with Maggie, sex wouldn't be an issue between them. Hell, for all he knew, she wasn't even attracted to him.

Liar! a voice inside his head shouted at him. Jackson shrugged in dismissal. He'd caught her looking at him with more than professional interest a few times. He'd noticed that her eyes lit up whenever she saw him, and she smiled at him in a way that always made him aware of his masculinity. So what?

Maggie didn't strike him as a woman who gave herself lightly. She knew she'd be leaving in a few weeks. He doubted she was any more interested in starting an affair than he was. She'd probably deck him if he tried to kiss her.

That thought wasn't nearly as comforting as it should have been, but Jackson figured that was just his ego talking. He'd already promised his uncle he would get to know Maggie better, and he would. He might even allow himself to develop a friendship with her. But he wouldn't go one step farther than that. He just couldn't afford to do otherwise.

So why did he still have this awful, sinking feeling in his gut that the decision might not be his alone to make?

Five

After leaving Jackson's office, Maggie grabbed a set of casual clothes she'd stashed in the car and changed in the women's rest room at the tribal center restaurant. The aromas of french fries and hamburgers sizzling on the grill made her stomach rumble. She glanced at her watch, noting with surprise that it was almost noon. Heavens, where had the morning gone?

She hurried back out to her car, dumped her suit and pumps into the back seat, then returned to the restaurant. Three people nodded and smiled at her as she seated herself in a booth by the window, and with a jolt she realized she was beginning to feel as if she belonged here. That was silly, of course. She would be going back to Washington in a few weeks to resume her career and her "real" life.

And yet, when she considered it for another moment, the idea of belonging at Laughing Horse didn't seem quite so ridiculous. These people didn't see someone "different" when they looked at her; they simply saw a woman who looked like themselves. She was one of them. It was a liberating concept, in a place few people would have associated with freedom.

Maggie glanced around, met with more nods and smiles, and felt a warm glow ignite deep in her chest. These people were *her* people. She'd known that intellectually from the beginning, but this was the first time she'd actually *felt* it.

That was why she'd taken up the teenagers' cause. Why she'd felt such a strong sense of accomplishment when she told Jackson and Frank about her morning's work. Why she'd risked her job when her boss reprimanded her.

Though she rarely held a grudge, the memory of that phone call still rankled. She hadn't thought Congressman Baldwin could ever be so insensitive to any of his constituents' needs, not to mention their civil rights. But after what he'd said to her, she had to wonder if perhaps Jackson was right to be suspicious of Baldwin's sudden interest in the tribe's welfare.

A waitress came and took her order. While she waited for her cheeseburger and fries, Maggie tried to sort out her troubled thoughts. She had always considered herself a loyal employee. She'd thoroughly enjoyed researching the political issues the congressman dealt with, and she'd seldom questioned how he would use that information or how his actions would affect peoples' lives. Now, for the first time in her career, she had to question both of those things.

Just where did her own responsibilities for what happened in the political process begin and end? And where did her loyalties lie in this instance? With Congressman Baldwin and the U.S. Government? Or with the Northern Cheyenne? If they were really *her* people . . .

"Hey, the food's not *that* bad here," an amused male voice said from somewhere above her head.

Startled, Maggie looked up and found herself gazing into Jackson Hawk's dark, dark eyes. Her stomach did a little flip that had nothing to do with hunger. Sweet, merciful heaven, when he smiled, he was one handsome hunk of man.

"Mind if I join you?" he asked.

Maggie gestured toward the opposite bench seat in invitation. "By all means."

Suddenly nervous, she cleared her throat, then sipped from the glass of ice water the waitress had brought her. Jackson's long legs bumped against her knees as he settled himself in the booth. The resulting jolt of sexual awareness raised her temperature five degrees. She took another sip. Oh, this was absurd. She saw handsome men every day on Capitol Hill without getting hot and bothered.

Propping his forearms on the table, he leaned closer. She caught a whiff of a clean, outdoorsy scent. His braids hung down in front of his shoulders, and she had a sudden urge to reach out, tug off the leather strings tied to the ends and see what his hair looked like unbound. Judging from the plump, shiny coils of his braids, she suspected it would be thick and smooth. It would probably glide through her fingers like warm—

"You were on top of the world this morning," he said. "What put that frown on your face?"

She shook her head, trying to dispel the pleasurable, caressing effect his deep, quiet voice had on her ears. Lord, it made her think of darkened bedrooms and murmured intimacies between lovers. *Get a grip,* she told herself, praying he hadn't already noticed her reaction to him.

Jackson had been friendlier than usual since yesterday, but she couldn't forget he'd already called her stupid, naive, and an apple. She doubted he even thought of her as a woman. It would be absolutely humiliating if he knew she was sitting here lusting after his bod.

"Nothing important," she said. "I was just thinking about something."

He looked as if he wanted to question her further, but the arrival of her lunch provided a distraction. Jackson ordered an identical meal, then sat back and watched while Maggie piled condiments on her cheeseburger. His intent regard made her feel jittery inside and turned her fingers into uncoordinated sticks at the ends of her hands.

"I liked your uncle," she said, hoping to distract him again. "Is he your mother's brother, or your father's?"

"My mother's. He liked you, too."

"Good. I want to interview him, when he's well enough."

"He's well enough now," Jackson said. "In fact, he's coming back to work tomorrow. That's why I tracked you down. I've got a proposition for you."

"Oh, really?" she asked, raising an eyebrow at his word choice. "Would you care to explain that?"

Jackson grinned and pointed at her plate. "Go ahead and eat while it's hot, Maggie. Mine'll be coming in a minute. I'll talk while you chew."

She dunked a french fry in a puddle of ketchup and popped it into her mouth, then looked at him expectantly.

"Since Uncle Frank's coming back, I'll have some free time," he said. "You haven't seen much of the res beyond the tribal center. I'd be happy to drive you around, so you can see the rest of it and meet more of the people. Are you interested?''

An hour ago, she would have eagerly accepted his offer. Given the way her attraction to him appeared to be getting out of hand, however, she wasn't at all sure she wanted to be cooped up in a vehicle with him for hours at a time. On the other hand, she needed to explore the outer reaches of the reservation. She'd probably spend half her time being lost if she tried to travel those lonely back roads alone.

For heaven's sake, she chided herself, dithering about this was ridiculous. She was an adult, and a professional. She could handle this...infatuation or hormonal surge or whatever the heck was wrong with her. The way they tended to fight with each other, she'd be over it in no time.

"Yes, I'm interested," she said. "Thank you."

"You're welcome. We'll start tomorrow afternoon."

The waitress arrived with Jackson's order. He put his cheeseburger together and bit into it enthusiastically. A drop of mustard squirted out the side and clung to the corner of his mouth. Maggie stared at that little yellow dot and gulped.

She'd never thought there was anything even slightly erotic about watching someone eat, but at this moment, she wanted to lick that drop of mustard away and then kiss him. Long and hard. Until he gasped for air. No doubt about it, she was losing her mind.

And then, bold as any hooker in downtown D.C., Jackson looked up, winked at her, and went back to munching his burger. He knew! Oh, God, the wretched man knew exactly what she'd been thinking all along! She didn't know whether to laugh or cry or howl with mortification.

A fourth option—hitting him over the head with the ketchup bottle—held enormous appeal. Unfortunately, Al Black Bird, one of the tribal policemen she had interviewed, was sitting at a nearby table. She didn't particularly want to tangle with all six foot six and two hundred and fifty pounds of him.

Jackson continued to eat as if nothing unusual had passed between them. Promising herself she'd get even one of these days, Maggie picked up her own burger and forced her concentration onto her meal. When they were finishing, a short, wiry-looking white man wearing a dark gray uniform entered the restaurant. The room suddenly fell silent as everyone turned to stare at him. His face flushed beneath his curly blond hair, but he murmured something to the cashier, then walked quickly to Maggie's booth.

"Excuse me, ma'am," he said, "are you Maggie Schaeffer?"

"Yes, I am."

"My name's Harvey." He pointed to the white letters embroidered on his shirt.

Hoping to ease his obvious tension, Maggie smiled. "It's nice to meet you, Harvey. May I help you?"

He pulled an envelope out of his hip pocket and handed it to her. "I have a delivery for you, ma'am. If you'll sign that top form, and tell me where you want the stuff, I'll unload it for you and be on my way."

Mystified, Maggie opened the envelope and found a bill of lading from Conway Electronics in Billings. She gasped at the listed inventory, then quickly flipped the top sheet over and read the note her father must have faxed from Denver to the store. Barely suppressing a delighted whoop, she stuffed the papers back in the envelope and grinned at Jackson, who was staring at her with a perplexed frown.

Then she stood, stuck one hand out and wiggled her fingers at him. Lowering her voice, because everyone else was staring at her, too, and listening with avid interest, she said, "Your keys, Jackson. I need to get into the Indian school."

"What for?"

"I don't want to explain it here," she said. "It's sort of a surprise for the kids."

"Do you mind if I tag along?"

"You'll get put to work if you do," she warned him.

He slid out of the booth and plunked his Stetson on his head. "I'll take my chances."

Harvey headed for the exit as if he couldn't get out of there fast enough. Maggie followed him, leaving Jackson to bring up the rear.

"Hey, Maggie, what about your check?" the cashier called as she hurried past.

Maggie looked over her shoulder and grinned at the woman. "Give it to Jackson, Gretchen." It wasn't much of a payback for that outrageous wink, but for now it would have to do.

Jackson paid both checks, then left the restaurant, chuckling to himself. He knew exactly why she'd stiffed him with her bill, and he figured he deserved it.

He really shouldn't have winked at her like that, but he hadn't been able to resist. How anyone with a face as expressive as hers had ever survived in Washington was beyond him. Her reaction to their knees' bumping under the table had confirmed his suspicion that she was attracted to him and stroked his ego at the same time. The fun part had been watching her try to hide what she was feeling. And fail miserably.

If he had any smarts at all, he wouldn't have found it so amusing. Or so endearing. But, hey, it was no big deal. Just a little harmless teasing between friends, right?

Ignoring the jeering inner voice that shouted *Liar!* at him again, Jackson shoved his sunglasses on his face and left the restaurant. Maggie and the delivery man stood beside a long white van parked at the curb, talking about the great spring weather. When Jackson joined them, they all piled into the front seat of the vehicle, with Maggie in the middle. She gave the driver directions, then shot Jackson an excited grin.

"You want to tell me what this is all about?" he asked.

"Computers." She handed him the envelope she'd received from Harvey. "Take a look."

Holy smokes, Jackson thought as he studied the bill of lading. There must be thousands of dollars' worth of equipment in the back of this rig. Tens of thousands. Then he flipped over the top sheet and found a note that explained the situation.

Dear Maggie,

Kids who work as hard in school as the ones you described to me last night deserve a helping hand. The goodies are for the after-school program. Let me know if they need anything else. Take care of yourself, honey, and God bless.

Dad

Playing for time, Jackson carefully folded the papers, poked them back into the envelope and handed it to Maggie. She smiled at him expectantly. Damn. She obviously thought he'd be as delighted as she was to get this equipment for the kids. He wished he could be, if only to keep that smile on her face.

The driver pulled over in front of the Indian school. Jackson leaned across Maggie and said, "Sit tight for a minute, Harvey. We need to talk about something."

He climbed down and offered Maggie his hand. Shooting him a wary look, she scrambled out of the van without his assistance. Her refusal to touch him was irritating, but he clamped down on his annoyance and walked toward the building, turning to face her when he was sure they wouldn't be overheard.

Her chin raised to a challenging angle, she propped her fists on her hips. "All right, what's the matter?"

Oh, brother, Jackson thought grimly, here we go again. Aloud, he said, "I'm not sure the tribal council will want to accept this stuff."

She gave him a perplexed frown. "Why on earth wouldn't they? It's just a gift. And a pretty darned nice one."

Jackson shrugged one shoulder. "Sometimes gifts come with strings attached. We've learned that the hard way."

Her frown deepened. "When my father gives a gift, that's exactly what it is, Jackson. A *gift*. He doesn't expect anything in return. What could he want from the tribe, anyway?"

"He's into motels, isn't he? Other tribes have them. Maybe he wants to build one here."

"Would it be so awful if he did? Laughing Horse could certainly use one, and it would bring in jobs and tourist money."

"Yeah, it probably would," Jackson said. "But that isn't the kind of decision we make lightly, Maggie. We have to consider the negative effects it might have, too."

"Such as?"

"More garbage and sewer problems. Strangers coming onto the res, bringing in drugs, and who knows what else?"

She rolled her eyes at him. "Oh, come on, Jackson, don't you think you're reaching a little bit? Why are you really worried about this? Because my dad's white?"

Jackson shrugged again. "That's part of it. Rich white guys usually try to take something for nothing, not give it. We've learned that the hard way, too."

"My father is a kind, generous man. He would never try to force a business deal on anyone."

"How can you be so sure of that?"

"I grew up with the man!" She glared at him for a second, then gave her head an impatient shake. "All right, think about it logically. Dad doesn't need any more motels. Certainly not enough to try to bribe an Indian tribe with a few computers."

"A *few?*" Jackson jerked his thumb toward the van. "I saw the list, Maggie. There must be twenty computers out there."

"And printers, software, modems and CD-ROM players," she agreed with a fond smile—for her father, no doubt. "If I know Dad, there's probably a case of computer paper and extra printer ribbons out there, too. Believe me, he can afford it."

"But why would he give all that stuff away?"

"That's just the way he is. He was always donating things to the schools I attended."

"Why would he do this for *us,* Maggie? He's never been here. He doesn't know anyone on this reservation but you. Why would he care that much about a bunch of Indian kids he's never met?"

"Has it ever occurred to you that you might have a problem with bigotry, Jackson?" She exhaled an angry huff, then shook her head again and continued before he could defend himself.

"Dad's always tried to help people take charge of their own lives. Half of his executive staff didn't have high school diplomas when they started working for him. I couldn't begin to tell you how many employees he's sent to college over the years. He never cared what color they were, either.''

"Look, I didn't mean to offend you, or accuse your father of anything,'' Jackson said slowly. "It's just pretty damned unusual for anyone to be so generous.''

"Well, he's a pretty damned unusual man. Perhaps you should meet him before you judge him the way you judged me.''

Jackson winced inwardly when that remark struck home, but he refused to let her sidetrack him. "It's not that simple.''

"Why not? You've accepted corporate donations before, haven't you?''

"Yeah, and sometimes that's hurt us more than it's helped us. We've depended on the white man's charity for too long. At some point we've got to start depending on ourselves and solve our own problems.''

"And you think *this* is that point?'' she demanded.

"It's as good as any,'' Jackson shot back. "I don't want these kids to think all they have to do to get what they want is whine to some rich white guy about how poor they are. I want them to understand they've got to work for it.''

"That's a noble sentiment, but how are they going to work if they don't have the skills to get jobs that will pay them a living wage?'' Jabbing her finger toward the van, she said, "There are *jobs* in those boxes. And not just for the kids. Some of the unemployed adults could learn to use those computers while the kids are in school.''

"It's still charity, damn it. We'll never regain our pride as a people until we learn to provide for our own needs. There's a principle involved here.''

"If you want to use a principle, try the one that says if you give a man a fish, you feed him for one day. If you teach a man to fish, you feed him for a lifetime. That's all my dad's trying to do here. And I don't think it's the people's pride you're worried about, Jackson. It's your *own*.''

"That's not true.'' He shoved his hands into his pockets to stop himself from shaking her senseless. Why the hell did she always have to make such a big deal out of everything?

"It's a question of values. *Indian* values, which you obviously can't understand."

"Because I'm an apple?" She snorted in disgust. "Please try to explain it to me, and I'll do my best to follow along."

"It's looking for a quick fix. Taking the easy way out. Whatever you call it, it does nothing to build character."

"You think poverty *does?*"

Jackson closed his eyes for a moment and sucked in a deep breath. Beating down this woman's arguments was like swatting mosquitoes in a swamp. Every time you squashed one, three more appeared to suck your blood.

"The point I'm trying to make," he said, opening his eyes and glaring at her, "is that *real* Indians, *real* Northern Cheyenne, are more concerned with values and character and the long-term survival of our tribe than we are with chasing the almighty dollar. That's why we haven't built a casino here. Another good example is the way our cousins over at the Lame Deer reservation handled the coal companies a few years ago."

Maggie crossed her arms over her chest and leaned one shoulder against the building. "What did they do?"

"They weren't much better off economically than we are now, but they're sitting on one of the world's biggest coal deposits," Jackson explained. "Nobody paid any attention to it until the energy crisis hit back in the seventies. Then, all of a sudden, the coal companies and power companies started offering them millions of dollars for the privilege of strip-mining on the reservation. Can you imagine how tempting it was for them to grab that money and let Mother Earth take care of herself?"

Maggie nodded "But they didn't?"

Jackson shook his head. "Nope. There was a big legal hassle, because the tribal council had already signed leases, on the advice of the BIA. But when they saw what was happening to the environment a few miles north of the reservation, at Colstrip, the tribe raised hell until they got those leases canceled. If they ever do develop their energy resources, it'll be on their own terms, and in a way that won't destroy their land."

"That's fascinating," Maggie said. "But I still don't see why you're being so pigheaded about the computers. They're not going to harm the environment or anything else."

"It's the *principle*, Maggie. Accepting this huge gift will not help us learn to manage our own resources, any more than taking the coal companies' money would have helped our cousins learn to manage theirs. If our kids need computers, then the tribe should find a way to provide them."

She studied him for so long, he began to hope he'd finally gotten through to her. Then she dashed his hopes with a firm shake of her head.

"You couldn't find time to confront Ed Reese for the kids. How long will they have to wait for the tribe to help them? Until it's too late to graduate with the rest of their class?"

"Probably. But it won't be the end of the world. They can get their GED certificates and still go to college."

"Oh, yeah? And how will they feel about it, Jackson? Don't you think they'll feel cheated? Damn it, it's not fair."

"Grow up, will you?" Jackson snapped. "Life is rarely fair for anyone, much less Indians."

"But this time it could be," she insisted. "Those kids have *earned* their diplomas. Denying them the chance to walk across that stage with their classmates is only going to teach them that their hard work *won't* be rewarded. The only thing it will motivate them to do is give up. Can't you see that?"

Jackson didn't want to, but when she put it that way, he had to admit she might have a point. Graduation night was always one of the worst nights of the year for underage drinking on the res. Last year, five Laughing Horse kids had been killed in an alcohol-related car accident. Grudgingly giving in to the inevitable, he fished his keys out of his pocket and beckoned to Harvey to start unloading.

"All right," he said as he unlocked the door. "You win this time, but don't solicit any other donations unless you clear it with the tribal council first."

"No problem. I didn't solicit *this* one. But if I ever get the urge, I'll leave it up to the *real* Indians. God knows I wouldn't want to taint anyone with my inferior white values."

Surprised at the pain he detected behind her sarcasm, Jackson shot her a quick look. Oh, man, her chin was trembling, and her long eyelashes were moving at top speed, undoubtedly blinking back tears. She always fought him so fiercely, he tended to forget the possibility of hurting her feelings.

She turned her back to him, yanked the door open wide and flipped down the doorstop for Harvey. Then she stepped inside, switched on the lights and marched down the hall to the tutoring center. Cursing under his breath, Jackson hurried after her.

When he entered the room, she was systematically pulling chairs away from the study tables. He cleared his throat. If she heard him, she ignored him.

"Look," he said, approaching her with a tentative smile. "I didn't mean anything personal."

She shoved a chair into his path, but didn't speak. He set the chair aside and, stepping closer, put his hand on her shoulder. She jerked away as if he'd stabbed her with a needle.

"Hey," he protested. "I'm trying to apologize for whatever I said that hurt your feelings."

Refusing even to look at him, she yanked another chair out of the way. "Forget it. Thanks for unlocking the door. I'll handle things from here."

"You said you were going to put me to work."

"I changed my mind."

"It's not like you to hold a grudge, Maggie."

"How would you know?"

"We've fought before, and you never did. It's one of the things I like about you."

She shot him a disbelieving glare. "Yeah, right. Why don't you be honest, Mr. Hawk, and admit you don't like me at all?"

"Because it's not true." He walked around the end of the table, smiling to himself when she straightened to her full height and faced him, like a boxer bracing for the next round. Well, fine. He'd rather have her come out swinging at him than see her in tears. "You want to tell me what I said that upset you so much?"

"No. Go away. I've got work to do."

As if to prove her point, Harvey entered the room, pushing a dolly loaded with boxes. "Where do you folks want these?"

Maggie pointed to the nearest wall. "Just stack them over there, Harvey."

Jackson waited for the other man to leave, then approached her again. "Come on, out with it. It won't be much fun touring the res together if you're mad at me."

"I've changed my mind about that, too. Thanks for the offer, but I'd prefer to drive myself."

"Don't even think about it," he said, feeling his temper starting to heat up again. "This is rough, desolate country. You've got no business being out there alone."

She opened her mouth as if she would argue the point. Fortunately, Al Black Bird walked into the room, cutting her off before she could get out a syllable.

"What's goin' on in here?" the big tribal policeman asked.

Maggie gave him a brief explanation, then went back to banging chairs around.

"Did you need something, Al?" Jackson asked.

Al tipped his baseball cap back and stuck his hands in his jeans pockets. "Yeah. Somethin's happened I think you'd better be in on, Jackson."

"What is it?"

Al glanced at Maggie, then raised an eyebrow at Jackson, as if asking whether or not he should talk in front of her. Jackson nodded.

"George Sweetwater was huntin' rabbits in the brush about ten miles past your place this mornin'," Al said. "He found some bones out there, and he thinks they're human."

Staring at his friend, Jackson said, "Human bones?"

"Yeah. An arm and a hand." Al shrugged his beefy shoulders. "George said they look like they've been there for years. There's an old burial ground out that way, but I couldn't tell from his description whether the bones came from there. If they didn't, we could be lookin' at a homicide.''

"Any idea who it would be?"

"Nope. We don't have any outstanding missing-persons reports on file. But I think you should come check it out with me. It never hurts to have a credible witness, you know?''

"Go ahead, Jackson," Maggie said quietly. "I can handle the rest of this.''

He didn't doubt she could handle damn near anything, but it didn't feel right to leave her with this dispute unresolved.

"Really," she insisted. "I'll just set up a couple of the computers, and let Sara and the kids help with the rest.''

Al lumbered to the doorway. "Let's go, Hawk. I want to get out there before the Feds do. I don't want them touchin' anything until we can figure out if those bones belong to an ancestor. I want to call in your old pal, Tracy Roper, 'cause I know she'll shoot straight with us.''

"I'll be right there," Jackson answered. Turning to Maggie, he said, "Let's meet at my office at one tomorrow. We can finish sorting this out then, okay?''

He walked to the doorway and turned for one last look at Maggie. She stood there, staring at him with those big dark eyes of hers. There was a wounded sort of vulnerability about her that reached down into his chest and gave his heartstrings a hard yank. He gulped, searching for something to say that would make things all right between them again.

He finally settled for an unsatisfying but practical warning. "Don't turn on more than three computers at one time until we can get an electrician in here to check out the wiring.''

Her only response was a nod. Biting back a frustrated curse, Jackson left. Al waited for him at the front door, grinning like he'd just won a medal for marksmanship.

"Whoo-whee," he said. "That was some tension between you and the Little Fed in there.''

Jackson brushed past the policeman. "Shut up, Al."

Al caught up with him in two strides. "Oooh, touchy, are we? You got the hots for her, or what?"

Jackson scowled at him over the top of the four-wheel-drive wagon that served as a cruiser. "Mind your own damn business."

Al slid into the driver's seat and fired the engine while Jackson climbed in on the other side. "Can't say as I blame you," he said, as if Jackson hadn't spoken. "That Maggie's somethin' else. I really like the way she smiles, you know? Kinda lights up the whole room. She sure wasn't smilin' at you, though, buddy. Whatcha do to her?"

"Damned if I know," Jackson muttered. Then he put on his sunglasses, dragged the brim of his hat down over his face, crossed his arms over his chest and slid down until his head rested on the back of the seat.

"Hey, if you don't wanna talk, all you have to do is say so." Chuckling, Al grabbed the microphone, radioed his position to the office and drove away from the curb.

Jackson tuned him out, his thoughts immediately returning to Maggie. Damn it, he knew better than to let a woman manipulate him with tears. So why did the memory of Maggie struggling not to shed them make him feel so stinkin' guilty? Especially when she was too immature to just come out and tell him what he'd done? Talk about manipulative!

But the hurt in her eyes and in her voice had gone deeper than that. Just picturing the way she'd looked before he left made him feel like he'd kicked a defenseless puppy. Which was about the most ridiculous notion he could imagine.

Maggie was hardly defenseless. She'd taken on both Reese and Baldwin this morning, and she'd still had plenty of steam left to rake him over the proverbial coals. That woman could take on a tank and win, for God's sake.

The funny thing was, in the everyday scheme of things, she didn't come across as a combative sort of person. Too many people on the res liked her for that to be true. In fact, other than their first meeting, when he'd deliberately provoked her, the only times he'd seen her temper flare had been connected with her efforts to help the teenagers.

He could hardly blame her for that; in fact, he admired her protectiveness toward those kids tremendously. Because of it, he'd actually started to look forward to showing her the rest of the res, in spite of his ambivalent feelings toward her.

Maybe his ambivalence was the key to this whole mess. He'd been trying so hard not to like her more than he should, he'd convinced her he didn't like her at all. Aw, hell, now that he thought about it, it wasn't hard to see how she'd come to that conclusion.

He'd treated her like she was nothing but trouble on the hoof from the beginning. Even when it had become perfectly clear that she was only trying to help, he'd questioned everything she did, not to mention the integrity of her boss and her father. And he'd been damn suspicious and condescending, because . . . well, because he was scared spitless to trust his reactions to her.

It hadn't *really* been necessary to make such a big stink about those computers. While he believed wholeheartedly in the principle of self-reliance, he could bend a principle when circumstances warranted it; building self-esteem in the tribe's young people warranted almost any amount of bending.

He could have just said thank-you on behalf of the tribe and accepted Maggie's father's generous gift. But had he? No, he'd thrown it back in her face, and made all kinds of nasty remarks about a man she obviously loved a lot.

It was time to stop acting like a jackass. As Uncle Frank had said, women like Maggie didn't come along every day. He'd fought his attraction to her for as long as he could, but he might as well admit it was no use.

Maggie challenged him, intrigued him, infuriated him and confused the hell out of him. If he allowed himself to get close to her, she might well break his heart. But damn it all, whenever he was with her, he felt more alive than he had in years. And somehow, some way, he just had to find out what made her tick.

Six

When the hollow sound of Jackson's bootheels hitting the tile floor had faded away, Maggie swallowed at the lump in her throat. Then she gritted her teeth, squared her shoulders and went back to work. She would *not* cry over that man. And she was *not* going to tour the res with him, either. She'd rather get lost out in the boondocks and never be heard from again than accept the tiniest scrap of help from that arrogant jerk.

By tomorrow she would have her emotions back under control, and she'd tell him what he could do with his proposition and where he could put his *real* Indian values. With anger fueling her energy, she rearranged the room, set up three of the systems and loaded the software onto the computers' hard drives, finishing as the school buses arrived from Whitehorn.

A moment later, the building's main doors crashed open and an excited babble of voices filled the hallway. Wanda Weasel Tail burst into the room, followed by a herd of other teenagers.

"Miss Schaeffer! Miss Schaeffer!" Wanda called, gleefully racing over to Maggie. "You'll never guess what happened today. We got library books!"

"I don't know what you did to those librarians," Nina Walks Tall said, "but I wish I'd a been there to see it."

Janie Brown Bear dumped her backpack on the big round study table, headed after the other girls, then stopped and did a double take when she spotted one of the computers. Her mouth fell open, and an awed expression came over her face as she looked around the room. "Hey, where did all this stuff come from?"

The other girls stopped chattering for a second, shooting irritated glances at Janie. She pointed at a gleaming monitor. Wanda and Nina followed the direction of her finger. Then, as if they'd communicated some signal only teen-agers could hear, all three girls started jumping up and down and shrieking in delight.

More kids rushed in to see what was going on. Their sur-prised and happy shouts brought people running from all over the building. Luckily, Sara Lewis was among the new-comers. After assuring the crowd that everyone would eventually have a chance to use the machines, she shooed out the folks who were supposed to be somewhere else with the skill of a born organizer.

Then she organized those who remained into a work de-tail to set up the remaining systems. When Maggie relayed Jackson's warning about the wiring, Sara called the em-ployment office at the tribal headquarters. Two unem-ployed electricians arrived in short order.

For the next two hours, Maggie hurried from group to group, checking connections, demonstrating how to load software and marveling at how well the kids cooperated with each other. They were so appreciative and eager to learn, she wanted to hug them all. Their excitement over the new equipment provided a sorely needed balm to the emotional wounds Jackson had inflicted.

By the time the last reluctant straggler left for home at dusk, however, she felt wrung out. She wanted a hot shower and solitude. Hours and hours of solitude, and at least twenty-four hours of sleep. She nearly groaned out loud when Sara suggested a celebration as they walked out of the building together.

"I'm really whipped, Sara," Maggie said. "Would you be offended if I asked for a rain check?"

"After what you've accomplished today, you couldn't offend me if you tried," Sara replied with a sympathetic grin. "As long as you promise to tell me what you did to Reese. I want to hear every gory detail."

Maintaining a deadpan expression, Maggie shrugged. "Oh, it was nothing. I just walked into his office, shoved a gun in his face, and he caved right in."

Sara laughed. "Yeah, right. Do you realize all the teach-ers in Whitehorn are wondering why they suddenly got orders to take their Indian kids to the library today? Some of my friends called me to talk about it. And I'll bet we can get the school district to set up evening or weekend keyboarding classes out here for the kids and the adults. This is really going to open up some opportunities, Maggie. It's just wonderful.''

"I'm glad I could help, but it wasn't that big of a deal."

"It was a very big deal to the kids," Sara said. "Now, tell me, where did all of that stuff come from?''

Fearing Sara would react as Jackson had if she knew the source of the new equipment, Maggie said, "It was a corporate donation, Sara. I just happened to mention the kids to a C.E.O. friend of mine, and he sent the computers right out.''

"We should all have such friends," Sara said with a grin. "You'd better watch your step, though. You've made a big impression on the kids. I wouldn't be surprised to see every one of those girls walk in with short hair tomorrow.''

Recalling her conversation with Jackson, Maggie winced. "Lord, I hope not. I'm not exactly great role model material for Indian kids.''

"How can you say that?" Sara demanded, scowling at her. "You gave them hope, and showed them one person can make a difference. Sounds like pretty good role model material for any kind of kids to me.''

Wishing she'd kept her mouth shut, Maggie shook her head dismissively and forced a smile. Sara was not about to be put off so easily, however. Pausing beside her car, she studied Maggie through narrowed eyes.

"You should be higher than a kite. The library books were a major victory by themselves, but to get the computers, too, is a miracle.''

"Look, I've really got to go," Maggie said. "The road to Whitehorn's bad enough in the daytime. I'd rather not tackle it when it's any darker than it already is.''

Sara grasped Maggie's arm when she would have turned away. "Wait a minute. What's wrong, Maggie?''

"It's nothing. Really. I've just had a long day."

Though she raised a doubtful eyebrow, Sara released Maggie's arm. "Okay. I can understand that, I guess. But if you ever want to talk or anything, you know where to find me."

"Yeah. Thanks, Sara. I'll see you later."

Maggie headed on toward the tribal center. The last rays of the sunset had faded to a deep navy blue, and the stars were coming out. Maggie slowed to look at them, suddenly feeling terribly small and alone. Seeing her little rental car sitting all by itself where she'd parked it in front of the tribal offices this morning reinforced the feeling.

Sara honked and waved when she drove away from the school, dispelling Maggie's blue mood for a moment. She waved back, then nearly had a coronary when she turned around and saw a man step out of a doorway on the other side of the street. She was always ultracareful about being out alone at night in Washington, but Laughing Horse had such a small-town ambience, she hadn't thought much about her personal security.

She stopped walking, hoping he would go the other way. The man didn't. He looked big and dark, and his face was obscured by the deep shadows cast by the brim of his Stetson. And he was walking straight toward her, as if he meant business. Adrenaline surging, she backed up a step, then another, struggling to stay calm and remember what she'd learned in the self-defense class she took last year.

"Relax, Maggie, it's me," Jackson said.

She halted her retreat, pressing one hand over her heart, as if that would still its frantic pounding. He stopped less than a foot in front of her, tipped back his hat and looked down at her, his forehead creased with concern. "Are you all right?"

"Fine. You just scared the devil out of me," she said with a shaky laugh. She took two steps back to put a more comfortable distance between them. "What are you doing here so late?"

"Waiting for you."

"Why?"

He spread his feet farther apart and stuck the tips of his fingers into his back pockets. "I wanted to talk to you."

"Oh, please," she said. "Couldn't it wait? I don't have enough energy to fight with you again today."

"I said talk, not fight."

"We don't seem to be able to do one without doing the other." She sidestepped around him and made a beeline for her car.

He followed her, easily catching up with his longer stride. "Yeah, I know. I wanted to apologize for that."

Maggie shot him a skeptical look, then stuck her key in the door lock. "Don't bother. I know you don't like me, and that's your privilege, Jackson. Believe me, I can handle it."

"It didn't look that way to me," he said. "When I left, you were damn near ready to cry."

Nuts. She'd hoped he hadn't noticed. "I got over it."

"Well, I didn't." Raising one hand, he brushed the backs of his knuckles across her cheek. "I felt guilty all afternoon."

She pushed his hand away, not because his touch felt bad, but because it felt too good. "I cry sometimes when I'm really angry. It's embarrassing, but it's no big problem."

"You weren't just angry. You were hurt."

"Even apples have feelings, Mr. Hawk."

He smiled at that. "So do bigots, Ms. Schaeffer. You know, when we start arguing, neither one of us knows when to shut up. Were you ever on a debating team?"

His question pulled a reluctant grin from her. "How did you know?"

"Just a wild guess." He chuckled, then gazed at her for a long moment, his expression turning sober. "But you've got one thing wrong, Maggie. I don't dislike you."

She rolled her eyes at him. "Give me a break. I don't feel like getting into that again now, so—"

He laid one finger across her lips. "This is one of those times you should shut up. I tried to tell you this before I left, but you weren't ready to listen. The truth is, I like you a lot. I'm even . . . attracted to you."

Maggie raised her eyebrows in disbelief. Chuckling again, Jackson traced her upper lip with his forefinger. Soft as dandelion fluff, his touch left a trail of tingling nerve endings behind it.

"You don't believe me?" He stepped closer, crowding her against the side of the car, framing her face between his big hands when she tried to lean away from him. "Well, I guess I'll have to prove it to you."

Staring in stupefaction, she watched his head slowly descend, the brim of his hat blocking out what little light there was on the deserted street. Though she'd literally seen it coming, she started when his mouth brushed against hers.

"Easy, I won't bite..." he murmured. He slid his right hand into her hair, above her ear, and curved his long fingers around the back of her head. "Close your eyes, Maggie."

His voice was so low, so gentle, she obeyed automatically. And then his mouth closed over hers with a passion that stole the oxygen from her lungs and demanded a response.

"God, you're sweet." He tilted his head in the opposite direction, then took her mouth again, as if he had all the time in the world.

Kissing Jackson was better than anything she'd imagined, and she'd fantasized enough about him to have imagined plenty. She'd thought it would be hot and exciting, maybe a little dangerous and overpowering. It was all of those things, and more. It was like her first dive off the high board, like taking on raging white water in a flimsy rubber raft, like the great shrieking rush you get just before you hit the end of a bungee cord.

She opened her mouth, eager for the taste and feel of his tongue stroking hers. He accepted her invitation with a muffled groan. She raised her hands to his chest. Her fingertips pressed into his hard muscles, and she felt his heart hammering beneath her palms. She heard his harsh, choppy breaths—or maybe they were hers. She didn't know or care. The only thing she knew for certain at the moment was, she wanted to get closer. Much, much closer.

As if he'd read her mind, he dropped his left arm to her hips and pulled her flush against him. Her mouth went dry and her knees went weak when the rigid length of his arousal pressed into her belly. It felt...intimate. Too intimate. Too fast. Too out of control.

Wrenching her mouth from his, she said, "Jackson, no. Stop. Please, stop."

His arm around her hips loosened, but he didn't let her go completely until she found the strength to push against his chest. He shook his head, as if to clear it, then dropped his arms to his sides and turned away from her. Well, damn, she thought, shivering from the sudden lack of warmth. Knowing Jackson, he'd probably add being a tease to her long list of faults.

To her surprise, however, he looked over his shoulder and gave her a rueful grin. "Now do you believe me?"

"About what?"

"That I'm attracted to you."

"Oh, uh, well...sure," she stammered, fighting to suppress the fit of hysterical laughter bubbling up inside her. God, how had she gotten herself into this situation, with Jackson Hawk, of all people? "I, uh, I guess so..."

"You only *guess* so?" Turning back around, he waggled his eyebrows at her. His rueful grin became wicked. "You want more proof? I'll be happy to give you another demonstration."

"No, Jackson." She wrapped her arms around herself and backed away from him. "Thank you, but one was, uh, sufficient."

He held up both hands in a classic gesture of innocence. "I know things got a little carried away there for a minute, but you don't have to be afraid of me."

"I'm not, really. I'm just a little, uh...stunned."

"You didn't hate it, did you?"

"No." Her voice came out in a hoarse croak. She cleared her throat and tried again. "No, I didn't hate it."

"Does that mean you liked it?"

"Do you really expect me to answer that?"

He gave her another one of those wicked grins. "If you don't, I may have to try it again. Just to make sure I didn't get the wrong signals, or anything."

She couldn't help laughing at such a blatant attempt at manipulation. She couldn't resist taking a poke at his ego, either. "It was okay. On a scale of one to ten, I'd give it about a...four."

"Only a four, huh?" He hung his head, then looked up at her and winked. "I guess I'll have to practice."

"Why this sudden change of heart, Jackson?"

"It's not really sudden." He rested his hip against the side of her car and crossed his arms over his chest. "You were right about some of the things you said today."

"What things?"

"Bigotry, for one. I don't like it in other people, and I sure don't like it in myself. But it's there, all right." Sighing, he shook his head. "You've been catching the brunt of some things that happened a long time before I met you. I'm sorry, Maggie. You didn't deserve it."

There was no doubting his sincerity this time. Maggie gazed into his dark eyes and saw stark memories of pain. Feeling privileged that he had trusted her enough to let her see it, she stepped closer. "Do you want to talk about it?"

"Not right now." He reached out and caressed her cheek with the tips of his fingers. "I know you're tired. We'll have lots of time to talk when we're driving all over the res."

She pulled back, scowling at him. "Is that why you kissed me? Because I said I'd changed my mind?"

Jackson straightened away from the car, dropped a quick, hard kiss on her lips, and opened the door for her. "No. I kissed you because I damn well wanted to. In fact, if you don't get out of here in the next thirty seconds, I'll probably do it again, because I still want to."

Maggie slid into the driver's seat, then rolled down the window when Jackson shut the door for her. "I'm not comfortable with this. I don't mix business relationships with personal ones. If you're expecting—"

"I'm not expecting anything," Jackson said, interrupting her. "Why don't we pretend we just met, and try to be friends, for starters?"

"Do you really think that's possible? Just being friends?"

His wicked grin returned. Bracing one hand on the window opening, he leaned down until they were eye-to-eye. "I like my women willing. You won't have any problem resisting me, if my kisses only rate a four, Maggie."

Oh, you wretch, she thought, smiling in spite of her better judgment. "That sounds like a challenge."

"You started it. But, hey, if you don't think you can handle it . . ." Allowing his voice to trail off, he shrugged as if it didn't matter to him whether or not she accepted it.

Though she wasn't at all certain she *could* handle his challenge, Maggie wouldn't have admitted it to him under torture. "All right. I'll see you tomorrow at one."

She started the car and backed out of the parking slot as Jackson raised one hand to wave her off. Tapping the brake, she stuck her head out of the window and called to him, "Hey, Jackson? That kiss was closer to a six."

Then she drove away, with the sound of his laughter echoing in her wake. She smiled all the way to the junction with highway 191, the road back to Whitehorn. In truth, that kiss had been more like a fifteen, but she didn't want him to get any more conceited than he already was. Besides, it would be fun to see how hard he was willing to work to improve his score.

As she turned south and the miles passed, however, doubts about the wisdom of getting more personally involved with Jackson crept into her mind. Whether or not either of them wanted to admit it, they were heading in that direction. He was the most complicated, fascinating man she'd ever met, and by far the best kisser. Knowing he was as physically attracted to her as she was to him had given her ego a nice boost.

What worried her was that if Jackson continued to be as charming as he'd been tonight, it might not be all that difficult for her to fall in love with him. She couldn't afford to do it. There was the promise to her mother, for one thing. For another, much as she was enjoying her time at Laughing Horse, she didn't want to live there permanently. It was impossible to imagine Jackson living anywhere else.

Her mother had consistently advised her to stand on her own two feet and never depend on a man to support her. Maggie had taken the advice to heart, and she had no regrets for having done so. While she was starting to have some uneasy feelings about Congressman Baldwin, she loved her work a great deal. She wanted to get married and have children someday, but not at the expense of her career.

"Wait a minute, Schaeffer," she muttered. "You're getting way ahead of yourself. Jackson didn't say anything about love or marriage. He just wants to take you to bed."

It was a disheartening thought, but one she couldn't ignore. She hadn't been living in a convent, after all. She'd dated enough to know what men wanted from women, and it usually wasn't a commitment. Her unwillingness to engage in sex without one had ended more than a few promising relationships.

She hadn't mourned over her lost relationships, though. Not for long, anyway. Her life was busy and fulfilling, and only one of those men had ever turned her on enough to tempt her into bed with him in the first place. Of course, if any of the others had ever kissed her the way Jackson had, she might not be feeling quite so virtuous.

Lord, just thinking about it was enough to make her toes curl and her heart pound with anticipation of the next one. And there would, undoubtedly, be a next one. Oh, drat the man. He certainly had a gift for keeping her in a constant state of confusion about *some*thing. How did he manage to do that?

Reducing her speed as she entered the Whitehorn city limits, Maggie heaved a weary sigh. Well, it was too late to back out now. When she arrived at the motel, she would go straight to bed and get a good night's sleep. She had a feeling she would need every bit of strength she could muster in order to deal with Jackson Hawk tomorrow.

Jackson spent the next morning helping his uncle catch up on tribal business. The hours passed in a flurry of paperwork and arguments over how he'd handled this problem or that one, but Maggie was never far from his thoughts. After a long night of too little sleep and too much reflection, he had come to the brilliant conclusion that he never should have kissed her.

He honestly hadn't intended to. He'd only meant to make sure she was okay and try to reestablish a decent working relationship. But then he'd watched her come out of the school with Sara and heard almost every word the two women had said.

Knowing Maggie *had* been higher than a kite when she came back from her confrontation with Reese, that she'd been high again when the computers arrived, and that he'd smashed her pleasure in both events, had made him feel like a mean bastard all over again.

His guilt had grown when she left Sara and crossed the street, looking so discouraged. Then he'd unwittingly scared the hell out of her; he didn't even want to imagine what a woman from a crime-ridden city like Washington must have felt when he came at her out of the darkness the way he had. And when she'd stood there in the street, fiercely rejecting his apology... well, damn, he'd have done almost anything to earn her forgiveness.

Like an idiot, he'd gone too far, of course. But then, he seemed to overreact to just about everything when he was with Maggie. He knew he'd overreacted to the power of that kiss, too. He would have rated it higher than a four or a six, but it hadn't really been all *that* spectacular. Had it?

The only way to be absolutely sure, of course, was to kiss her again. He wanted to. Oh, yeah, he wanted to do it so bad, his lips itched. But what if it *had* been as spectacular as he remembered? He could get addicted to that kind of pleasure. And then he'd want more and more and more. Oh, hell, who was he trying to kid? He'd already made love to her in his fantasies at least fifty times.

No matter where he was or what he was trying to do, Maggie nagged at the edges of his mind, like a pesky fly that wouldn't go away, but wouldn't land anywhere so he could swat it. Like a TV with the sound turned low enough he couldn't quite hear it, but loud enough that he couldn't quite ignore it, either. Like a song whose melody haunted him, but whose lyrics he could only half remember.

She was just always *there*. He didn't know if he really wanted to resist her. Or if he even *could* resist her if he really wanted to. Now, if that wasn't a confusing mess for a supposedly rational lawyer to find himself in, he'd like to know what was.

"I don't know where your brain is, nephew, but it sure as hell ain't here," Frank said, scowling at Jackson. "What's goin' on with you?"

"Nothing."

Frank threw down his pen, shoved back his chair and stood. "Well, I'm starvin' to death. Let's get some lunch."

"I can't, uncle. I'm taking Maggie for a tour of the res this afternoon."

A knowing smile spread across Frank's face. "Well, I guess that explains it."

"Explains what?"

"The nothing that's goin' on with you." Chuckling, Frank walked out the door, calling, *"Ne-sta-va-voomatse,"* as he left.

"Right, I'll see you later, uncle," Jackson replied.

He glanced at his watch and felt a sharp surge of anticipation in the center of his chest. Since it was almost one o'clock, and Maggie operated on white man's time, she should be here any minute. Would she be nervous about seeing him again? he wondered. As nervous as he was about seeing her?

Disgusted with himself for that admission, he gathered up the papers he'd been working on, muttering, "For God's sake, it was just a kiss."

His heart lurched when he heard the outer door open, followed by muffled footsteps. And then Maggie appeared in the doorway of his office, wearing jeans, sneakers, and a bright purple shirt with intricate beading on the collar under her jacket. Her shy smile warmed him, driving every rational, self-preserving thought from his head. Damn, but he was glad to see her.

"Hello, Jackson," she said.

"Hello, Maggie."

She paused just inside the doorway, as if she weren't sure what to expect from him. "Are you ready to go?"

Smiling at her, Jackson pushed himself to his feet. Before he could say anything, however, the outer door opened again.

"Hello?" a feminine voice he didn't recognize called from the end of the hallway. "Is someone there?"

Maggie looked at Jackson, her eyebrows raised in a silent query. When he shrugged to let her know he wasn't expecting anybody, she stepped back into the hallway and said, "Down here, ma'am. May I help you?"

"Well, actually, I was hoping I could help you," the woman said, her words accompanied by the staccato clicking of high heels striking the tile floor.

Maggie shot Jackson an amused glance. A second later, he understood why. The woman who walked into his office was a delicate, fortyish blonde who looked as if she ought to be heading for a ladies' luncheon at a country club.

She wore a pastel-pink suit with a short, straight skirt, a white scoop-necked blouse, and pearls at her ears and throat. She carried a small handbag the same color as her shoes, three-inch spikes that had, no doubt, been dyed to match her outfit. Her makeup was subtle and flattering, every strand of her shoulder-length hair was combed into place, and her perfectly manicured fingernails told him any work she did with her hands was rarely more strenuous than arranging flowers.

The woman stood in the middle of the room for a moment, glancing from Jackson to Maggie and back to Jackson, obviously trying to figure out which one of them was in charge. Impatient to learn her business and get on with his afternoon with Maggie, Jackson said, "What can we do for you, miss?"

"Oh, it's Mrs.," she said, raising her left hand to her necklace, flashing a ring with a diamond the size of an acorn in it. Then she gave him a sweet smile and offered her dainty right hand to him. "Mrs. Dugin Kincaid. But please, call me Mary Jo. Everyone does."

"Jackson Hawk," he said, reluctantly shaking her hand. Oh, great, he thought grimly, *Maheo* knew he'd always wanted to be on a first-name basis with Jeremiah Kincaid's daughter-in-law. Maggie came forward and offered the woman a chair.

"It's a pleasure to meet you, Mary Jo," she said, shooting Jackson a warning scowl. "I'm Maggie Schaeffer. I'm working with the tribe on a temporary assignment for Congressman Baldwin."

The woman settled herself on the straight-backed wooden chair, responding graciously to Maggie's efforts to make polite small talk. After five minutes, Jackson had heard all the get-acquainted chitchat he could stand. He cleared his throat to gain the women's attention.

"What brings you to Laughing Horse, Mrs. Kincaid?" he asked.

"Well, I know this may sound a bit strange, but if you'll bear with me, I'll do my best to explain," she said. "You see, Duggie and I were having dinner at the club last night, and I heard this rumor about you folks out here, and I just *had* to find out if it was true. I mean, I didn't really know if I'd be welcome, or anything, but then I thought, why not? It never hurts to ask, does it?"

Jackson broke in when she finally paused to take a breath. "Excuse me, Mrs. Kincaid. Would you mind telling us what the rumor was?"

"Oh, silly me, didn't I tell you?" She let out a giggle that was annoyingly girlish for a woman her age, tipped her head to one side and batted her eyelashes at him. The effect was less than charming, as far as Jackson was concerned, but he answered as patiently as he could.

"No, I don't believe you did."

"Well, what I heard was that you folks will be starting a children's library out here soon, and I just happen to be a children's librarian. You see, I used to work at the library in town, but I had to quit when I married Duggie, because he's on the library board and he didn't really think it was proper for his wife to work for money. We have a certain... position to maintain in the community, you know."

Her light, breathless chatter grated on Jackson's nerves almost as much as the ultrafeminine little gestures she made with her hands did. Honest to God, watching her talk was like watching hummingbirds zipping from flower to flower in his mother's garden. He caught another warning scowl from Maggie, however, and decided to keep his mouth shut for the moment.

"Anyway," Mary Jo rattled on, "I just love children, and since it's all right if I volunteer to work for a worthy cause, I hoped you might be willing to allow me to organize your new children's library. I really am a very good librarian."

"We've discussed the idea of starting a children's library, but I'm afraid we're still at the thinking stage," Jackson said. "We don't have any definite plans."

"Oh," Mary Jo said, her shoulders slumping, as if she were terribly disappointed. "I see. Then it was just a rumor."

"That was an awfully kind offer," Maggie said. "Organizing a library must be a huge undertaking."

Mary Jo gave her a sad smile. "Well, yes, it is, but I would have loved doing it. I'm just not used to being idle, and I miss being around children so much."

"There's an after-school tutoring program you might enjoy," Maggie suggested. "We can always use volunteers to help the children with their homework."

Mary Jo perked right up, beaming at Maggie as if she'd offered her a winning lottery ticket. "Really? That sounds wonderful. Could I work with the little ones?"

"You'll have to talk to Sara Lewis about that," Jackson said, sending Maggie a warning scowl of his own. It was bad enough this woman was a Kincaid, but her personality alone would drive him to drink, if he had to be around her much. "She's in charge of the program."

Mary Jo flashed him a brilliant smile. "I'll do it today. Oh, this will be such fun. You know, I've always been fascinated with Indians, and they talk about you folks in town all the time. Why, this morning one of our neighbors told me you found a body out here yesterday. Is that just another rumor?"

"No, it's partly true, Mrs. Kincaid," Jackson said, hoping to scare her off for good. "We've only found a skeletonized arm and hand so far, but Dr. Hunter has assured the tribal police they were human remains."

Mary Jo shuddered delicately. "How gruesome. Do you think there was ... murder involved?"

Encouraged by her shudder, Jackson decided to lay it on good and thick. "We won't know for certain until we find the rest of the skeleton, but I wouldn't be surprised if it was. We've had such a bad history of violence at Laughing Horse, the FBI is sending in a forensic specialist to study the case."

"Really? Do you think they'll be able to solve it?"

Jackson studied Mary Jo for a moment. Nuts. The woman seemed to be more interested in learning the gory details of a crime than scared. This was one weird lady. She made all the right noises, but somehow, they just didn't ring true.

"I guess we'll see," he said. "You should be extremely careful when you come out here, Mrs. Kincaid. If there was foul play attached to those bones, the murderer is probably still running loose, right here on the reservation."

"Oh, my goodness," Mary Jo murmured. She shuddered again, then stood and said, "Well, I must go now, but I'll be back to work with the children. And I will be careful, I promise. Thanks again. I'll see you later."

With a cheery wave, she left the room, trailing a cloud of expensive perfume. Jackson waited until he heard the outer door bang shut before looking at Maggie. Arms folded across her chest, she was studying him as intently as he'd studied Mary Jo Kincaid. Uh-oh. It didn't take a psychic to tell him he was in for it again.

Seven

Maggie met and held Jackson's challenging gaze for the space of a heartbeat, then lowered her hands to her sides. She had spent the morning in her motel room, organizing her notes and thinking about him. After analyzing their stormy relationship to date, she had decided to take Jackson at his word and accept his suggestion that they start over and try to be friends.

In the spirit of that decision, she was determined to reserve comment on his behavior toward Mary Jo Kincaid until he asked for her opinion. And maybe, with luck and patience, they could learn to have calm, rational discussions, instead of fierce, energy-draining debates.

"I'm ready to leave, if you are," she said with a smile. "Do you want to take your car or mine?"

His eyebrows rose halfway up his forehead, and he stared at her for a moment. Then his face and shoulders relaxed, and the corners of his mouth curved into a grin. He grabbed his hat from the top of the bookshelf behind his desk, plunked it on his head and motioned for her to precede him through the doorway.

"We'll take my truck. I want to show you the grazing leases first, and the roads are rough out there."

Neither of them spoke again as they headed out of Laughing Horse in his battered red pickup, traveling southwest on a gravel road. Maggie settled back in the seat and gazed out the side window. The homesteads gradually came fewer and farther between, bearing little resemblance to the well-kept farms and ranches she'd seen on the outskirts of Whitehorn.

There were no stately red barns, no satellite dishes, no elaborate sprinkler systems. Many of the houses were unpretentious clapboards with faded and peeling paint and the

Spartan, cookie-cutter sameness of government construction. Others were little more than log cabins or tar-paper shacks surrounded by sagging fences and the rusting carcasses of junked vehicles, farm machinery and appliances. Some had a few chickens scratching at the dirt in the front yard, a privy and a sagging clothesline out back. Occasionally she saw a horse or a mangy-looking dog, but if there were people around, they remained out of sight.

Maggie had seen plenty of urban poverty before, but she found this rural variety wrenched her heart with equal, if not greater, force. Americans frequently heard about the problems of the poor in their cities on the nightly news. These grim, isolated pockets of dreariness were much easier for the media to ignore; the people who struggled to survive out here were all-too-often forgotten.

In stark contrast to the homesteads, the landscape provided a backdrop of breathtaking scenery. To the west, the jagged, snowcapped peaks of the Crazy Mountains soared into the clear blue sky like a prayer reaching for heaven. The grass covering the foothills was turning green. A large bird, probably an eagle or a hawk, floated on the air currents high overhead.

Such poverty in the midst of so much rich natural beauty struck Maggie as some kind of a cruel joke. Did her mother's family live in a ramshackle place like that one? Did Jackson? He finally broke the silence, startling her out of her reverie.

"Well?" he asked.

Maggie looked at him, raising one eyebrow at the gruff demand in his voice. "Well, what?"

"Aren't you going to tell me what a paranoid bigot I am again?"

"Do you really want me to?"

"Not particularly, but I know that's what you're thinking. You might as well go ahead and say it."

Chuckling at his disgruntled tone, she shifted around on the seat until she was partially facing him. "I think you're hearing the voice of your own guilty conscience, because you fibbed to Mrs. Kincaid."

A grin tugged at the corners of Jackson's mouth. "No, I didn't. Nothing I said was really a lie."

"Oh, huh! The story I heard, was that the elders were pretty darn positive those bones came from the old burial ground, which was why they've locked them up until the FBI's forensic specialist can get here. And you deliberately led that poor woman to believe there's a vicious killer on the loose."

He shrugged. "She can believe whatever she wants. But tell me, what did you really think of her?"

"I'm not sure," she said. "She was nice enough, I guess, but maybe a little... strange."

"Only a little?" he shot her a disbelieving look, then turned his attention to the road again and shook his head.

"Well, actually, I thought she was pretty ditzy," Maggie admitted with a laugh, "but I thought she seemed sincere about wanting to help."

"She wants something, all right, but I doubt it has anything to do with the library, or the kids."

"Why, Jackson?"

"For starters, good ol' Duggie and his father despise Indians. I can't believe either one of them would approve of her volunteering to work out here, no matter how worthy the cause. It just doesn't fit, unless there's some other motive involved."

Maggie opened her eyes wide and lowered her voice to a spooky whisper. "Maybe she's on a mission to infiltrate the tribe and spy for Jeremiah. Maybe she's a pervert who gets off on kiddie library books. Maybe she's a commie pinko rat!"

Jackson snorted with laughter. "Stop makin' fun of me, Schaeffer. There's something weird about that woman, and you know it."

"Agreed, but can you really imagine that ditzy little woman being involved in Jeremiah's business affairs? And if he wanted to send in a spy, wouldn't you expect him to be more subtle than to use his own daughter-in-law?"

"Who knows what to expect from that guy?"

"What if Mary Jo's last name was Smith or Jones, instead of Kincaid? Would you still be suspicious of her?"

"Probably. Does that make me a bigot?"

"I didn't call you a bigot," Maggie said, struggling to hold on to her patience. "I said you might have a problem with bigotry. For whatever it's worth, I think we all have a touch of it somewhere in our souls."

"Okay. So why do you think I have such a problem with it?"

"Because you seem to suspect the motives of every white person who offers to do anything good for the tribe. Why don't you trust any of them?"

"Why do you trust all of them?"

Maggie shook her head in exasperation. "I don't. But I at least try to give people the benefit of the doubt until they prove me wrong, Jackson."

"That's fine on a personal basis. But when you're responsible for the well-being of two thousand people, you can't afford to make mistakes."

"Somebody must have really hurt you to make you feel that way," Maggie said quietly.

Jackson laughed again, but there was no humor in it this time. "Don't try to psychoanalyze me. I'm not one bit more suspicious of whites than anyone else who grew up on the res."

"Yes, you are, and it's really a personal thing with you. Come on, Jackson, talk to me. If we're going to be friends, I need to understand."

He pulled over to the side of the road, switched off the ignition and turned to face her. "Look, Maggie, I'm not saying this to be insulting, but I don't think anyone with your background really *can* understand."

Maggie opened her mouth to protest, but he held up one hand like a traffic cop. "Give me a minute, and then you can yell at me all you want. The truth is, you've had a rich white daddy smoothing the way for you with his money and influence. My guess is, all the stuff he donated to your schools probably bought you a lot of acceptance from the teachers and the other kids."

"You mean, they didn't all love me for my charm, intelligence and good looks?" Maggie asked, her tongue firmly planted in her cheek.

He shot her a quelling glance. "Your intelligence and good looks, maybe. I wouldn't bet on the other one. Anyway, what I was trying to say is, the rest of us weren't that lucky. We couldn't even go to school in Whitehorn back then."

"Where did you go?"

"To a BIA boarding school in Oklahoma."

"What was it like?"

"I guess it was better than my parents had it, but I thought it was worse than being sent to prison." Jackson's eyes took on a faraway cast. "My father was a traditional medicine man. He was determined we would know our own culture, and we spoke very little English at home. The teachers at the school were equally determined to turn us into little white people. We weren't allowed to speak anything *but* English there. Since I was more afraid of the teachers than I was of my dad, I focused on English. My Cheyenne vocabulary is still at a six-year-old's level."

"It must have been hard for your parents to let you go so far from home, when you were still so little."

"They didn't have a choice. If they wanted to receive any of the government benefits they needed to survive, all of their children had to be enrolled. It was blackmail, really, and it broke my father's heart to see his children being systematically stripped of everything he'd tried to teach us."

"How often did you get to go home, Jackson?"

"Once a year. For about six weeks in the summer. All year long, I'd live for those few days at home, but then I'd get here and everything would feel so strange, I couldn't relax. My father would try to undo all the damage he thought my teachers had done to me, and we didn't get along very well. It became a classic Catch-22."

"In what way?" Maggie asked.

"At school I was too Indian. At home I had too many white ideas. Wherever I was, there was always somebody ready and willing to tell me there was something wrong with me."

Jackson gave Maggie a lopsided grin that made her want to weep for the sad little boy he must have been.

"How did you ever cope with that?" she asked.

He studied her face for a moment, then scowled at her. "Don't feel sorry for me. I was one of the lucky ones. At least I was tough enough to survive."

"Some of them didn't?"

Jackson grimly shook his head. "There were always kids who couldn't stand the homesickness and the regimentation. Some of them decided suicide was the only way out. Others ran away and died of exposure before anyone found them, or they just plain vanished. Who knows what happened to them?"

"God, that's awful. You didn't ever think about..."

"Killing myself? Sure I did. I was just too damned mean to give anybody the satisfaction of getting rid of me."

"Oh, Jackson, that's a terrible thing to say."

"That's how it felt sometimes, Maggie. Especially after they shook up the whole system and I had to come back and go to high school in Whitehorn. Believe me, I was one screwed-up kid. I don't know how my parents tolerated me at all."

"Most teenagers rebel at one time or another," Maggie said.

"Yeah, well, I did more than my share. Most of the other kids got into alcohol or drugs, but I chose the one way guaranteed to hurt my father the most."

"What was that?"

"I turned my back on the tribe. I let everybody know I couldn't wait to leave the res, and that I never intended to come back. If I had to choose between the white world and the Indian one, by God, I was gonna go with the winners."

"Is that why you went to law school?"

He nodded. "I thought if I could study hard enough, assimilate enough and make enough money, it wouldn't matter who I was or where I'd come from. People would have to accept me, whether they wanted to or not."

"So, I'm not the only apple around here," she said.

"Not hardly. It takes one to know one." Uttering a bitter laugh, he shook his head again. "That's why you bugged me so much the first time we met. You reminded me too much of myself. I guess I owe you another apology for that."

She nodded in acceptance, then asked, "Why did you come back here, Jackson?"

"I finally realized I'd been fooling myself and selling my soul at the same time. Whites will accept you to the degree you can assimilate, but sooner or later, you'll slip up and remind them you're an Indian. When you get right down to it, equality's just a myth."

"You really believe that, don't you?"

He shrugged one shoulder, as if to say it didn't matter what he really believed. "That's what I experienced. When I figured that out, I decided to come home and learn how to be the man *Maheo* created me to be. I am Northern Cheyenne, and I will always *be* Northern Cheyenne, and if I have anything to say about it, this tribe will never be at the mercy of whites again. When it comes to Indians, they don't have any mercy to spare."

"They're not *all* like that, Jackson," Maggie said, quietly chiding him.

"Oh, I'm sure there's a few good guys out there. But I haven't had much luck in separating the good ones from the bad ones. I'm not willing to risk being wrong anymore."

"So you hate the whole bunch. Don't trust anyone. Is that the way you want to live your whole life?"

"I didn't choose it, Maggie. But I've learned the hard way that if you stick your neck out with whites, the chances are too damn high you're gonna get your head chopped off. Maybe you're just too young to understand betrayal."

"I'm not too young or too naive to understand anything," she said. "I've been betrayed by whites and other Indians, and I know how much it hurts. But if you go into every new relationship expecting betrayal, you're setting yourself up for a self-fulfilling prophecy. That's a defeatist attitude."

He gazed at her for a long moment, his expression completely unreadable. "I prefer to think of it as realistic. And one of these days, you're gonna find out I'm right."

When she made no reply, he started the engine and drove back onto the road. Releasing a resigned sigh, Maggie turned to her window. So much for ending their fierce debates, she thought with a wry grin. But, while their discussion had become more heated than she would have liked, Maggie believed she and Jackson were making progress toward understanding each other.

She was beginning to understand him, anyway, she thought, sneaking a sidelong glance at him. He'd put his aviator glasses on, and she wondered whether it was for protection from the sun or to shield his eyes from her view because he felt he'd revealed too much. Well, he'd better get used to it. By telling her about his childhood, he'd only whetted her appetite to learn more about him.

Somewhere inside that big, strong, sexy man, there was a hurt, confused, lonely little boy who had never really felt accepted. Her childhood had undoubtedly been easier than his, and maybe she couldn't relate to everything that had happened to him. But she knew more than he thought she did about feeling lost and left out. And wondering if she would ever really belong anywhere. Perhaps they could find some answers together.

The road deteriorated into a rutted path, forcing Jackson to concentrate more on his driving and less on Maggie, but she still occupied a large part of his mind. She'd drifted into a thoughtful silence about five miles back, and he'd give a small fortune to know what was going on in that head of hers. Nuts.

He shouldn't have told her all that stuff about boarding school. It wasn't relevant to anything going on with the tribe now, and he'd probably sounded like a big baby, whining over a scratch that should have healed and been forgotten a long time ago. She was such a good listener, he'd have to watch himself, or he'd wind up boring her to tears with the story of his whole damn sad life. The idea made his skin crawl.

Spotting the turnoff he'd been looking for, he shifted into a lower gear, warned Maggie to hang on and gunned the engine. The pickup jolted and bounced violently over rocks and potholes, but ultimately conquered the track, which ran straight up the side of a steep hill. Knowing the top of it ended in a cliff, he slammed on the brakes as soon as the truck leveled out.

Maggie shot him a wild-eyed, indignant look as the dust settled. He grinned at her, then climbed out of the cab and hurried around to open the door for her. She jumped to the ground and stalked away from him, hands curled into fists at her sides. She came to an abrupt halt a moment later and gazed off into the distance as if entranced.

He walked over and stood beside her, his face turned toward the sun, allowing Maggie a modicum of privacy while she absorbed the view he had seen so many times before. Though he had few of the spiritual powers of his father, Jackson knew this ground was sacred. He silently offered prayers to *Maheo* and each of the four directions, then glanced at Maggie.

Her eyes shone with the awed wonder of a child. When she spoke, her voice held a hushed reverence. "Oh, Jackson, this is so... beautiful."

For once, they were in complete accord. As if Mother Earth had chosen this particular spot to display her most impressive gifts to their best advantage, a lush valley stretched for miles before them, reaching all the way to the point at which the mountains blocked the horizon. Sunlight sparkled on a blue ribbon of water cutting a lazy, serpentine path through the center of the valley. Clumps of aspen and cottonwood trees along the river would soon provide shade for sleek Hereford cows and their recently born calves.

"What is this place?" Maggie murmured.

"It's ours," he said. "The land we're trying to get back from the Whitehorn Ranchers' Association."

"No wonder they want it. It looks like Eden."

"It's a paradise for cattle, all right. It's got all the best grass and water. Kincaid and his friends have gotten rich off this valley."

"What will you do with it?" she asked.

"The same thing they're doing. Raise cattle. So many of our people have worked for the white ranchers, we've got plenty of expertise to draw from."

"Won't it take an awful lot of money to get started?"

Jackson nodded. "We're already working on grant proposals."

"Let me know when you're ready to submit them. Perhaps I can speed up the process."

"I'll keep that in mind," he said, smiling at her. "I may need your help first to settle a disagreement among the tribal council members."

"Me? How could I do that?"

"Sweet talk your buddy Earnest Running Bull into giving up the idea we should raise buffalo instead of Herefords."

"Buffalo?"

"Sure. This whole area was a bison feeding ground long before the white men showed up. Our people used to hunt here every summer. We're standing on a buffalo jump right now."

Maggie looked up at him, her eyes wide with surprise. "You're kidding."

"Nope. The men would climb up into those hills back there," Jackson said, pointing over his right shoulder with his thumb. "They'd bunch up as many buffalo as they could, and drive them off this cliff. The animals would break their necks when they fell, and the women would be waiting down below to finish them off and start the butchering."

Leaning out, Maggie peeked over the edge of the cliff. A huge chunk of dirt in front of her toes broke loose and smashed on the boulders below. Arms flapping wildly for balance, she teetered for an instant, and would have pitched forward to disaster if Jackson hadn't grabbed the back of her Windbreaker and yanked her back to safety.

"That," she said, uttering a shaky laugh, "was close."

Jackson couldn't have agreed more, but since his heart was still stuck in his throat, he didn't try to talk. Instead, he wrapped his arm around her shoulders, urged her farther back from the ledge and held her against his side, while he waited for his lungs to start working again. She threw both arms around him and buried her face in the front of his shirt.

A fierce sense of gladness washed over him. Gladness she hadn't fallen. And gladness that, despite their previous disagreement, she had felt she could turn to him for comfort.

Vivid pictures of what would have happened if he hadn't grabbed her in time flashed through his mind, and suddenly none of the things they'd argued about seemed important.

"It's all right, Maggie," he said, stroking her glossy hair with a hand that was none too steady. "It's all right."

She felt good in his arms. It had been so long since he'd held a woman like this, he'd almost forgotten what pleasure a simple human touch could bring. She turned her face to the side. With her ear still pressed against his chest, she gazed up at him from under her long lashes.

"Your heart's pounding like crazy," she said.

"That's because you scared the hell out of me."

"You saved my life, Jackson."

"Next time you're mad enough to strangle me, remember that."

"I'd probably kiss your whole face right now, if you weren't so darn tall."

"Is that a fact?"

"You betcha, kemo sabe."

Tickled by her ridiculous reference to the Lone Ranger's faithful Indian friend, Tonto, and the way she wrinkled her impish little nose at him, Jackson put his hands on Maggie's waist, picked her up and carried her back to the pickup. Then he plunked her tush down on the hood, braced his hands on either side of her and looked her right in the eye.

"I'm not too tall now, am I?"

Returning his challenging grin with one of her own, she lifted his Stetson off his head and set it behind her. She took his sunglasses next, carefully laying them on his hat brim. Finally she linked her fingers at the back of his head and pulled him closer.

His heart started racing again as she kissed his eyes shut. Her breath struck his face in sweet little puffs as she moved on to his nose, his cheekbones, his forehead. His lips tingled, wanting their turn, but she playfully denied them in favor of his temples, jaw and chin.

"You missed a spot, Schaeffer," he grumbled, opening one eye to glare at her.

She kissed it shut again. "Don't be so impatient," she said, punctuating each word with another soft kiss, retracing her previous route. "I'll get there eventually."

It was the gentlest form of torture, but torture nonetheless, especially when she started stroking her thumbs behind his ears, while her fingers massaged the back of his neck. He didn't know why he tolerated it, except that it was... fun. Like Maggie. He'd bet his truck she'd been one of those adorable little girls who loved to flirt and tease and giggle.

And suddenly she "got there," reminding him in no uncertain terms that she was all woman, not a little girl. Her lips brushed tentatively over his, then zeroed in for a kiss that sent blood rushing to his groin in one hell of a hurry. She clasped the sides of his head, as if she feared he might try to escape, and slid her tongue into his mouth.

Damn. It was even better than the last time. All of his senses were on overload, but he couldn't taste enough, feel enough, breathe in enough of her essence. A primitive part of him wanted to seize control—just grab her and lay her back on the pickup's hood, strip off her jeans and bury himself to the hilt in her softness. But another part of him was enjoying her gentle seduction too much to risk frightening her into ending it. Or, worse yet, never doing it again.

Her hands were on his chest now, stroking and petting, and the sweet, hungry little sounds she was making were driving him out of his mind. She took the kiss hotter, wetter, deeper. He *had* to touch her with his hands. *Had* to pull her closer and feel her breasts rub against his chest. *Had* to nuzzle the side of her neck.

It was like racing down a mountain on a runaway train—too fast and powerful to stop, both exhilarating and terrifying while the ride lasted. And all along you knew it would have to stop sooner or later, and the end wouldn't be pretty. Already it was starting to happen.

She was calling his name, trying to get his attention, slamming on the brakes. Damn it, she wanted him. He felt it in the way her body clung to his, even as her hands halfheartedly pushed at his shoulders. He could silence her

protests with another kiss, overwhelm her silly female re-
straint with passion.

It wouldn't be rape. Not even close. But it wouldn't be
right, either. Eventually she would regret her loss of control, and come to hate him. And then he would hate himself.

Forcing himself to release her, he stepped back. His chest
heaved like a bellows as he sucked in head-clearing oxygen.
When his thundering pulse finally subsided, he looked at
Maggie and felt his heart contract.

Still sitting on the pickup's hood, she had her hands
clasped in her lap, her shoulders hunched and her eyes focused on the ground. Then, with agonizing slowness, she
raised her gaze to meet his. The wariness he saw in her eyes
made him feel like crawling under a flat rock.

"I'm sorry," she said. "I never intended for it to get
so..."

"Hot?" Jackson suggested. "Wild? Crazy? Passionate?"

Her cheeks flushed. "All of the above."

"I didn't either, Maggie." Shrugging one shoulder, he
crammed his hands into his pockets and tried to give her a
grin. "Some chemistry, huh?"

"Yeah." Her answering grin was crooked to start out
with. A second later, it vanished, leaving her with a somber
expression. "But it can't happen again."

"Because you don't mix business and personal relationships?"

"Yes. I'll only be here a few more weeks, so there's no
future in pursuing this for either of us."

"You have to have a future with every guy you kiss?"

"Not if I'm sure it'll stop with kissing. That's not true
with you, Jackson."

"Are you afraid of me?" he asked. "Is that what this is
all about?"

"No." She slid off the hood and, with her feet planted
firmly on the ground, faced him squarely. "I'm more afraid
of myself. I don't usually get so, um...carried away."

"You think I *do?*" he demanded.

"That's beside the point. We were supposed to be starting over as friends, and I can't afford to be anything more than that with you." She walked around to the passenger door, opened it and put one foot on the running board. "This game with the kisses is too risky for me. It has to end now."

"What do you want to do?" Jackson asked, propping his hands on his hips. "Pretend it never happened?"

"That's right. Otherwise, I'll have to drive myself."

The look in her eyes told him more clearly than words that she meant exactly what she'd said. Which didn't leave him much choice. The crazy, stubborn damn woman was liable to get herself killed if she went off alone, and his uncle would skin him alive if he let her do it. Of course, he'd never forget that kiss, and neither would she, but if this was how she wanted to play it, he'd go along with her. For now.

"Okay, Maggie," he said. "We'll do it your way."

She climbed into the cab, shut the door and fastened her seat belt. Jackson followed suit and carefully turned the pickup around so that he wouldn't have to back down the hill. Neither of them spoke, even after they'd bounced and jolted their way to the bottom. He turned right, heading farther out, to show her the actual boundary to the leased land.

Maggie asked an occasional question, appearing to be completely at ease with him. Now that she'd settled the issue of their sexual attraction to her satisfaction, why shouldn't she be at ease with him? Jackson smiled to himself and kept on driving. As far as he was concerned, they had settled nothing. In fact, that second dynamite kiss had changed everything.

He had no clear vision of where he wanted their relationship to go. He sure as hell wasn't ready to declare that he loved her, or propose marriage. But for the first time in a long, long time, he felt there were possibilities to be explored, and he damn well intended to explore them all.

Granted, on the surface, he and Maggie didn't have much in common. He could have named a whole handful of barriers to having a meaningful relationship with her. None of them had stopped this powerful attraction, however, probably because there was a hell of a lot more to it than just sex. Not that he had any objection to sex for its own sake, but he'd found he liked it better if he had an emotional attachment to his partner. He suspected the same was true for Maggie.

He also suspected there was more to her reluctance to get involved with him than a simple desire to keep her business and personal relationships separate. She might not be afraid of him, but she was afraid of something, all right. One way or another, he intended to find out what it was.

Eight

"Come on, you've done enough for one day."

"Give me ten more minutes." Maggie tossed a quick smile over her shoulder at Jackson, then turned to the computer monitor again. "I've only got one more page to go, and Wanda needs to start editing tomorrow."

"I need to work in the office for a couple of hours before we take off tomorrow," Jackson said. "You can finish it then."

Out of the corner of her eye, she saw his hand sneak toward the keyboard, his index finger aimed at the save button. "Stop that," she said, rapping his hand with her knuckles. "I want to see how she wraps this up."

Sara Lewis chuckled. Pushing her chair away from the computer next to Maggie's, she stood and rubbed the small of her back. "You might as well give it up, Jackson. When the Little Fed's on a mission, she won't quit till she's good and ready."

"Tell me about it," he said in a dry tone. "She runs my butt all over the res all day, and then drags me in here to type research papers until my fingers bleed at night. She's wearin' me down to a nub."

"So, go on home to bed," Maggie suggested without taking her eyes from the screen.

"No way," he said. "Shut up and keep typing."

Maggie lifted both hands from the keyboard and looked over at Sara. "Has he always been this bossy?"

Sara chuckled again. "He can't help it, Maggie. It runs in his family."

"Well, tell him he doesn't have to escort me all the way in to Whitehorn every night. I'm a big girl now, with a driver's license and everything. I can get back to the motel all by myself."

"Oh, no." Sara held up crossed forefingers in front of her face, as if warding off a vampire. "I'm not getting in the middle of one of your spats. Leave me out of this."

"Wise move, Sara," Jackson told her. "I wouldn't listen, anyway. She thinks just because she's not in D.C., there aren't any dangers for a woman traveling alone at night."

Maggie rolled her eyes in exasperation and went back to typing. Honestly, ever since she'd almost fallen from the buffalo jump two weeks ago, Jackson had been driving her batty. Not that he'd given her a single legitimate reason to complain.

There had been no unnecessary touches, no teasing innuendos, no more kisses. While she still suffered the pangs of the strongest sexual attraction of her life every time she got within six feet of him, being around her didn't seem to faze him a bit. He was invariably helpful and solicitous of her comfort, but for all the notice he took of her as a woman, she could have been his sister or an elderly aunt.

Of course, that irritated Maggie to the roots of her hair, but after the way she'd told him to back off, what could she possibly say? *Hey, Jackson, I've changed my mind. Why don't you start hitting on me again?* Not in this or any other lifetime.

As if the physical attraction weren't enough to contend with, the wretched man kept revealing new, utterly appealing sides to his personality. Last week, for instance, they'd called on a young woman who had four-month-old twins. While the mother was pouring her heart out to Maggie about the problems her husband was having in finding a steady job, both babies had started fussing.

Jackson had scooped the kids into his arms and left the kitchen. When her conversation ended half an hour later, Maggie had followed her hostess into the living room, where they'd found him sitting in an old wooden rocking chair, with a sleeping baby draped over each shoulder and a smug grin on his face.

And take yesterday. They had visited an elderly man who was crippled with arthritis and lived in a trailer with a dilapidated porch attached to the front. While Maggie conducted her interview, Jackson had poked around in the old fellow's garage, found a hammer and nails and repaired the wobbly steps leading up to the porch.

Today he'd merely chopped wood for over an hour and milked a cow for a harassed grandmother who was baby-sitting four grandchildren and tending to her husband, who was dying of lung cancer. Who did he think he was? The Mother Teresa of the res?

Maggie found it extremely difficult to remain emotionally aloof from a man who did things like that and then acted embarrassed when simple gratitude was offered in return. She couldn't even indulge in the cynical suspicion he was only doing those things to impress her. She'd heard too many stories about Jackson's previous kindnesses, from too many people, to believe that of him.

"Earth to Maggie. Yo, woman, wake up!"

Startled out of her reverie by the sound of his voice right next to her ear, she looked up into Jackson's dark, amused eyes, and discovered she couldn't look away. Lord, she must be more tired than she'd realized. Because at that moment, she wanted nothing more than to wrap his long braids around her hands and pull him down for a bone-melting kiss.

As if he'd read her thoughts, his gaze dropped to her lips and lingered there. Her throat constricted in an involuntary swallow. Then he grasped the back of her chair and unceremoniously dragged her away from the keyboard. Before she could gather a coherent protest, he'd hit the save key, backed out of the word-processing program and turned off the computer.

"That's it, Schaeffer. We're outa here. You're gonna be too sleepy to drive if you wait any longer."

Unable to argue, she climbed to her feet, stretched out the kinks in her shoulders and exchanged a weary grin with Sara. "The kids are going to make it, aren't they?"

"You'd better believe it. They've done excellent work in the short time they've had to pull these papers together," Sara said. "They're getting so excited about graduation."

"That's great," Maggie said. "We should be thinking about a party for them. Maybe we could hire a disc jockey, or—"

Jackson barged between the two women, grabbed each of them by an arm and hustled them down the hallway to the exit, scolding them as they skipped to keep up with his long strides. "Think we're on Indian time around here? Get a move on, ladies. It'll keep till tomorrow."

He practically shoved them outdoors, then went back to turn off the lights and lock up the building. Maggie shot him a dirty look, which sent Sara into gales of laughter.

"Listen," Sara said when she'd regained her composure, "there's no reason the two of you have to go through this every night."

"I know," Maggie retorted. "But that big dope in there must have flunked listening in kindergarten. I just can't get him to understand I can take care of myself."

"That's not what I meant," Sara said. "I've got a spare bedroom you can use, if you're interested."

"You mean tonight?"

"Tonight, and any other night you want. You're spending so much time out here, you might as well move in with me. It's nothing fancy, but I'd be glad to have you."

"That's a great offer, Sara, but I couldn't impose on you."

"If I thought you'd impose, I wouldn't have offered," Sara replied.

"Are you sure you wouldn't mind?" Maggie asked. It really would be a godsend to skip the awful drive back and forth to Whitehorn every day.

Sara shrugged. "I grew up in a house smaller than mine is, with my grandmother, mother, older brother and father—at least until he ran off. One skinny little Fed isn't gonna get in my way." As if that settled the issue, she dug around in her purse and pulled out a key.

Maggie tucked it into her jeans pocket and gave Sara a quick hug. "Thanks, pal. I'll move in in the morning."

Sara got into her car and rolled down the window. "It's the little blue house right behind the jail. Your room's the one off the living room."

"See you tomorrow night." Maggie waved as her friend drove off, then turned when the door to the building opened behind her.

No matter how much she tried to convince herself otherwise, she always felt her heart lift at the sight of Jackson coming her way. Just this once, she allowed herself to enjoy the sensation. She liked the way his broad shoulders moved with his loose-limbed cowboy walk. She liked the scruffy clothes he wore that allowed him to do nice things for people without worrying about getting himself dirty. She even liked that tired, scowling expression on his handsome face.

If circumstances had been different, she would have opened her arms to him, hugged him for being the big-hearted man he was beneath that gruff, cranky exterior he often hid behind, and soothed away his weariness with kisses. She'd learned so much about him in the past few weeks, but there was much, much more she wanted to know. More than she could ever learn in the time she had left at Laughing Horse. Maybe more than she could learn in a lifetime.

Fearing her thoughts and emotions would show on her face, she turned away and climbed into her car. When Jackson had done likewise, she backed out of her parking space and headed for Whitehorn. She tried to put him out of her mind, but with his headlights shining a constant reminder in her rearview mirror, it was impossible to forget he was right behind her.

And with each passing mile, the conviction grew that, with or without his headlights in her mirror, no matter how much time or distance she put between them, she would never be able to forget Jackson Hawk.

Gripping a mug of coffee in his left hand, Jackson steered the pickup with his right on his way into Laughing Horse the next morning. As usual, his thoughts were on Maggie. Also as usual, they were confused and frustrated.

Keeping his hands off her the past two weeks hadn't been easy, but he'd done it. The question uppermost in his mind at the moment was whether or not it was time to change tactics. There'd been a second last night, just after he caught her zoning off at the computer, when he could have sworn she wanted him to kiss her. If Sara hadn't been there, he would have done it, consequences be damned.

In the clear light of a new morning, however, those consequences seemed a hell of a lot more important. The more he'd worked with Maggie, the more he'd come to appreciate just how special she really was. They'd visited some people and seen some situations that had made *him* want to throw up his hands in defeat—battered wives; children abandoned to grandparents who were too old to keep up with them; angry, bewildered young men and women who couldn't find anything better to do with their lives than to try to drown their despair in alcohol or drugs.

Considering the privileged background she'd grown up with, Maggie's capacity for empathizing with these people was nothing short of astonishing to Jackson. No matter how poor the household, she treated each person with dignity and respect, and graciously accepted whatever hospitality was offered. Time and time again, he'd watched sullen, bitter people fall victim to the magic of her smiles.

She had a unique gift for focusing her attention on the person in front of her and responding without defensiveness or judgment. The pattern that followed had become as predictable to Jackson as the sun rising in the east. Before long, the interviewees would be sitting up straighter, dropping their flip or sarcastic answers to her questions, speaking with more assurance and conviction as they finally began to believe that whatever they said honest-to-God mattered to her.

What they didn't know was how much all that warmth and understanding cost Maggie in emotional terms. Oh, she didn't let on about it. She didn't rant and rave, the way he often wanted to, or cry, which seemed more appropriate for a softhearted woman like her. But day after day he'd seen it—a slow, steady drain on her energy, leaving behind a quiet, tense little ghost in place of the bubbly little elf he'd come to love.

Love? a voice inside his head inquired. *Did you say love?*

Jackson's response was both automatic and emphatic. No. It couldn't be love. He felt a lot of emotions toward Maggie—admiration, gratitude for her efforts on behalf of the tribe, lust, and even a certain amount of affection. But he was only exploring the possibilities of a deeper relationship with her at this point. He didn't love her as in "falling in love with." Uh-uh. No way.

Why the hell not? the voice demanded.

"I don't know her well enough yet," Jackson muttered.

Bull. She's perfect for you, and you know it.

His gut clenched, and every muscle in his back and shoulders tightened. "She doesn't love me."

How do you know? Have you asked her?

"Of course not. I just know, all right?" A clammy sweat had broken out on his forehead and the back of his neck. "Even if she did, it wouldn't work out."

Oh, you're psychic now, huh? You can read her mind? See into the future?

"I didn't say that."

Then why are you being so negative? Don't you think you're man enough for her?

"I didn't say that, either."

But you're too damned chicken to find out, aren't you?

"Now, look," Jackson said, forcing the words out through gritted teeth. "She's got a career and a life of her own in Washington. She even said there's no future for us—"

And you're just gonna take her word for it? Sheesh! Women change their minds all the time. If you had the balls to go after her, you could help Maggie change hers.

The clammy sweat was moving down to his palms. Jackson tightened his grip on the steering wheel. "She wouldn't stay here."

You don't know that. Cluck, cluck, cluck.

"She'll leave me like Nancy did."

She's not Nancy. Cluck, cluck, cluck.

"There's not enough time," Jackson insisted.

And you're wasting what little you've got left, pretending to be her buddy. You've gotta do something, you big jackass. And you'd better do it damn fast.

"Do what? Seduce her? Kidnap her? Hold her hostage?"

How the hell should I know? But you'd better think of something, or she'll leave for sure, and you'll end up alone and clucking for the rest of your life.

With that thought reverberating in his mind, Jackson pulled up in front of the tribal offices, put the pickup in Park and set his empty mug on the dash. Drumming his fingers on the steering wheel, he considered the situation from every possible angle.

Maggie was scheduled to return to D.C. in a month—six weeks, if he was lucky. While that really didn't give him much time, he couldn't rush her, either. They'd made a good start on building a friendship, but if he pushed her too hard to deepen it, she was liable to finish her assignment and get the hell out of here. Okay, so he had to be careful.

On the plus side, he was certain she'd begun to identify with the people of Laughing Horse. On the minus side, her father and her career represented powerful ties to the white world.

Could he find a way to break those ties? Not likely. The best he could probably hope for would be to neutralize them with equally strong ties to him and to the tribe. Was it possible to do that in a month?

Jackson didn't know the answer, but he'd fail for sure if he didn't try. Maggie had spent all of her time here documenting the reservation's most desperate problems. Maybe if she saw some of the better parts of life on the res, she'd find the idea of staying more attractive. And maybe it was time for him to be more open about himself.

If he'd learned anything from his divorce, it was that it wouldn't do any good to pretty things up for her. If she ever did fall in love with him, it had to be with the "real" him. With the Indian him. He couldn't deny who and what he was for anyone, ever again. Not even Maggie.

The thought made him nervous as hell, but he was not without weapons in this fight for her affections. What he had to do now was put them to good use. The question was, where should he start?

After a busy morning spent checking out of the motel, moving into Sara's house and typing the rest of Wanda's research paper, Maggie climbed into the passenger seat of Jackson's pickup. She sat back and took a moment to catch her breath while he drove west out of Laughing Horse, on the same road he'd taken to go to the buffalo jump.

He took the north fork this time, however. Ten miles beyond it, he made a left turn onto a dirt lane cut into a stand of towering ponderosa pines. Since Jackson appeared to be in one of his quiet moods, Maggie contented herself with watching the scenery. The lane twisted and turned back into the trees, growing narrower and more weed-choked the farther they went.

"Whose place is this?" she asked after fifteen minutes of bouncing from one pothole to the next.

"Mine."

"Did you forget something this morning?" she asked.

"Nope."

"Then why are we stopping here?"

"Because I think it's about time you interviewed me," he said, giving her a smile that was far too bland to be completely innocent. What the heck was he up to, anyway?

"Do you really think that's necessary?" she asked. "We've spent a lot of time together."

"And we've spent all of it talking about other people. Don't you want to hear about my ideas for the tribe's future?"

"Don't I already know most of them?"

"Maybe. But I want to be officially on the record."

Jackson slowed down. Maggie glanced away from him, then felt her mouth drop open when she caught sight of the clearing ahead of them. He braked to a complete stop, as if he knew she needed a moment to absorb the entire scene.

Sheltered on two sides by the pines, the two-story log home perched at the top of a small rise, facing east. Front picture windows looked out over a broad field of native grasses. Solar panels covered the roof, and a rock chimney protruded at the north end of the building. A detached two-car garage sat fifteen feet to the south. A pair of pinto horses grazed in a fenced pasture beyond the garage.

"It's lovely, Jackson," she murmured, giving him a bemused smile.

He muttered a soft "Thanks" and drove on up to the garage. He climbed out of the cab, hurried around the front of the pickup and opened her door for her. When she stepped down beside him, he took her hand and led her inside.

Most of the main floor had been left in one large, open space, with room divisions suggested by the placement of furniture rather than interior walls. A sofa and two easy chairs were grouped around an oval braided rug in front of the fireplace. A trestle table and matching chairs created a dining area, which was separated from the kitchen by a freestanding work island.

Sunlight poured in through the large windows in each exterior log wall, accenting the warm golden tones in the wood used just about everywhere—the built-in bookcases, the kitchen cabinets, the banister flanking the stairway to the second floor. Thriving green plants, fat pillows covered in calico prints and an overflowing box of toys in the living room added vivid colors to the cozy atmosphere.

Jackson hung his Stetson on a peg mounted by the door, then led the way to the kitchen. "Come on. Let's see what we can find for lunch."

Maggie followed at a slower pace, pausing in the dining area to study a small but intricately carved wooden statue of a hawk, its wings spread as if it were poised for flight.

"My father made that for me when I was six," Jackson said. "He told me it was a little piece of home I could take to boarding school with me."

"It's beautiful. He's very talented."

Leaving the statue, Maggie walked slowly to the work island.

"He was," Jackson said. He took a can of chili out of a cupboard and set an aluminum pot on the stove. "He died four and a half years ago."

"I'm sorry. I know how much it hurts to lose a parent."

With swift, economical movements, he dumped the chili into the pot and switched on the burner, then went to the refrigerator for a block of cheese and an onion. "The hurt, I can handle. I have a harder time coping with the guilt."

"Why do you feel guilty?"

"Because I helped to kill him."

Jackson turned away from her undoubtedly shocked expression and rummaged in drawers and cupboards, coming up with a knife, a cutting board and a grater. He left again and came back with a couple of bowls, shoving one of them, the cheese and the grater across the countertop to Maggie. She eyed him with exasperation for a moment, then picked up the cheese and went to work while he attacked the onion.

"I don't believe that, Jackson."

He gave her a long, steady look. "I didn't do it with a knife or a gun, but I helped kill him, all right."

"What happened?"

Jackson cleared his throat and went back to chopping the onion. "When I told you I turned my back on the tribe, I wasn't kidding. After I started college, I never came home if I could avoid it. And I was damn good at avoiding it."

"Because you didn't get along with your father?"

"That was part of it," he agreed. "But it was more because of the pressure I always felt from everyone to come back to the res. Have you ever watched the boys play basketball after school?"

Though she felt confused by the abrupt change of subject, Maggie nodded. "I'm no expert, but some of them look awfully good out there."

"They *are* good. Good enough for full-ride basketball scholarships, but the recruiters don't offer them to Indian kids anymore."

"Why not?"

"Because they won't stay in school. They get stuck in some big dorm with a bunch of white strangers. They're scared and lonesome and their classes are harder than they expected. They come home for a weekend and go out drinkin' with their buddies, and all they hear is how they're never gonna make it, and how they think they're better than everybody else. It's like the friends who got left behind can't stand to see them succeed."

"That's a shame," Maggie said.

"It's a damn waste. Every high school basketball star I saw leave this place for college before I did ended up right back here before the first year was over. I decided that wasn't gonna happen to me. I'm the only guy from this reservation who actually got a degree out of sports, and I never could have done it if I hadn't stayed away.''

"Was that hard for you?"

He stirred the bubbling chili, then brought two more bowls to the work island and poured the contents of the pot into them.

"The first year was the worst, because my family kept begging me to come home. After that, they kinda gave up. It got to be a real pride issue. I wasn't like those drunks on the res. I was this tough guy who could make it on his own.''

"That's a perfectly understandable reaction," Maggie said. "Don't be so hard on yourself.''

"Thanks for the sympathy," he said with a wry smile. He carried the bowls to the table, and pulled out a chair for her. "But that's not why I'm tellin' you all of this.''

"Okay, I'll bite," Maggie said, bringing the cheese and chopped onion to the table. When they were both seated, she asked, "Why are you telling me this?"

"Because I want you to understand why the tribe's welfare is so important to me. It's more than a convenient career choice.''

"I figured that out a long time ago," she said. "But go ahead and finish your story.''

"There's not much left. I went to law school at Georgetown, married a white woman, and went to work for a big Wall Street firm.''

"Whoa, back up one," Maggie said, hoping her eyes weren't bugging out as far as she thought they were. She'd heard he was divorced, but nobody had ever mentioned that little tidbit of information about him before. "You married a *white* woman?"

"I told you I was an apple, didn't I?" he said, raising one shoulder in a half shrug.

Maggie glanced toward the living room. "Whose toys are those, Jackson?"

He laughed. "Relax, I don't have any kids. I keep the toys around for my nieces and nephews. I've got a bunch of 'em.''

"Oh. Go on, then. What happened next?"

"We were a nice yuppie couple. Nancy was a stock trader. We raked in all kinds of bucks, and had one hell of a good time. Then, one day, my youngest sister tracked me down and told me our father had suffered a coronary. He was in intensive care in Billings, and he was asking for me."

"Did you get home in time to say goodbye?"

Jackson nodded. "Yeah. He was stabilized by the time I got there, and everyone seemed to think he'd be all right. But then he demanded to see me alone. He begged me to take care of my mother if he didn't make it. I promised I would. Hell, I'd have done anything to ease his mind. But he had another heart attack right then, and they couldn't bring him back. He'd never even met my wife."

Her eyes stinging with unshed tears, Maggie reached across the table and laid her hand over his clenched fist. "Sometimes those things just happen. It wasn't your fault."

"Yes, it was. If I'd come home once in a while, or at least stayed in touch, I would have known he was having health problems and refusing to go to the white man's doctor. Hell, I could have paid his doctor bills with the money I blew on tickets for Broadway shows and numbered prints. He was the tribal council chairman, and I could have used my law degree to help him the way I'm helping Uncle Frank now."

"It's always easy to see those things in hindsight, Jackson, but you can't change anything. What good does it do to beat yourself up like this?"

He pulled his hand out from under hers. "It helps me to remember what my pride and selfishness caused, and appreciate the beauty of the tribal system. When my father died, I found out I wasn't one bit different from those drunks on the res. I'd be one of them, if Uncle Frank hadn't straightened me out in time."

"So, you're working for the tribe as a way to atone for your father's death?"

"There's no way I could ever do that. But when I cut myself off from the tribe, I hurt myself as much as I hurt anyone else, including my father. At this point, I'm still tryin' to get my own identity back."

"I'm not sure I understand what you mean."

"It goes back to the issue of values, Maggie. To a Cheyenne, preserving the tribe is a sacred responsibility. We're taught from an early age it's more important to share and get along with the group than it is to seek personal glory and achievement. Competing successfully in the white society meant I had to deny almost every lesson my parents had taught me. It took my father's death to make me realize my values were so screwed up, I didn't know who I was anymore."

"Is that when you moved back here?"

"About six months later. My wife hung in there as long as she could, but my sudden search for my native roots seemed pretty bizarre to her. When she filed for divorce, I came home."

Maggie winced. "First your father, then your wife. That must have hurt."

"It did at the time. But in the long run, I think it was for the best that my marriage ended when it did. At least there weren't any children involved, and now I'm where I belong."

Jackson pushed back his chair and cleared away the empty bowls. Sensing he needed a moment's privacy, Maggie stayed at the table. A lump grew in her throat as she let her gaze roam from one end of the room to the other. This was by far the nicest house she'd visited on the res, but it was obviously meant for a family.

Did Jackson ever feel lonely here? she wondered. As lonely as she sometimes felt in her Washington apartment? Or did the tribe offer all the companionship he wanted? He was so self-contained, she couldn't be sure, but she had the impression he hadn't made as complete a transition back to his native roots as he had led her to believe. Perhaps he'd found a measure of contentment, but he didn't really seem . . . happy.

He returned to the dining area. "You look too serious, Schaeffer. Why don't we take a break and go for a walk?"

"That sounds great." Standing, she rubbed her fanny and gave him a rueful grin. "We've been sitting too much lately."

Chuckling, Jackson went back to the refrigerator, pulled out a couple of carrots and pointed them toward the rear of the kitchen. "We'll go out that way and visit the horses first."

Glad to see his mood lightening, Maggie followed him outdoors. "Oh, wow..." she said, pausing at the bottom of the steps to study his backyard.

There were crooked hopscotch boxes drawn in colored chalk all over the small cement patio. A sandbox filled with toy trucks and plastic pails sat off to the right. A wooden jungle gym filled the space between a couple of spindly-looking trees she couldn't identify, and beyond that was a vegetable garden that had been tilled, but not yet planted. A huge cottonwood tree grew behind the garden.

"This is quite a spread ya got here, Mr. Hawk," she drawled, hustling to catch up with him. "Looks like your nieces and nephews visit a lot."

"Yeah, they do," he said. "The rest of my family lives about five miles up the road. I try to make it fun for the kids to come visit Uncle Jackson."

"Why don't you live with the rest of your family?" Maggie asked. "Everyone else around here seems to do that."

"When I first came back, I wasn't welcome. It's taken time to heal the wounds I caused, and earn my family's respect again." He grinned suddenly and looked back at the house. "They all thought I was nuts when I started building this place."

"You built it yourself?"

"Most of it. Uncle Frank helped me clear the trees and put up the walls. I think he figured if I stayed busy enough out here, I wouldn't be tearin' up the bars in Whitehorn."

"It's a beautiful house, Jackson, but why did you make it so big?"

"I intended to give it to my mother, but she was too attached to the house my dad built for her. She let me help her fix that one up, though. And, you know, I guess there's still enough apple left in me, I kinda like havin' my privacy."

"Have all the wounds with your family been healed, then?"

"You'll see for yourself next week. I've been given strict orders to bring you over for supper when we're done typing the kids' papers. Would you mind?"

"Why would I mind?"

He turned to her with a broad smile. "Because they've all been tryin' to marry me off for the last couple of years. You'll be a prime candidate as far as they're concerned."

"How big of a group are we talking here?" Maggie asked, silently ordering her heart to stop its sudden thumping. He hadn't said *he* thought she'd be a prime candidate, only that his family would. Since she had no intention of staying here, what did it matter, anyway?

"I have two younger sisters and two brothers. They're all married and have at least three kids apiece. Then there's Uncle Frank and Aunt Sally and their four kids and their families. My mother also has two younger sisters, who'll probably bring their whole families along, and on my father's side—"

"Enough, enough!" Maggie said with a laugh. "I get the picture."

"I doubt it. They're about as subtle as a bunch of terrorists with machine guns when it comes to matchmaking."

"Would you rather I declined the invitation?"

"Nope. Just givin' you fair warning, so you won't feel embarrassed."

If he only knew how many of the elderly members of the tribe had already extolled his virtues to her when he'd been out chopping wood and the like, he wouldn't worry about that, Maggie thought with a grin. They arrived at the fenced pasture. Jackson called the horses over and gave Maggie a carrot. She fed it to one of the mares, while he fed the other one.

"They're beautiful," she said, stroking the animal's smooth neck. "Do you ride them much?"

He shook his head. "They're not broke yet. I got 'em about a week before you came, as payment for some legal work. I'm really gonna have to watch the kids this summer. Some of the boys are gettin' to the age where they'll try to ride anything with four legs."

The horses lost interest when the carrots ran out. Jackson and Maggie strolled along the fence line toward the trees. At the end of the pasture, they came to a small creek. Maggie spotted a ring of stones with a pile of ashes in the middle. Next to it was a waist-high dome-shaped frame built with saplings and fishing line.

"Is this going to be a tent for the kids?" she asked, walking closer to inspect it.

Jackson laughed. "Aw, come on, Maggie. Haven't you ever seen a sweat lodge before?"

"Uh, no. We didn't have too many of those in Denver. Is it like a sauna?"

"Yeah. We use it to purify ourselves and to pray. It's part of our religion."

"Are you really into this religion thing?"

"I'm learning about it. Uncle Frank helped me with a vision quest when I'd been home for a year. I pierced for the first time at the Sun Dance last summer."

Sweat lodge, vision quest, Sun Dance? Maggie shook her head in amazement. Every time she thought she was starting to see him clearly, he tossed out some new thing that blurred her image of him all over again.

"What?" he asked, sitting on a log near the campfire ring. "You look confused."

She ambled over to join him, collecting her thoughts as she walked. "All of this sounds kind of... mystical," she said, for lack of a better word.

The corners of his eyes crinkled with amusement. Clutching one hand to his chest as if he'd been mortally wounded, he said, "You don't see me as a great Indian mystic?"

"No."

"Why not?"

Chuckling, she rolled her eyes at him. "You're too hard-headed for that. Too much of a lawyer. Too modern."

He accepted her description of him with one of his half shrugs. "It's not easy to shed all those years of living in the white world, Maggie."

"They're a part of who you are, Jackson," she said. "Why would you want to shed them?"

"They're what makes it so hard for me to grasp all the mystical stuff that came so naturally to my father. He wasn't stupid, by any means, but he was a very simple man in a lot of ways. I mean, he didn't have to stop and think about right and wrong in any situation. He just always seemed to know what was best for the family and for the tribe."

"He lived in simpler times. He probably didn't have to make as many choices as you do," Maggie said.

Giving her a sad smile, Jackson nodded in agreement. "You're right. He didn't have many choices to make, because Indians had very little control over their lives back then. But he had such... vision. He was a true spiritual leader. I wish I'd listened to him more."

The regret in his voice tore at Maggie's heart. It sounded to her as if Jackson had set up his father as some kind of a saint whose standards he could never meet.

"Jackson," she said softly, continuing only when his gaze rose to meet hers. "Different times call for different skills and styles of leadership. The tribe desperately needs your particular skills right now, and you were only able to develop them because of the years you spent in the white world. Don't deny those years. And don't discount the contribution you're making because it's not what your father's might have been."

"Thanks," he said, his voice equally soft, equally sincere. "I hadn't thought of it that way before."

She turned toward him, lifting one knee to balance more comfortably on the log. "So tell me about *your* vision. What do you want to see happen for the tribe in the next ten years?"

His mouth curved into a thoughtful smile, and he gazed into the distance. "I want to see economic security and independence, our own businesses and entertainment facilities. I want us to have a real hospital, staffed with our own doctors, nurses and medicine men. I want us to have our own schools, where our kids can learn to be proud of who they are before they have to deal with whites. I want our young people to have job opportunities right here on the res. They shouldn't have to choose cultural annihilation or welfare to survive."

"What else?" Maggie asked, when he paused for a moment.

"I want to see more tribal unity. People taking more pride in themselves and more responsibility for themselves. We've got to find some answers to the drug and alcohol problems before they damage another whole generation. And I want us to stop seeing ourselves as a conquered people. As powerless victims."

"How would you accomplish that?"

"I like what I've seen happening since you've been here, Maggie. Especially with the kids. But I think we need to focus more attention on the old ways, too. Our religion has a lot to teach about living a meaningful life."

"And you think you don't have vision?" Maggie asked, raising both eyebrows at him. "That's a pretty tall order for only ten years, Jackson."

He shot her a self-conscious grin. "You think it's too much?"

"My dad always told me you might as well shoot for the stars. It seems to me, though, that what you're really wanting is for the tribe to withdraw from the white world even more than it already has."

"Absolutely," Jackson said. "We need to rebuild our strength from within. In order to do that, we've got to limit the amount of white interference in our affairs. The grazing leases are one example. The Whitehorn schools are another."

"I can see that," Maggie said, searching for words to suggest an alternative view that wouldn't raise his hackles.

"I can already hear the 'but' in your next sentence," he said, heaving an exaggerated sigh that made her smile.

"But," she said, "I think you'll need to maintain a careful balance there, Jackson. The tribe can't employ everyone, and the white world is not going to go away while you're rebuilding from within. You'll need people who can cope effectively in both worlds."

"I agree." He leaned closer, gazing so deeply into her eyes, she felt as if he could see down into her soul. "We'll need people like you, Maggie. Why don't you quit working for Baldwin and come to work for the tribe? You could coordinate our social programs and help us develop new ones. Write grant proposals. Help us plan economic development.''

Unable to believe she'd heard him correctly, Maggie stared at Jackson in stupefaction. He calmly returned her regard, as if he expected her to be pleased with his suggestion. And the really astonishing thing was, she was almost tempted to consider it. But, of course, she couldn't. Not without breaking her promise to her mother, which she would never, ever do.

"That's impossible," she said, forcing a flat note of finality into her voice.

"Why?" he asked. "Uncle Frank's crazy about you. A word from him to the tribal council, and—"

She stood, cutting him off with a vehement shake of her head. "No. Don't even think about it, Jackson. And don't you dare bring it up with your uncle."

"Maggie—"

"No."

He rose to his feet and held out his hands, as if in a plea for a reasonable discussion. "Just think about it for a second."

She backed up, shaking her head even more vehemently. "Which part don't you understand, Jackson? The *n* or the *o*? I already have a career."

"So, you'll have another one. You wouldn't make as much money, but—"

"Money is not the issue."

"Then what *is* the issue?"

"I don't belong here. You've said it yourself often enough."

"That was weeks ago. And I was dead wrong, Maggie. You could belong here just fine, if you wanted to."

"I *don't* want to," she said, knowing, even as she said them, that those words were not entirely the truth.

"Okay," Jackson said, shoving his hands into his jeans pockets. "It was just an idea."

Eyes narrowed with suspicion, she studied him for a moment. "Why are you giving up so easily?"

"Isn't that what you wanted?"

"Yes." She stepped closer, frowning at him in confusion. There was something seriously out of whack with this conversation, but she couldn't quite grasp what it was. It was almost as if she were talking to a slightly different Jackson from the one she was used to. "But it's not like you to be so agreeable."

"Excuse me?" he said, giving her a wounded-puppy look. "Are you saying I'm a disagreeable kind of a guy?"

"Usually."

Laughing, he casually slung his arm around her shoulders and turned her toward the house. "Okay, be that way, Schaeffer. Come on. Let's go back to work."

She walked along beside him, telling herself there was no need to feel so threatened. If Jackson had been more willing to be open about himself today, it was simply the logical result of their growing friendship. He wouldn't suddenly challenge the boundaries she'd demanded, after he'd accepted them for weeks.

And yet she couldn't deny a nagging suspicion that something important had changed. Call it a premonition, an intuition, or plain old instinct, she knew darn well he was up to something. Something he knew she wasn't going to approve of when she figured it out. It really wasn't like him to be so agreeable.

Nine

A week later, Maggie sat at Sara's kitchen table, working at her laptop computer. Sara had gone to bed hours ago. Maggie knew she should have done likewise, but there didn't seem to be much point. She would only thrash around all night, as she had every other night since her visit to Jackson's house.

There was simply no ignoring the growing urgency she felt about finishing her report and getting back to her own life— her *real* life—now, while she still could.

She paused to rub her burning eyes and stretch her stiff shoulders, muttering, "Oh, damn the man."

Her insomnia was all Jackson's fault, of course. If he hadn't suggested she go to work for the tribe, she'd be sleeping at this very moment, instead of sitting here in the dead of night, racing to finish her rough draft. Trying not to think about him or his insane job offer.

And it *was* insane. Why couldn't she remember that? Why did the notion of staying here tantalize her imagination to the point of making her question her goals, her life-style, even her own conscience? Was it the job itself she found so attractive—the thought of helping Jackson to achieve his goals for the tribe? Or was it really the possibility of staying close to him?

"Damn the man," she muttered again, burying her face in her hands.

A vision of his face appeared in her mind's eye, and she didn't know whether to burst into hysterical laughter or weep with frustration. He was up to something, all right, and the word for it was *temptation*. If she hadn't experienced it herself, she never would have believed he could be so diabolically cunning. The sneaky wretch had her right where he wanted her.

And what, exactly, had he done? Nothing! That was the worst part—feeling the subtle, relentless pressure to do what he wanted, but not being able to call him on it, because he never did anything overtly out of line.

He hadn't tried to kiss her again, or made any suggestive remarks. But a woman would have to be blind to miss the masculine admiration in his eyes whenever he looked at her now. She'd have to be deaf not to hear the new warmth in his voice when he spoke to her. She'd have to be unconscious or dead to be unaware of the sexual vibrations he'd been putting out all week.

He hadn't mentioned the job offer again, either. Instead, he had taken a more active role in the interviews she conducted, painting seductive word pictures of what Laughing Horse could be like as he elaborated on his dreams for the tribe's future. And he always managed to make her feel as if those dreams would never come true without her help.

It was blatant manipulation, but she had precious few defenses against it. When she was with him, she felt sexy, intelligent and wanted—hardly the kind of emotions to put any woman in a mood to resist. But did he want her as a mate for himself, or as an employee for the tribe? And could he ever really accept her for who and what she was, including her white background and father?

Ah, yes, now those were excellent questions, weren't they? They were also the only things that had kept her from tumbling head over heels in love with Jackson. If she wasn't extremely careful, he would turn her entire life upside down. Shaking her head in disgust at her own confusion, she went back to work.

A moment later, she heard a noise at the doorway and jerked her head up in time to see her hostess enter the room. Wrapped in a green terry bathrobe, Sara scuffed the toes of her slippers across the floor, filled the teakettle with water and lit a burner. Then she turned around, crossed her arms over her breasts and leaned back against the counter.

"All right, Schaeffer, what's going on with you?"

"I'm just getting in a little extra work," Maggie said, resisting the urge to squirm beneath Sara's probing teacher's gaze. "I'm sorry if I woke you."

"I haven't been to sleep yet. Too many weird vibes coming out of this kitchen. Are you and Jackson feuding again?"

Maggie wished the problem was that simple. "No, we've been getting along fine."

"I thought you had three more weeks to finish your report."

"I do," Maggie admitted.

"Then what's the big rush?" Sara demanded.

The teakettle shrieked. Sara moved it to a cold burner, spooned decaffeinated instant coffee into two mugs and filled them with hot water. Then she carried them to the table and sat down across from Maggie.

"Do you want me to move out?" Maggie asked.

"Of course not. I just want to know what's bothering you. Maybe I can help."

While she was tempted to unburden herself, Maggie was all too aware that Sara had to get up early for work the next morning. "I'm okay."

"Uh-huh. That's why you're typing at 2:00 a.m.? Because you're okay?"

"It's not a big deal," Maggie insisted. "And it would take too long to explain."

"I'm not goin' anywhere," Sara said dryly. "Certainly not to sleep, while you're out here actin' like a speed freak. You might as well spill your guts."

Sighing with resignation, Maggie told Sara about Jackson's invitation to work for the tribe.

"I think it's a great idea," Sara said. "Why does it upset you so much?"

"It's ridiculous, Sara. I can't just quit my job and move clear across the country."

"Why can't you? Is there a man you don't want to leave?"

"No."

"Is it the people here? I know some of them can be cantankerous, but—"

"No. They've been wonderful, and I'd really like to help them."

"Is it Jackson?"

"What about him?"

"You *know* what about him," Sara told her in a chiding tone. "You're falling in love with him, aren't you?"

Maggie opened her mouth to utter a third denial, but found she couldn't force the short syllable past her lips. Too agitated to sit another second, she shoved back her chair and paced across the room. Sara silently watched her make three round-trips to the doorway and back, then started to chuckle.

"It's not funny." Maggie wrapped her arms around herself in an effort to ward off the chill sinking into her bones. "I feel like I'm getting into something way over my head."

"You're really good for him, you know," Sara said in a mild tone. "Everyone's noticed it."

"Noticed what?"

"He smiles and laughs more when you're around. He's more relaxed. He's even putting up with that weird white lady you recruited for the tutoring program."

"Mary Jo's not weird," Maggie protested.

Sara simply stared at her with a deadpan expression. "She keeps asking about those bones George Sweetwater found. Don't you think that's a little weird?"

"Well, maybe a little. But she shows up regularly, and the kids like her, don't they?"

"I'm not sure they do. It's more like they're trying to figure her out. She's not always very patient with them."

"Do you want me to talk with her about that?"

Sara shook her head. "I can handle her. Now, stop trying to change the subject. What I want you to talk about, is Jackson. Are you falling in love with him or not?"

"I'm getting there, I guess," Maggie grumbled. "That's why I have to finish this report and get the heck out of here."

"That doesn't make any sense."

"I'm not sure how he feels about me, Sara. Even if he was in love with me, we could never make a relationship work. It's just ... futile."

"I can't believe I'm hearing this garbage from you, of all people," Sara said. "We all thought it was futile to try to get our kids fair treatment in the Whitehorn schools. You marched in there for one measly hour and showed us we were wrong."

"That was different."

"Hah! If you can get Reese to toe the line, Jackson'll be a cinch. I'll admit I was a little surprised when I first noticed there was something going on between you two, but trust me, the sparks are flying in both directions. It wouldn't surprise me if he took you home to meet his family any day now."

Feeling the blood draining out of her head, Maggie returned to her chair and collapsed into it. "I'm having dinner at his mother's house tomorrow night. The whole family is supposed to be there."

Sara slapped the table and hooted with delight. "See? What'd I tell ya? No man in his right mind takes a woman to something like that unless he's serious about her."

Maggie groaned and shook her head.

"Aw, c'mon, Maggie. We're talkin' about love here, not a funeral. You're lookin' at this all wrong."

"Am I? What about my career, Sara? It happens to be very important to me, it's not portable, and I'm not going to give it up just because some man crooks his finger at me."

"If it was just any old man, I might agree with you," Sara said. "But it's not. It's Jackson. If you really love him—"

"Damn it, Sara, you don't understand. I *can't* love him. I *can't* live on a reservation. I shouldn't even be here now."

Sara straightened up and studied her as if she'd finally heard at least a hint of the desperation Maggie was feeling. "Okay," she said softly. "Then why don't you explain it to me?"

"It has to do with my mother." Maggie paused to swallow the lump that had suddenly formed in her throat, then recounted what little she knew of her mother's background.

"Speaks Softly," Sara murmured, when Maggie had finished. "I've heard that name before, but I can't remember where." She shrugged after a moment. "Well, I'll think of it someday. So what does this have to do with Jackson?"

"My mother died from cancer five years ago. The last time I saw her when she was still lucid, she made me promise I would never go back to the blanket."

Sara jerked back as if she'd been slapped. Her nostrils flared, and her eyes took on a frosty expression. "Go back to the *blanket?* Did she actually *say* it that way?"

Maggie nodded. Before she could speak in her mother's defense, however, Sara stood, grabbed her empty mug and carried it to the sink. She banged it onto the drain board with such force, Maggie was surprised it didn't shatter. Then she returned to the table, sat down and crossed her arms over her breasts.

"Sara, I didn't mean to offend you."

"I know you didn't, but it makes me angry, and very, very sad, to hear that phrase. And coming from one of our own people, well, it reeks of self-hatred and shame and denial of who we are. *We* were here first. This was *our* land, but we were willing to share it with the whites. *We* didn't violate the treaties we made with them. Was it our fault we ended up with only blankets?"

Not knowing what else to say, Maggie whispered, "I'm sorry."

Sara shook her head. "It's not your fault, Maggie. I feel sorry for you, though. What your mother did to you wasn't fair."

"What do you mean?"

"She denied you your heritage while you were growing up. And then she made you promise to give it up permanently, when you had no idea what you were surrendering."

"I don't think you really understand, Sara."

"No, Maggie. *You* are the one who doesn't understand. If you honor your mother's last request, you'll never know who you really are. You will have given up the right to be a real Indian. A real Northern Cheyenne."

Maggie felt her temper starting to flare, and made no effort to control it. "You know, Jackson has said things like that to me, too, and I find them extremely offensive. What is this *real* Indian stuff, anyway? Do I have to earn a merit badge to get into the club? Buy a membership card? What do I have to do to prove myself to you people? Huh?"

"You don't have to prove anything to anyone but yourself," Sara said quietly. "If you're happy with yourself and the way you live, it's nobody's business but yours. But I've been watching you ever since you came here, and I don't think you're all that happy."

"Why not?"

"Why did you come here in the first place?"

"It was my job, Sara."

Sara leaned forward, pinning Maggie with an unblinking stare. "It was an excuse. An excuse to break your promise, just a little bit, so you could learn about your own people. If you're honest with yourself, you'll admit you *like* being with us, and you *want* to belong here. You *want* to be a part of this tribe. You're just afraid to make the commitment."

"I didn't know you had a degree in psychiatry."

"Can the sarcasm," Sara said. "It's not me you're really mad at."

Maggie glared at her for a moment, then sighed and shook her head. "You're right. I'm just all . . . confused."

"Welcome to the human race. It seems to me, though, that you're trying to figure out two issues at once. Maybe if you separated them, it wouldn't be so hard to figure out."

"You mean the, uh, Indian thing and Jackson?"

"Yeah. There's really no point in worrying about a relationship with Jackson until you decide whether or not you're willing to go back on your promise and become a part of the tribe. He's here to stay, Maggie. He's committed to his eyeballs, and I think you know that."

Maggie nodded. "It's one of the things I admire most about him. And you're right about something else. I *do* like being here. I can see so many things I could do for the tribe, and I *like* being a part of things. But I feel guilty about it."

"Because of your mother."

"Yes. I always knew she loved me, Sara. Whatever she did, she only did it to protect me. She wasn't a bad person."

"I never thought she was," Sara said. "I think she was misguided, but she had to have been a pretty special lady to raise a daughter like you."

"Thanks. But where does that leave me now?" Maggie asked. "If you were in my place, what would you do?"

"I'd find her family and see if anyone could tell me why she left and why she never came back."

"What difference would that make?"

"I'm not sure," Sara admitted. "I'll tell you one thing, though. Jackson Hawk is no saint, but he's one of the finest men I've ever known. If I was in love with him the way I think you are, I wouldn't give him up without a damn good reason."

"That assumes, of course, that he's in love with me, too," Maggie said. "Big assumption, Sara."

Sara grinned. "Aw, he'll get around to telling you one of these days. Are you okay now?"

"Yeah. I'm better, anyway. Go get some sleep."

"Right. See you tomorrow, Maggie."

Maggie waited until she heard Sara's bedroom door shut, then exhaled a ragged sigh. It was time to make a decision. Countless times, she had considered asking Jackson to introduce her to her relatives. She'd always chickened out, because it had felt like an invasion of her mother's privacy, at best. At worst, outright disrespect.

But so many of the things Sara had said were on target. What if she was right about Jackson's feelings for her, too? Her heart skipped half a beat, then lurched into high gear as the truth finally hit her.

Oh, God. She had to meet her relatives as soon as possible. Had to resolve her guilt over her promise to her mother. She wasn't just falling in love with Jackson Hawk. That was already a done deal.

Fighting the worst case of nerves he'd suffered in years, Jackson parked in front of Sara's house the next evening and willed himself to calm down. It was only a dinner, he told himself. His family would like Maggie, and she would like them. No need to get himself all worked up.

If he knew what had been troubling her all day, he'd have an easier time believing his own assurances, but he hadn't been able to coax anything out of her. Damn, he hated trying to guess what was going on in a woman's mind. One of the things he liked most about Maggie was that she usually told him exactly what she thought, with little or no encouragement. But not today.

He'd never seen her so distracted. While he knew it was probably a sign his recent tactics had shaken her up, he couldn't tell if he'd made any real progress toward his goal. Had he been putting too much pressure on her? Not enough? The wrong kind?

Well, he'd had enough of the indirect approach. As soon as this damn dinner was over, he'd have a talk with her and get the whole thing out in the open. Then they'd both feel better. At least he hoped they would.

Muttering under his breath, Jackson climbed out of the pickup, hurried up the walk and knocked on the door. Maggie opened it a moment later and smiled at him, and his heart rolled over like a well-trained pup. She'd traded in her jeans for a pair of slim-fitting black slacks. With them, she wore a red long-sleeved silk blouse, cinched in at the waist by a black leather belt. Dainty silver earrings complemented her short hair, and a matching pendant winked at him from the V neckline of her blouse.

She looked casual and classy, sweet and sexy, all at the same time. And if he didn't get to kiss her again soon, he was gonna go totally out of his mind. Knowing he couldn't trust himself to keep his hands off her if they spent much time alone, he declined her invitation to come inside. Once he got her settled in the passenger seat, he made a U-turn and headed straight for his mother's place.

As he'd expected, the simple family dinner had escalated into a full-fledged party. Luckily, the weather had been unseasonably warm during the past two weeks, making a picnic possible tonight. The air was fragrant with the scent of the pine trees and smoke from the barbecue pit. Vehicles of every kind and vintage lined both sides of the long driveway. The big yard surrounding the house teemed with people.

The teenagers had taken over the front porch. One group of women hustled back and forth between the kitchen and the rows of picnic tables, setting out food and fussing over the arrangement of salads, baked beans and frybread. Another group cooed over the babies and gossiped between frantic dashes to keep the more adventurous toddlers away from the irrigation ditch that formed the southern boundary of the yard.

The men played their traditional role of helping the women by staying the hell out of their way. Translated into action, that meant occasionally tending the barbecue pit or gathering around a metal horse trough filled with ice, beer and soft drinks, smoking cigarettes and swapping lies and jokes. The kids charged around in packs of five and six, laughing, yelling and generally adding to the commotion.

Meeting a clan as large and diverse as his would have been daunting for anyone. The one time his ex-wife had been here, she'd acted like she was afraid of catching a disease if she touched anyone or anything. Maggie couldn't have been more gracious. The longer Jackson watched her chatting and laughing with his relatives, the more convinced he became that she belonged here. With him. He could hardly stand to wait until dinner was over to start trying to convince her.

When the time finally came, he casually offered to take her for a walk, and guided her away from the party. They strolled past the barn in silence. Once they were out of sight and earshot of the others, he led her over to the corral fence.

Maggie rested both hands on the top rail. "What's up, Jackson?"

"I thought you might like a break from the horde. Are they driving you crazy yet?"

She laughed. "No, your family's wonderful."

Turning toward her, he braced his elbow on the rail, buying a little time to search for the right words. "I'm glad you feel that way. It makes it a little easier to confess something."

"Oh? What have you done now?"

"It's more what I haven't done," he said, returning her teasing grin with a rueful one of his own. "For the past week, I haven't been very honest with you."

Her grin faded. "In what way?"

"I really haven't given up on the idea of your coming to work for the tribe. I've been trying to put you in situations where you'd see how much we need your skills."

"Is that all?" she asked with a chuckle. "I hate to tell you this, Jackson, but you're about as subtle as your family."

He gave her an unrepentant wink. "Well? Did it work? Have you thought about it at all?"

"Yes."

He prompted when she didn't go on. "And?"

"And, I'm . . . intrigued with the idea."

"How intrigued?"

She looked away from him, pausing, as if she were wrestling with some inner decision. Impatience clawed at Jackson's gut, but he forced himself to remain silent. Then she looked at him again. Though her eyes held an anxiety he'd never seen before, her voice was filled with conviction.

"There's something I need to do before I can seriously consider any kind of a future relationship with the tribe."

"What is it, Maggie?"

"I need to understand what happened to my mother. I need to meet her relatives."

Jackson released the breath he'd been holding, in a silent sigh of relief. This he could help her with. "I'll set up a meeting tomorrow, if you want."

She grimaced. "That soon?"

"Frankly, I've been wondering why you haven't wanted to meet them before this."

"It's not that I haven't wanted to." Biting her lower lip, she hesitated, then glanced away again. In a hoarse whisper, she finally admitted, "But I'm scared."

Needing to touch her, he cupped the side of her face with his palm and forced her to look at him. "Why, Maggie?"

"What if they don't want to meet me? I mean, what if they hated my mother, for some reason? Don't you think they might hate me, too?"

"Hate you?" Stroking her cheek with the backs of his knuckles, he laughed softly at the absurdity of any such notion. "Honey, believe me, that won't happen."

"How can you be so sure? Do you know why my mother left and never came back?"

"No. But you've already met your grandmother, and she likes you just fine."

"I have a grandmother?"

He nodded. "Yup. You also have three aunts, two uncles and a slew of cousins on your mother's side of the family."

"Oh, my," she murmured, her voice sounding so wistful it wrenched Jackson's heart.

"Don't you want to know who they are?"

She shook her head. "I don't think so. If I ran into one of them before the meeting, I'd probably freak out or something. Do you, uh, know anything about my biological father's family?"

"Yeah. I was curious about why he wasn't listed on the tribal rolls with you and your mother, so I did a little discreet checking."

"What did you find out?"

"He was from Lame Deer. You've got a bunch of relatives over there, too. I'll be glad to go with you, if you want to make contact."

"Thank you. That's awfully sweet of you."

"Yeah, that's me, all right. I'm always a real sweet guy."

Her low, husky chuckle wrapped around him like a warm blanket on a frigid night. Her eyes caressed his face with shared humor, and her teasing grin was as blatant an invitation to a kiss as he'd ever seen. Then she wrinkled her sassy little nose at him.

Uttering a half laugh, half groan, he said, "Aw, Maggie," and gathered her into his arms.

She didn't seem to mind. When he lowered his head to capture her mouth, she went up on tiptoe and met him halfway. Her arms slid around his neck. Her lips parted. She welcomed his tongue with eager little moans.

The magic was still there, sweeter and more intense than the last time he'd kissed her. God, how had he lived without doing this for so long? He held her tighter, reveling in the sensations created by her body pressing against his from chest to thighs.

Her name pounded in his head in rhythm with the thundering of his heartbeat. Maggie, Maggie, Maggie... Determined to stay more in control this time, he shifted his mouth to the right and contented himself with peppering quick, light kisses across her cheeks, her eyelids, her temples and, finally, the tip of her sassy little nose. Then he rested his forehead against hers.

"Hey, Maggie, ya know what?"

"What, Jackson?"

"Pretending we're just friends doesn't work for me."

She sighed, but didn't open her eyes. "It doesn't work for me, either, but I don't know what else to do. Maybe we should stay away from each other."

"Is that what you really want?"

Slowly shaking her head, she looked up at him. "I like being with you, Jackson."

"I like being with you, too. I like it a lot. I like kissing you even more."

"Yeah, me too." She dropped her gaze. "Whenever it happens, though, I, uh, seem to forget that it's not nice to be a tease. I'll understand if you'd rather keep your distance."

"That's the last thing I want," he said. "I'd like to see you stay here for the tribe's sake, but that's not the only reason I've been pressuring you, Maggie. You know that, don't you?"

"I thought there might be more to it, but I wasn't sure."

"Well, now you are. I want you so bad, I ache with it."

She gulped, then looked up at him again. "I don't think I can handle an affair with you, Jackson."

"Did it ever occur to you I might want more than an affair?"

"What are you saying? Is this a... proposal?"

"What if I said yes?"

She pulled out of his loose embrace. "I don't know."

"Relax," he said. "It's not a proposal, but my intentions aren't completely dishonorable. For now, I'd just like to give our relationship a chance to grow and see what happens. Know what I mean?''

Her eyes narrowing with suspicion, she backed up a step. ''I'm not sure I do.''

''C'mon, Maggie, lighten up a little, will ya? All I'm askin' is for us to admit we're more than pals and do some of the things other couples do. Like hold hands, or hug or kiss once in a while. It might even be fun to go out on a date and talk about something besides work. Now does that sound so damn bad?''

Feeling foolish for practically yelling at her when he'd been trying to woo her, Jackson scowled while he waited for an answer. Honest to God, he thought he'd behaved pretty well when she called a halt to their kissing before. Considering how much he wanted her and how fiercely she'd responded to him, he'd damn near been a saint.

The corners of her mouth twitched, then slowly curved up in a smile that was worth every bit of aggravation she'd caused him. ''No, Jackson, it doesn't sound bad at all. As long as you understand that's as far as I can go until I find out about my mother.''

He held out his hand. She slid hers into it. And without another word, they set off for his mother's house again. It was a far cry from where he hoped to end up with her, but at least it was a start.

Ten

The next afternoon, Maggie climbed into the passenger seat of Jackson's pickup, fastened her seat belt and clamped her hands between her knees to stop them from shaking. Jackson slid behind the wheel and drove north on a gravel road they'd never taken before. She wished she had a pair of aviator sunglasses like his to hide behind.

"Nervous?" Jackson asked.

"Yes. You know, it's weird, but I wasn't half as nervous when I went to see Mr. Reese."

Jackson shot her a teasing smile. "Hell, he's lots meaner and uglier than your grandmmother."

"My head knows that." Maggie wiped her damp palms on her jeans. "But the rest of me hasn't gotten the message yet."

Steering with his left hand, he reached across the bench seat with his right, grabbed her left hand and laced their fingers together. "You're only gonna meet your grandmother and one of your aunts today. I promise, it'll be okay. Annie was tickled to death when I called her this morning."

"Annie?"

"Yeah. Annie Little Deer is your grandmother. And Rose Weasel Tail is your aunt."

"Then Wanda's..."

"Your first cousin," Jackson finished for her. "You couldn't have asked for nicer relatives, so stop worrying."

Maggie digested that information for a moment, then blew out a quiet sigh. "You weren't supposed to tell me, Jackson."

"You were gettin' so tense over there, I was afraid you were either gonna pass out or barf all over my pickup. Besides, if I didn't tell you now, there wouldn't be any time for you to settle down. We're almost there.''

Her stomach lurched. She yanked her hand away from Jackson's and held it over her eyes. "Lord, I won't know what to say to them. Turn around. I can't do this.''

He pulled to the side of the road and turned off the engine. Then he unfastened his seat belt, slid over next to Maggie and hauled her onto his lap. "It's okay,'' he murmured. "I'll be right there with you. They're probably just as scared as you are, Maggie.''

"I'm being ridiculous, aren't I?''

"A little. But I won't tell a soul.''

Smiling at her own foolishness, she rubbed her cheek against the front of his shirt, taking comfort from his warmth and the strong, steady beating of his heart beneath her ear. She wished she could stay here all day. But, of course, she couldn't. Her grandmother and aunt were waiting.

She gave him a quick, hard kiss for luck, then scooted off his lap and ordered him to drive on before she lost her nerve again. In what seemed like only a few seconds, he turned into a rutted driveway. Gnarled old cottonwood trees flanked both sides of the lane. When the house came into view, Maggie's heart sank.

Small and shabby, it had the peeling paint and junk-filled yard of almost every other house on the reservation. But it wasn't just any other house. Her mother had been born, taken her first steps and said her first words there. It was difficult to believe anyone, much less her own mother, could have started out in this decrepit little cottage and ended up in a gorgeous home in one of Denver's most exclusive subdivisions.

"Are you ready?'' Jackson asked as he shut off the engine.

No. She would never be ready for this, but it was too late for retreat. The front door opened. Two women stepped out onto the sagging porch and stood there, silently watching and waiting. Though they didn't touch, an aura of unity surrounded them, as if they had stood on that porch many times, lending each other strength while they watched and waited for a loved one to return.

Maggie inhaled a deep breath, clutched her purse and the carton of cigarettes she'd brought as a traditional gift of tobacco for her grandmother to her chest and said, "Let's go."

She popped the door latch, climbed down and slowly crossed the yard, unable to take her gaze off the women whose blood she shared. Annie was an inch shorter than Rose, her face heavily lined by at least seventy years of sun and struggle. Her hair had a liberal sprinkling of gray among the darker strands, and she wore it pulled back in one long braid. She was thin to the point of gauntness, but she held her back straight and proud, and a keen intelligence shone from her black eyes.

Rose was a rounder, younger-looking version of Annie. She wore her hair in a similar style, but it was a thick, lustrous black that reflected the bright sunshine. She had the same proud bearing as her mother, and she studied Maggie with the same intense interest.

Maggie stopped at the foot of the steps, raising one hand to shade her eyes. Her mouth was as dry as the parched ground. Her heart was thumping so hard, everyone must be able to hear it. Then she felt a hard, reassuring arm wrap around her waist, steadying her.

She looked up at Jackson, found empathy and support in his wink, and abruptly felt her anxiety fade to a manageable level. It was the strangest sensation, as if by his mere presence he'd replenished her depleted supply of courage. She gave him a grateful smile, then turned back to her grandmother and aunt.

Finally able to see past her own fear, she suddenly noticed her grandmother's. Annie's chin was quivering. Her lips were clamped together. Her fingers were clasped in a tight knot in front of her abdomen. All those small clues formed a picture of a woman fighting to control a powerful emotion. And there was a desperate eagerness in Annie's misty eyes that told Maggie the emotion was not rejection.

Clearing her throat, she climbed the first step. "Hello, Grandmother."

As if those two quiet words had unlocked a set of flood-gates, tears spilled from Annie's eyes, leaving glistening tracks down her lined cheeks. Her hands jerked apart. She opened her arms in a silent invitation. Maggie ran up the last two steps and squeezed her eyes shut as her grandmother's bony little arms closed around her in a fierce hug.

A moment later, Annie pulled back and raised her hands to Maggie's face, tracing her features with trembling fingertips, smiling through her tears.

"Welcome, little one," she whispered. "I never thought I would be blessed to see you again. You look like my Bevy."

"Thank you," Maggie murmured, blinking back tears of her own. "She was a beautiful lady."

"Quit hoggin' her, Mama," Rose said. "I want a hug, too."

Laughing, Maggie turned to her aunt and received another warm welcome. Then Rose took over, drawing Annie, Maggie and Jackson inside, leading the way to a cozy kitchen at the back of the house, talking constantly, as if she intended to make up for all the lost years in one afternoon.

Jackson elbowed Maggie in the ribs, gestured toward Rose with his thumb and whispered, "That's where you got your gabbiness."

"Oh, hush," Maggie whispered back, but the thought pleased her immensely.

She'd noted many times before that no matter how poor a Cheyenne home might look on the outside, the inside was invariably neat and clean, and whatever food the people had was generously shared with visitors. Annie Little Deer's home was no exception. Feeling too excited to eat, Maggie almost groaned when she saw the kitchen table.

Big dishes of vegetables and salads fought for space with heaping platters of beef, chicken and frybread. Four freshly baked pies sat on the counter beside the stove. Her grandmother and aunt must have been cooking nonstop since Jackson phoned this morning. The gesture touched Maggie deeply, and she did her best to do the meal justice.

Jackson and Rose carried most of the conversation while they were eating. When Rose stood to clear away the dirty dessert plates, however, Annie got up and brought a fat, dog-eared photo album to the table. Maggie and Jackson scooted their chairs closer for a better view of the book. Picture by picture, memory by memory, Annie revealed a part of Beverly's life Maggie had never known.

There were photographs of Beverly as a young child, with Rose and their other sisters, Carol and Susan, playing with dolls, lined up on a horse's back, having a water fight with their brothers, William and Henry. As the pages turned, the children grew into gangly adolescents and then into good-looking young men and women. Toward the end of the book, a heartbreakingly handsome young man began to appear in the photos with Beverly.

"Your father," Annie said, "Daniel Speaks Softly."

"What was he like?" Maggie asked.

"He was a good boy," Annie said. "Polite, smart, ambitious. He could fix any kind of a machine. He loved your mother very much."

"Then why did he leave her?"

"He got into an argument with his boss and lost his job. Couldn't find another one, because the boss spread lies about him all over Whitehorn. Then he felt ashamed and started drinkin'." Annie sighed and shook her head. "My Bevy, she tried real hard to make him stop, but it wasn't no use. He just up and left one day. Didn't even know you were on the way."

Jackson pointed to a photo of Beverly, smiling down at a squalling infant in her arms. "Is that Maggie?"

Rose peered over Jackson's shoulder and laughed when she saw the picture. "Oh, yeah. We were all crazy about that kid, but she had a set of lungs on her you could hear for miles."

Maggie smiled over her shoulder at Rose, who reached out and affectionately ruffled her hair.

"And from what Wanda tells me, she still makes a lot of noise in certain places," Rose said, with a wicked grin. "Like school district offices. We owe you big-time for that one, sweetie. Thanks."

"You're welcome," Maggie said.

Annie closed the album, then got up and pulled open a drawer. Returning to the table, she set a small, intricately beaded pouch shaped like a turtle in front of Maggie. "I made this for you when you were born. I want you to have it."

Maggie picked it up and studied both sides, feeling something hard, like a little stick, between the layers. "This is beautiful. What is it?"

"A charm to make you grow up healthy and protect you from evil. This is an old Cheyenne custom. When you have babies, I will make charms for them."

"What's inside it, Grandmother?"

"A piece of your navel cord. That's what makes the medicine work." Annie shot a sly grin at Jackson, then looked back at Maggie. "This Hawk kid, here—I think he might give you pretty babies. You like him?"

Maggie felt her face grow hot. She heard Jackson let out a deep, rough chuckle, but didn't dare look at him. "Yes, I like him, Grandmother, but we haven't known each other very long."

"Pah!" Annie said, waving aside Maggie's cautious words. "What's to know? He's a big, handsome fella. Got steady work, a nice house and a decent family. You could do a lot worse."

"Thank you, Annie," Jackson said.

She shook a bony finger at him. "Don't get all conceited, Jackson Hawk. She could do a lot *better* than you, too. You get this girl of ours, I'll expect you to take good care of her."

"Yes, ma'am," Jackson said.

"I don't need anyone to take care of me." Maggie shot him a warning look. "I can take care of myself."

"Yeah, sure," Annie agreed. "Most of us can. But it don't hurt to have a good-lookin' man around to give you them pretty babies."

"Don't give him any more ideas, Grandmother," Maggie complained. "He's got enough of his own."

"He's a randy one, eh?" Raising her eyebrows, Annie turned her scrutiny on Jackson again. "You behave yourself around our girl, Jackson Hawk. Show her respect, or her uncles will pay you a visit. You understand me?"

His eyes glinting with unholy glee, Jackson nodded solemnly. "Yes, ma'am. I understand."

Annie nodded back at him, then leaned forward, bracing her forearms on the table. "Tell me about your mother, Maggie. This Mr. Schaeffer she married—was he good to her?"

"Oh, yes," Maggie said. "He's a wonderful man. Would you like to see a picture of them together?"

"Please."

Maggie dug her wallet out of her purse and pulled a photograph from it's plastic sleeve. "This was taken at Lake Louise, up in Canada, about a year before she got sick."

Annie accepted the picture, holding it carefully by the edges. Rose came over and stood behind her, laying one hand on Annie's shoulder, as if in a gesture of comfort. Annie's face contorted with grief.

After a moment of silent struggle, her expression cleared, and she said softly, "My Bevy looks happy. Like when she was a little girl."

"Yeah, she does," Rose said. "See what pretty clothes she's wearing?"

Annie started to hand back the picture, but Maggie refused to take it. "I still have the negative. You keep that one, Grandmother."

"Thank you." Annie looked up at Maggie, then down at the photograph again. "You said she got sick?"

"She had breast cancer. The doctors did everything they could, but she never liked going to the doctor much, and they found it too late to help her."

Annie's voice softened to a hoarse whisper. "Did she . . . suffer?"

"It got bad toward the end," Maggie said, "but she had the best care Dad and I could give her. We still miss her a lot."

Gently laying the picture on the table, Annie said, "We also miss her, Maggie. I'm happy you finally came to see me. It's like having a little piece of my Bevy back."

"Did you know who I was that first day, when we met at the day-care center?" Maggie asked.

Annie nodded. "I was pretty sure."

"Why didn't you say something, Grandmother?"

"I didn't know how much you knew, and I didn't want to force a relationship on you, if you didn't want to know us."

"I didn't know if you would want to see me," Maggie said. "I only knew Mama came from this reservation, and that she never wanted me to come here. Can you tell me why she felt that way? Was there a family fight, or something like that?"

Annie stiffened, then turned her gaze away from Maggie. "It had nothing to do with the family. We loved Bevy and she loved us. She wanted you to have a better life. That is all I have to say."

"But—"

"We will not speak of this again." Annie pushed back her chair and stood, suddenly looking old and exhausted. "Thank you for coming to see me. You'll come back for Wanda's graduation dinner. You can meet the others then."

In other words, here's your hat, what's your hurry? Maggie thought grimly. She looked to Jackson for guidance as to whether or not she should push for more information. He shook his head and got to his feet. Maggie exchanged a stilted goodbye with her grandmother and walked back to the front door.

She had almost reached the pickup when the door of the house opened behind her and Rose came out, softly calling her name.

"Wait, Maggie. Please."

Maggie turned around in time to see her aunt reach the bottom step and jog across the short distance between them.

"I don't want you to leave like this," Rose said. "Mama didn't mean to hurt your feelings."

"I know she didn't, Aunt Rose. Don't worry about it."

Rose took Maggie's right hand between both of hers and held on as if she feared her niece would run away. Anxiously searching Maggie's face, she said, "Mama's got real old-fashioned ideas about some things. You're probably imagining something worse than what really happened to your mom."

"Will you tell me?" Maggie asked.

"Sure, honey." Rose looked over at Jackson. "This is kinda private, so we're gonna go for a little walk, okay?"

"No problem," he replied. "Take your time."

Maggie gave him a grateful smile, then walked around the side of the house with her aunt.

Jackson stood beside his pickup until Maggie and Rose were out of sight. Then he climbed in behind the wheel, rolled down the windows and stretched his legs across the seat. Rose had said Maggie was probably imagining something worse than what had actually happened to Beverly, but the admission that something *had* indeed happened to Maggie's mother worried him. Her remark about Annie's being old-fashioned about some things made him suspect sex had been involved.

Women everywhere were vulnerable to male predators, but Indian women had always been especially helpless when it came to dealing with white men. Having grown up on a reservation, Rose was bound to have developed a stoic attitude toward the indignities Cheyenne women had often been forced to endure. But Maggie had grown up in an environment where women didn't learn to accept such indignities. Would Rose understand that, if she was planning to tell Maggie her mother had been raped?

The longer they were gone, the more anxious he felt. After ten minutes, he climbed out of the pickup and rearranged the jumble of tools he always carried around in the back. After twenty minutes, he started to pace back and forth between the pickup and the gravel road. After thirty, he decided to go looking for them.

As he rounded the corner of the house, the women came out of a stand of willows fifty yards away. Rose had her arm around Maggie's shoulders, but from this distance he couldn't see much more than that. Wanting to give them the privacy they needed to finish their conversation, he backtracked before they spotted him and got into the pickup again.

Five minutes later Maggie climbed in beside him, her face pale and set. Reminding himself she would tell him what she'd learned if and when she felt like it, he turned the vehicle around and drove away. She sat utterly still, looking straight ahead with the unblinking stare of a shock victim.

Gritting his teeth against the rage he felt at seeing her so upset, Jackson stomped on the accelerator. She still hadn't spoken by the time they arrived at his house, and she made no objection when he took her inside. Her hand was so icy in his, he was surprised she wasn't shivering.

He led her to the sofa. She obediently sat at one end, pulled her knees up to her chest and hugged them to her with both arms. Swearing under his breath, Jackson raced upstairs for a blanket, raced back to the living room and wrapped her up. Then he hurried out to the kitchen and made her a mug of strong, sweetened tea.

When he offered it to her, she looked up at him with a blank, shattered expression for a heartbeat, then slowly shook her head. Jackson set the cup on the coffee table, sat beside her and took both of her hands between his.

Briskly rubbing them, he said, "Maggie, honey, talk to me. What did Rose tell you?"

Maggie shook her head again, but then her face crumpled and a harsh, racking sob shuddered through her body. He pulled her into his arms and held her, wishing he could take away her pain and knowing he couldn't. The tears came next, soaking his shirt while she gasped for air each time another sob shook her. And finally she raised her fists and pounded on his chest, crying, "No, no, no! Oh, Mama, no!"

Her energy spent, she sagged against him. Resting his cheek on the top of her head, Jackson held her, rocked her, murmured comforting words to her until even the silent weeping stopped. At last she pulled away, wiping her eyes with the backs of her hands.

"I'm sorry," she said, her voice still raw with emotion.

"You have nothing to be sorry for." He handed her the mug. When she'd taken a swallow, he asked, "Can you tell me what this is all about now?"

She took another swallow, then set the mug down and nodded.

"My, uh...my mother..." She choked, gulped, shook her head, as if in frustration.

"It's all right," Jackson said. "Take your time."

"When I was born, my m-mother had to go into W-Whitehorn to the hospital." She paused to inhale a deep breath. "She had to have a C-section because I was in the b-breach position."

A sick feeling invaded the pit of Jackson's stomach as he sensed what was coming, but he silently waited while she paused to take another breath.

"When, uh... when her periods still hadn't started again about eight months later, she went back to the doctor who had performed the operation. He laughed at her, Jackson. And he t-told her to f-forget about it."

"Why?"

Maggie's eyes suddenly glittered with fury. Her voice dripped venom onto every word. "Because that lousy son of a bitch had given her a hysterectomy while she was still under the anesthetic. Nobody had bothered to tell her about it."

Jackson uttered a vicious curse. Maggie nodded in agreement. Then she continued.

"He, uh...he said he had every right to do it to any dirty squaw who came to him expecting free emergency service. He'd made it his personal mission to save the taxpayers from having to support any more lazy damned Indians. Aunt Rose told me she knows of at least ten other women he sterilized involuntarily."

"Nobody ever took him to court?"

Maggie shook her head. "The women were all too ashamed to talk about it, and none of them thought they'd get any justice from the white courts if they did."

"He's not still practicing, is he?"

"No. If he was, I'd probably kill the bastard. Unfortunately, he's already dead. He murdered her, Jackson. It was because of him she wouldn't go to the doctor when she found the lump in her breast. I know it was."

"Damn, Maggie, I'm sorry that happened to your mother."

"Me, too. God, she must have felt so violated, and to him, it was like spaying a dog or a cat." Maggie turned to him, her eyes stark with pain. "I can't even imagine hating anyone that much. Can you?"

"No. But that kind of hatred's been out there for a long time," Jackson said. "After what she went through, I don't understand why your mother willingly spent the rest of her life with whites."

"I didn't, either. Aunt Rose said Mama blamed everything on her own ignorance of white people. I guess she thought she could save me from being that ignorant by raising me off the res. It was just pure luck she met Dad."

"How did that happen?"

"He hired her to clean the rooms in his first motel. She could have made more money as a waitress, but she took the motel job because he allowed her to bring me to work with her."

"He sounds like a nice guy."

"He is. Oh, God, I should call him. I don't think he knows any of this."

"Do it tomorrow," Jackson suggested. "You've had enough for one day."

"You're right." Leaning her head back against the sofa cushion, she closed her eyes. "You know what makes me feel the worst about this?"

"What?"

"When I was little, I used to beg my mother for a brother or a sister. Can you imagine how much that must have hurt her?"

"You were just a kid. You didn't know."

Tears trickled out from beneath her lashes. "I know, but she loved babies so much. After she was diagnosed, she used to go up to the hospital when she wasn't sick from the chemotherapy. And she'd rock and cuddle the babies who were born addicted to drugs. She said it comforted her as much as it did them. And that miserable excuse for a doctor took away her right to have any more babies of her own."

Jackson pulled her into his arms again. She clung to him for a moment, then pushed herself away. Refusing to look at him, she whispered, "I'm sorry. Knowing what he did to her makes me feel like I'm dirty inside."

"You're not the dirty one, Maggie. That damned doctor was."

"I know, but somehow I feel too...violated myself to touch anyone. I need to be alone for a little while."

Though he hated the thought of leaving her when she looked so forlorn, Jackson nodded and got up. "All right. I'll check on the horses and mess around in the garage or something. Call me if you need anything."

As he reached the back door, she called to him. "Hey, Jackson? Thanks."

"That's what friends are for," he said.

Then he walked into the mudroom, where he spied the stack of tarps and blankets he used for the sweat lodge. He hesitated for a moment, wondering if the idea forming in his mind would help Maggie put this painful episode into perspective.

Well, why not? he asked himself. Her spirit needed healing. While his idea might not be too kosher, she wasn't a traditional Indian. Hell, she wouldn't even know the difference. Grabbing the pile of blankets, he hurried out the back door.

Exhausted and numb, Maggie curled up in the blanket again. Jackson had been so sweet, she hoped she hadn't hurt his feelings by asking him to leave her alone. But it couldn't be helped. She'd learned so many things today, she needed some time to digest them all and regain her composure.

Gradually, the daylight faded. Her clamorous thoughts subsided, and the peace and quiet of the house sank into her bones. She lost all sense of the passage of time. Her eyelids grew heavy.

"Maggie," a deep, familiar voice said close to her ear. "Maggie, wake up."

She forced her eyes open and sat up. What she saw made her wonder if she was having a weird dream. Closing her eyes, she shook her head to clear it. When she opened them again, Jackson was still standing in front of her, wearing nothing but a pair of black gym shorts and sneakers. He held out what looked like a purple T-shirt. In a voice that sounded as if it were coming from the bottom of a well, he asked if she needed some help.

"Help with what?" she asked.

He waved the T-shirt under her nose. "You need to take off everything but your underwear and put this on."

"Why?"

"We're gonna do a sweat. It'll make you feel better."

At the moment, she seriously doubted anything could accomplish that. But Jackson had a determined look on his face, and she still felt too groggy and disoriented to argue with him.

"Okay, okay..." she grumbled, holding out her hand. "I'll put it on."

"Do you need some help?" he asked again.

"No. Just give me a second to wake up."

"All right, but don't take too long. Everything's ready, and I can't leave the fire unattended. I can see it from the backyard, so I'll wait for you there." He handed her the shirt and walked to the door, then added, "Wear your shoes, too, or you'll get stickers in your feet."

Moving slowly, she stood up. When she heard the door shut, she stripped down to her bra and panties and pulled the T-shirt over her head. The soft fabric covered her from her neck to her knees. It held a fresh scent, as if it had been dried on a clothesline. Then she obediently put on her shoes, made a pit stop in the bathroom and went out to join Jackson.

A cool evening breeze washed away the last vestiges of drowsiness. Jackson smiled at her as she crossed the patio, holding out a hand in welcome. It felt natural to slide her hand into his and walk beside him under a sky filled with stars.

Looking up at them, she said, "How long did I sleep?"

"Five hours," he said.

"Tell me about this sweat thing. Why is it going to make me feel better?"

"It's a purification ritual. It'll help you find your center of balance again, and connect you with Mother Earth. We usually have more people than this, but we'll do our best with just the two of us."

The sweat lodge came into view. A patchwork of blankets covered the sapling frame. The fire ring beside it held a pyramid of rocks surrounded by glowing embers. A pitchfork leaned against a nearby tree.

Jackson released her hand, then grasped her shoulders and turned her to face him. "It'll be pitch-black when we get inside the lodge and close the flap. I'll bring in the rocks four times, and it'll feel like you're being roasted alive."

"Gee, it sounds like fun," she muttered.

Ignoring her smart remark, he went on. "If you can't breathe, put your face close to the ground or lie down. It'll be cooler down there. You can leave anytime you need to, but try to stay with me through all four rotations. Okay?"

Following his directions, she ducked through the low canvas doorway and crawled to the far end of the lodge. She sat cross-legged and inhaled slow, deep breaths, reminding herself she was not claustrophobic. The only furnishings were a bucket of water with a metal dipper and a portable cassette player. Weird, she thought. Using a modern machine in an ancient ceremony was definitely weird.

A moment later, Jackson carried in a load of glowing rocks, balancing them on the tines of the pitchfork. He dropped them in a hole dug in the center of the floor.

Then he quickly shut the flap and crawled to a spot beside her, dragging the bucket of water behind him. The temperature rose immediately. When the glow of the rocks died down, Maggie couldn't see a blessed thing. She heard a soft click, and the sound of Indian drums touched her ears. Well, that explained the cassette player. The rocks flared again when Jackson sprinkled something over them. Wisps of smoke rose from the pit. A wonderful aroma filled the air.

"This is cedar, for purification," Jackson said, his voice low and reverent, blending with the drums. "Breathe it in. Take it with your hands and rub it over yourself."

Determined to give this a chance, she followed his instructions. He poured a dipper of water over the rocks next, creating a hissing cloud of steam. Suddenly it was hotter. Hotter than anything she'd ever felt before. Hotter than even hell could be.

Sweat gushed from her skin. The air was too thick to breathe. Panic seized her. She had to get out. Get out. Get out!

Jackson's voice reached out to her, calming and soothing her, even though she couldn't understand the words he was chanting. They must be in Cheyenne. She bent down as Jackson had instructed, finally succeeding in dragging the searing air into her lungs. The drumbeats echoed through her head in a steady, relentless rhythm.

Her mind whirled with half-formed thoughts and fleeting images. Her heart picked up the cadence of the drums. She clung to Jackson's voice as if it were her only link to sanity, while the heat continued to come at her in overwhelming waves. Just when it was about to become bearable, she heard Jackson moving toward the doorway.

Cool air rushed in, shocking her skin, raising goose bumps as high as the Rockies. He brought in another load of rocks and flipped the canvas flap shut, and the cycle of heat and steam started all over again, opening her pores to another cleansing bath of sweat.

Slowly, slowly, her mind cleared. Her anxiety merged with the steam and floated into the night. She felt the earth, hard and cool beneath her. Heard the drums and Jackson's voice as if they were somewhere inside her. Sensed a deep and expanding unity of spirit with him that was like nothing she had ever known.

The lodge became a womb, the steam a protective cushion of fluid, the drums her mother's heartbeat. She was safe here. Safe from guilt and grief and humiliation. Safe from rage and hurt and confusion. She was one with the darkness, one with Jackson, one with all of the people who had ever experienced this ceremony. Here, finally, was a place where she felt, to the bottom of her soul, that she belonged.

When the fourth cycle ended, she didn't want to leave. The world outside was too exposed and frightening and lonely. But when Jackson held out his hand to her from the doorway, she went to him.

He helped her to her feet, then enfolded her in his arms. And suddenly, as if by magic, she felt safe again.

Eleven

"Thank you," Maggie whispered. She hugged Jackson with all her strength, then leaned back and gazed up at him. "That was absolutely incredible."

He tucked a strand of her hair behind her ear. "I thought you were pretty incredible. Your first sweat can be intimidating, but you handled it like a champ."

"Hearing your voice helped." She shivered from the memory of the intimate connection she had felt with him.

Jackson released her, untied one of the blankets on the sweat lodge and wrapped it around her. "Can't let you get chilled. Why don't you go to the house and take a shower? I'll clean up here."

"No, I want to help. You went to a lot of trouble to do this for me."

"It was my pleasure."

He leaned down and dropped a playful kiss on her mouth. That brief contact wasn't enough. She wanted much, much more. When he started to straighten up, she raised one hand to the back of his neck and held him there. His muscles tensed. His gaze locked with hers, and in the black depths of his eyes she saw a fierce hunger that matched her own. Oh, God. The intimate connection was still there, and she wanted—no, *needed*—to feel it with her body, as well as with her heart and mind.

She lifted her other hand to his neck and pressed her lips to his. The blanket slid off her shoulders, hitting the ground with a muffled plop. His arms surrounded her, pulling her flush against him.

Conscious thought ceased. Ancient instincts took over. He was all hot, naked skin, hard bones and muscles, strong, seeking hands. Her senses feasted on him. The slickness of his tongue stroking hers. The salty taste of his neck. The aroma of wood smoke mixing with his own musky scent. His hoarse groans of need and want. The rough calluses on his hands when he slid them beneath her shirt and caressed her back and sides.

She strained closer. Cupping his hands under her bottom, he hiked her up. She wrapped her legs around his hips, clutched at his back with her hands, rubbed her breasts against his chest, reveling in the strength of his erection pressing into her most private parts. God, she loved being wanted like this. Needed to be needed like this. Never, ever, wanted these exciting sensations to end.

But suddenly he was pushing her hips away, untangling her arms from around his neck, denying her his mouth. Her feet touched the ground. He held her by the waist until her wobbly legs would support her. Then he let her go, curling his fingers into fists at his sides, as if to prevent himself reaching for her again. They stared at each other, chests heaving with ragged breaths that rent the night's stillness.

"We can't do this, Maggie," he said. "Not now."

"I want you, Jackson. And you want me. Don't deny it."

"I don't want to deny it." He glanced down at his groin, then gave her one of his half shrugs and a rueful smile. "I couldn't if I wanted to. But you've had one hell of an emotional day, and I don't want to take advantage of you when you're so vulnerable. I didn't bring you out here to seduce you."

"Fine." Grinning wickedly, she stepped toward him, her palms itching to touch him again. "I'll seduce you."

He grabbed her hands and held them together in front of her. "No, Maggie. Stop and think about this, before I run out of nobility. Believe me, I don't have much left."

"Jackson, I know what I'm doing."

He inhaled a deep breath, then released it with a shuddering sigh. "Humor me. I don't want you to have any regrets. Go up to the house and wait for me. If you still want to make love with me when I get there, we will. If you don't, there won't be any problem. Deal?"

Maggie knew she wouldn't change her mind. She had never felt so close to anyone, and nothing in her life had ever felt this right. Unfortunately, she could see that he had his heart set on protecting her, and she could hardly fault him for forcing her to make a clear and conscious decision. In fact, she loved him for it, more than she'd ever dreamed she could love anyone.

"Okay, deal," she said. "But don't take forever."

Releasing her hands, he stepped back. She turned and walked away, plotting wonderfully wicked things she would do to him the next time she saw him. Unbraiding his hair topped the list. After that, she'd think of something.

She entered the kitchen, turned on the lights and dutifully sat down at the table to wait. She even tried to think of reasons not to make love with him. But there weren't any.

Until now, she had spent her whole life looking toward the future, studying to achieve the goals her mother had set for her and working to become the kind of woman who would make her mother proud.

The sweat lodge had forced her to live in the moment. It had taught her the joy of feeling all her feelings, no matter how intense they might be. It had shown her how empty her heart had been before she met Jackson.

When she finished her report, she would have to choose between going back to Washington and staying here with her people. It would not be an easy choice to make. But she wasn't going to worry about that now.

No, tonight she was not Beverly's daughter. She wasn't the congressman's aide or the Little Fed. She was simply a woman who deeply loved a man. She didn't need or want promises, commitments or obligations. The future would take care of itself. At this moment, the only thing she really wanted was to spend one night in Jackson's arms. Whatever she had promised her mother, she deserved that much happiness.

The back door opened and closed. Standing, she turned to face the doorway. Her heart soared when Jackson appeared. Catching sight of her, he halted in his tracks and rocked back on his heels as if he'd run into an invisible barrier. His gaze locked with hers, and in his eyes she saw everything she could have wished for—longing, hope and hunger, all mixed up with a resigned acceptance of the possibility that she'd changed her mind.

Unable to speak past the lump in her throat, she held out her arms to him. He crossed the room with long, deliberate strides, dumped the cassette player he carried on the table and studied her face intently, as if he were searching for the slightest sign of doubt. She looked back at him just as intently, holding her breath, praying he would see the feelings she couldn't express with words.

Finally, a slow, sensuous smile moved over his face, and then she was in his arms, hugging, kissing, laughing with the sheer joy of holding him. He lowered one hand to the backs of her knees and lifted her high against his chest. Chuckling at her startled yelp, he carried her up the stairs and into the bathroom.

He kissed her as if she were a tasty morsel he intended to savor to the fullest. Then he set her on her feet, turned away to start the water in the shower, and came back to her as the room began to fill with a steamy mist.

Beneath his tender ministrations, her clothing fell away. She sighed with delight when he kicked his gym shorts into the corner, revealing himself completely for the first time. He was a proud, virile warrior, created with long limbs and sleek, hard muscles, perfect for hunting and fighting off enemies and pleasing the eyes of his woman.

The admiration in his eyes when he looked at her said he found her equally pleasing, allowing her to shed all modesty and inhibition. Boldly she stepped forward and tugged off the leather strings at the ends of his braids. His hair immediately began to unwind. She helped it along, sliding her fingers through the thick ebony sections, spreading it out on his broad shoulders.

"I've wanted to do that for a long time," she said.

He held the shower curtain open with one hand and offered her the other. "Come."

She stepped into the bathtub, lifting her face to the water while he climbed in behind her and enclosed them both in a warm, intimate world. A world not unlike the sweat lodge. Surrounding her with his arms, he urged her to lean back against his chest.

Then he rubbed a bar of soap over her breasts and belly with his right hand and followed it with his left, working up a frothy lather on her skin. He scrubbed her arms, her legs, even her feet, then turned her around and scrubbed her back and buttocks with the same gentle thoroughness. Each slick, circular stroke of his hands sensitized a new swath of nerve endings until she burned with wanting him.

She held out her hand in a silent demand for the soap, returning his wicked smile when he slapped it into her palm. Oh, she would make him burn the way she burned, need the way she needed, want the way she wanted. But while the act of scrubbing him elicited groans of pleasure from deep in his throat, it also intensified her own arousal until she could barely contain it.

At last he took the soap away and handed her a bottle of shampoo. When she poured a generous dollop into her palm, he went down on one knee, nuzzling her breasts and belly, stroking her back and buttocks with his hands, while she rubbed the shampoo into his scalp. Exploding shampoo bubbles released a scent of citrus into the air. His hair flowed between her fingers like ropes of wet silk.

He lapped at the drops of water that collected in the grooves of her collarbones, followed some that drizzled into the valley between her breasts with his tongue, flicked at others that clung to her nipples. His hands grew bolder, sliding up and down the backs of her thighs, then the fronts, coming dangerously close to the one place she most wanted to feel his touch, but never quite reaching it.

Her knees quivered. She clutched his head against her abdomen, fearing she would collapse if she didn't hold on to something. In one smooth motion, he rose to his feet, anchoring her with a strong arm around her waist. Murmuring soothing nonsense phrases, he massaged shampoo into her hair, then ducked them both under the spray for a final rinse before shutting off the water.

After a few swipes of a towel over his hair and torso, he lifted her from the tub and made short work of drying her off. Then he scooped her up against his chest again. She wrapped her arms around his neck and felt his heart thudding against her side. Her own heart picked up the rhythm, pounding with anticipation as he carried her to his bedroom.

She would not have been surprised if he'd dumped her in the middle of the bed and taken her immediately. Nor would she have objected; she couldn't imagine feeling any more aroused than she already did.

Jackson had other ideas, however, wonderful, inventive, erotic ideas that he proceeded to demonstrate one by one. Using his hands and lips, his teeth and his tongue, he explored her body with maddening patience. He knew when to linger and when to move on, when to tantalize and when to stimulate, when to soothe and when to incite.

As it had in the sweat lodge, time stretched out until it lost all meaning. Her world narrowed to the circle of light cast by the lamp on the nightstand, to the man in her arms and the incredible sensations created by his touch. By the time he retrieved a foil packet from somewhere in the headboard, she was filled with such a fierce need for release, she wasn't about to wait for Chief Slow Hand to take care of the precautions.

Grabbing the packet out of his hand, she ripped it open with her teeth, tossed the foil aside and rolled the condom onto his engorged shaft with a minimum of fuss. Then she kissed her way up his torso, giving him a taste of his own sweet medicine before she captured his mouth with an urgent demand for satisfaction. And then he was beside her, sliding his right arm under her shoulders, hoisting her left leg over his hip, entering her with a powerful thrust that nearly made her weep with relief.

But there was no time for tears. The man with infinite patience had vanished. In his place, she found a man determined to drive her out of control in the shortest time possible.

Murmuring dark, delicious words that would have shocked her under any other circumstances, he thrust into her relentlessly, like the echoes of the drums she could still hear pounding in her memory. He nipped at the juncture of her neck and shoulder, soothed it with his tongue, caressed her breasts with his free hand. And the drums beat on, harder and faster. Her hips found the rhythm, meeting each thrust with equal power.

Again she found herself clinging to his voice as she reached and strained for something elusive. Elusive, but desperately important. A oneness. A connection of spirits that could be found only in sweat-drenched flesh and the drumbeats and the steamy friction where their bodies came together again and again in a pleasurable sort of violence.

And still he urged her on, praising her, commanding her, invading every part of her consciousness, until there was only heat and light and the drumbeats. Always the drumbeats. Driving her up and up in an endless quest. Suddenly they were there, reaching that mystical, elusive peak together in a chorus of ecstatic shouts. And for one utterly sweet moment, their souls embraced.

The drums gradually faded into the strong, steady thud of Jackson's heart beneath her ear. Ragged breathing softened to contented sighs. She curled into his warmth, felt him brush a gentle kiss on the top of her head, then slid into a deep, exhausted sleep.

Jackson awoke to the first golden rays of dawn with an arm and shoulder that had gone numb and a warm, naked body plastered against his side under the covers. He lifted the sheet and felt a wave of tenderness threaten to swamp his heart. Maggie's head lay in the crook of his shoulder, her hair standing up every which way in adorable little spikes. She had one arm and a leg draped over him in a boneless sprawl, and her mouth was curved in a soft smile that suggested happy dreams.

Man, she was something else, he thought, grinning as he tucked the covers around her neck and shoulders. He'd expected her to be an enthusiastic lover, but he hadn't expected her to take him on like such a tigress. Just remembering the fire in her eyes when she'd snatched the condom out of his hand brought on an erection he could have used for a tent pole.

And to think he'd given her a chance to back out. He might have lived the rest of his days without ever knowing what real passion felt like. After all that had happened between them last night, surely she must love him.

There was no use trying to deny it. He was deeply and irrevocably in love with Maggie, and he wanted her to stay with him forever—as his wife, and the mother of his children. He hadn't realized how much he wanted kids until yesterday, when Annie had told Maggie he could give her pretty babies. God, yes, he could. And he would, if only she would let him.

But what if she didn't feel the same way about him? The only predictable thing about Maggie was that she always found a way to do the unpredictable. Last night there had been no promises, no commitments, no words of love spoken.

What if she'd only wanted one night with him? She'd said she didn't want an affair, but when he'd hinted at a proposal, she sure hadn't turned any cartwheels, either. He squeezed his eyes shut, hoping he could also squeeze out these nagging doubts. Damn.

He wanted to shake her awake and demand a commitment. Or, better yet, make love to her again, and seduce one out of her. But as stubborn and independent as Maggie was, he figured trying to manipulate her or crowd her in any way would be the worst mistake he could make.

Much as he hated to admit it, this was probably one of those times when a wise man would back off and allow his woman the time and space she needed to make her own decision. That didn't mean he couldn't do his damnedest to help her make the right one. But ultimately, she would only stay with him if that was where she honestly wanted to be.

Unable to lie still any longer, Jackson slowly eased his shoulder from under Maggie's head, replacing it with a pillow. A million tiny needles attacked his arm as the blood flowed back into it. Biting back a hiss at the discomfort, he gently removed her arm and leg and slid out of the bed.

A pouty little frown crossed her face, but she shifted around, wrapped her arms around the pillow and settled back to sleep. He stood there, filling his eyes with her, imprinting this moment on his memory until the temptation to crawl back in there and make love to her again became almost irresistible.

Promising himself there would be time for that later, he gathered up a clean set of clothes and left the room. He took a quick shower, dressed and braided his hair, then hurried downstairs to the kitchen. Since neither of them had eaten last night, breakfast in bed seemed like as good a place as any to start convincing Maggie she couldn't live without him.

Hot coffee and orange juice, buttermilk pancakes with his mother's homemade huckleberry syrup, bacon and scrambled eggs—what more could a woman want? He tossed a dish towel over his shoulder, loaded everything onto a cookie sheet and carefully hauled it up the stairs. Maggie hadn't moved a centimeter since he'd left, nor did she when he entered the room.

Setting the tray on his dresser, he poured a mug of coffee and carried it to the bed. He held it under her nose, letting the fragrant steam act as an alarm clock. Her nose twitched. She yawned and stretched. Finally, one eye popped open, studying the cup with considerable confusion.

"Morning, gorgeous," he said. "Think you could eat some breakfast?"

Her other eye popped open, and for a second she stared at him as if she'd never laid eyes on him before. Then she shook her head, started to sit up, and made a desperate grab for the sheet when she realized she was naked. Tucking it under her arms, she frowned at him, while a rosy blush raced up her neck and into her cheeks.

He set the cup on the nightstand and sat on the bed, facing her. Bracing one hand on the far side of her hips, he raised his other hand to stroke her flushed cheek.

"There was no shame between us last night. There's no need for any now."

Her eyes opened wide, and he could actually see the memories of what they had shared return to her. The blush intensified, but her frown slowly reversed itself into a sweet, sexy smile.

"Don't look at me like that if you're hungry for food," he warned her, stealing a quick kiss from her lips.

As if on cue, her stomach rumbled. She pulled away with an embarrassed laugh. "Could I please borrow a shirt? I need to visit the bathroom, and I'm not really, um, used to morning-afters. You know?''

Yeah, he knew what she meant, and in a way, her modesty pleased him, though it also amused him. Her curvy little body held no secrets from him, but if she wasn't comfortable strutting around naked in front of him just yet, that was okay. He went to the dresser and found her a bright red T-shirt.

She accepted it with a grateful smile, tugged it on over her head and climbed out of bed. The shirt should have looked silly on her. The shoulder seams hung halfway down her arms, and the hem almost reached her knees, but it draped her curves in a way that made his mouth go dry and his hands tremble with a fierce need to scoop her up, put her back in that bed and keep her there for at least a week.

His thoughts must have shown on his face. Maggie shot him a wary smile, then turned and scurried down the hallway to the bathroom. He let out a deep, shuddering sigh and told himself to get a grip. She was bound to have a lot of things on her mind today. The last thing she needed was sexual pressure from him.

But, damn it, he'd finally found a woman who had given him a taste of heaven. Why couldn't they just fall in love, get married and live happily ever after like anyone else? It didn't seem fair that this situation had to be so blasted complicated.

"So, who ever promised you life would be fair?'' he muttered, turning away to straighten up the bed.

The sheets were still warm from her body, and the pillow she'd been sleeping on carried her unique scent. His chest tightened. His throat closed up. An icy sweat broke out on his forehead. He couldn't lose her now. He just couldn't. And he couldn't play it cool and pretend to give her time and space. Jeez, that sounded like something his ex-wife would have said. Yuppie ideas, if he'd ever heard any.

Those asinine notions had no place in an open, honest relationship, which was the only kind he wanted. Either Maggie loved him or she didn't. Either she wanted to be with him or she didn't. She wanted to live with her people or with whites.

She had to make a choice. It was as simple as that. But would she make the one he wanted? And how hard did he dare push her to make it?

Maggie breezed into the room then, her face glowing from a scrubbing. Her hair still stood up every which way, but she'd combed out the spikes. And that damn red T-shirt still made him feel randy as hell.

Clearing his throat, he fluffed up the pillows, then held the covers open in an invitation for her to climb in. She did so, with a smile that seemed both polite and nervous. Biting back an impatient snort, he grabbed the tray from the dresser, settled it on her lap, then sat down facing her again.

He stripped off the tinfoil he'd wrapped around the plates to keep the food warm. She oohed and aahed and thanked him for going to so much trouble, but her bright chatter couldn't hide the shadows in her eyes. Not from him, anyway. Just as he couldn't hide his tension from her, which had, no doubt, put those shadows in her eyes in the first place.

Damn it, this was supposed to be fun! He'd wanted to pamper her and care for her, but she looked like a kid trying to choke down liver and onions and brussels sprouts. Heedless of the pitcher of syrup or the juice glasses or the coffee cups, he dropped his fork onto his plate with a clatter, leaned across the tray and gave her a long, hard kiss.

When he pulled back, he clasped his hands on either side of her head and looked into her eyes. "Are you regretting what we did last night?"

"No," she said softly, meeting his gaze without hesitation. "I could never regret that, Jackson."

Thank God, he thought, feeling one knot of tension in the pit of his stomach relax. Lowering his hands to his lap, he mustered a half smile. "Then what's wrong? Now that you've had your way with me, don't you respect me anymore?"

She laughed, and another knot in his stomach relaxed. "Of course I do, you silly man." Then her expression grew sober. "I'm just not sure where we're supposed to go from here. I told you, I'm not used to this."

"You weren't a virgin last night," Jackson said, frowning when he realized he might not have known it if she had been. After all, he hadn't made a practice of deflowering virgins, and Nancy certainly hadn't been one when he met her. "Were you?"

"Not quite," she admitted. "There was one guy back in college, but that relationship didn't work out. To tell you the truth, I wasn't impressed enough with sex to try it again. Until last night."

"How do you feel about it now?" he asked, his voice sounding strained and hoarse to his own ears. "Were you, uh, impressed?"

Her lips slowly curved into a knowing smile, and her voice took on a husky note. "Oh, yeah. Incredibly impressed."

Though another knot relaxed in his stomach, the tension didn't dissipate this time. It simply moved lower. Straight to his groin, in fact.

"I'm glad," he said. "I was impressed, too, Maggie. In case you're wondering, I don't feel casual about it. I mean, it . . . well, it really meant something to me."

"I know, Jackson. It meant something to me, too. I'm just not sure what to do about it."

She couldn't offer him an opening like that and not expect him to take advantage of it. Still, there was an air of skittishness about her that told him it wouldn't hurt to be cautious. The trick would be to find a way to give her a gentle nudge in his direction, instead of a shove. Tipping his head to one side, he forced himself to choose his words as carefully as he would if he was defending a client charged with murder.

"Listen, Maggie, I know you have a lot to think about, in terms of your mother and your relatives and your career. And I don't want to add any pressure to what you're already feeling. But if you're ever interested in negotiating that proposal we joked about at my mother's place, all you have to do is say so."

Not bad, he told himself as he watched another smile spread over her face. You've let her know you're serious about her, without backing her into a corner. But it wasn't enough, damn it. It was just more of that stupid yuppie thinking. Had he become such an emotional coward he would settle for less than a baby step, when what he really wanted was a giant leap? Not hardly.

Picking up her hand, he turned it over and placed a kiss in the center of her palm. Then he looked into her eyes and said, "Move in with me. My intentions are absolutely honorable, and I want every spare moment you've got to show you how good we can be together."

"Isn't that a little risky? It will offend some of the more traditional people, Jackson. Like your family."

"That's their problem. I'm falling in love with you, Maggie. I want to be with you."

There. He'd said it, and it hadn't even hurt much. At least it wouldn't if she didn't reject him out of hand.

"Oh, Jackson, I don't know." Biting her lower lip, she studied him with big, sad eyes. "I'm confused about so many things right now."

"But I'm not one of them. You love me, honey. You proved it last night." He leaned closer, until their lips lightly brushed. "Want me to help you prove it again?"

A strangled sound, somewhere between a laugh and a groan, came out of her mouth. She raised her hands to his chest, but didn't push him away. "I can't think straight when you get so close."

"Good." He licked her bottom lip. "Don't think. Just feel."

"The food, Jackson—"

He shoved the tray off the bed, chuckling at the way she flinched when it crashed to the floor. "To hell with the food and the mess and what anyone else thinks." Grasping her by the shoulders, he lay back, pulling her on top of him. "You belong with me, Maggie. Let me convince you."

She rested her forehead against his, giggling when he snuck one hand under the hem of her shirt and squeezed her bottom. "Oh, you fight dirty, Mr. Hawk."

"And you love it, don't you, Ms. Schaeffer?"

"I guess that will depend."

"On what?"

"Whether or not you can convince me."

He rolled her onto her back and gazed into her laughing eyes. Then he straddled her hips and nuzzled the side of her neck while he pushed the T-shirt up to her armpits. What followed was a joyous romp that left the bedclothes hopelessly tangled and both of them weak and satiated.

Raising himself up on one elbow, he tucked a finger under her chin, coaxing her to look at him. When she did, he said, "Move in with me, Maggie."

She studied him for a long moment, then nodded gravely. "All right, Jackson. But I don't want you to hover over me, or talk about my mother, or the future. Okay?"

"No. I don't understand."

She laid a finger across his lips. "I need time to think, Jackson. I want to finish my report and present it to the tribal council. When it's all done, then we'll see where we are. That's my best offer. Take it or leave it."

He didn't like her offer much, but he could see by the stubborn set to her chin that she meant every word. He might be setting himself up for another broken heart, but it was too late to back out now.

"I'll take it."

Twelve

Maggie moved in with Jackson later that afternoon, phoned her father to tell him about Beverly, and for the next two weeks enjoyed the sort of idyllic existence most people long for, but rarely achieve. When Jackson left for the office in the morning, she settled in at the kitchen table with her notes and her laptop computer. What had started as a monumental jumble of comments, complaints and vague impressions slowly began to take on a coherent shape.

She took a break at noon every day, driving into Laughing Horse to have lunch with Jackson and Frank if she needed to clarify something for her report. Other days, she visited her grandmother and Aunt Rose to learn more about her mother and the rest of her relatives. Then she went back to work, until Jackson came home and coaxed her away from the computer with a kiss and a hug, which usually led to more passionate pursuits.

They cooked together, took long, rambling walks together, worked in his yard and planned his garden together. If occasional doubts and worries about the future crept into her mind, it was easy enough to banish them in the haven of Jackson's arms. And while she knew similar doubts assailed him at times, he kept his promise and never mentioned them.

Instead, he taught her more about her people—their history, their religious traditions and beliefs, what he remembered of their language. He opened his heart and his mind and his life to her in a way no one had ever done before. Each day and each night, she fell a little more deeply in love with him.

The words of love and commitment she knew he desperately wanted to hear trembled on the tip of her tongue every time he made love to her. But something, some invisible force, or perhaps an unrecognized fear, continually held the words back. She couldn't understand or explain it. It seemed that all she could do was wait for some kind of a mystical sign that would tell her what she must do.

And so, she loved him and worked and waited.

Finally, on the twenty-third of April, the afternoon arrived that would tell her whether or not she had accurately captured the tribe's needs and aspirations on paper. Frank Many Horses reserved the gymnasium at the Indian school for a special meeting of the tribal council. Any other interested members of the tribe were invited to attend and participate, as well.

Maggie surveyed the crowd during Frank's introduction. Realizing practically the entire population of the res had come to hear what she had written, she felt her palms grow damp. She looked at Jackson, who was sitting beside her, and found him looking back at her with such love and support in his eyes, her throat tightened with emotion.

Of course, that was the precise moment Frank chose to end his introduction. Taking a deep breath for courage, Maggie rose to her feet and approached the microphone. Her voice trembled a little at first, but gradually the rows and rows of faces became elders she had interviewed, teenagers she had tutored, friends and relatives. They listened with rapt attention, encouraging her with solemn nods and sporadic applause.

When she finished, a thoughtful hush filled the big room. When she asked for questions or suggestions for revision, fifty hands shot into the air. Jackson brought her a glass of water. Frank came to the podium to help her call on people by name.

For hours, the people debated point after point, amazing Maggie with their recall of the details in the report and their determination to be heard. She wished the members of the U.S. Congress could see this living example of participatory democracy in action. Though individual concerns were passionately expressed, the discussion remained doggedly focused on what was best for the tribe as a whole.

By the time the meeting adjourned, Maggie felt as if the people had made her report their own and accepted her into

their hearts. She walked across the street to the tribal offices with Jackson and Frank, alternating between exhaustion and exhilaration. While Frank went into his office to
check the answering machine, Jackson pulled her into his
arms and kissed her as if he were starving for the taste of
her.

Then he moved on to nibble at her earlobe, murmuring,
"You were wonderful today."

"Yes, I was," she agreed, taking giddy delight in sharing
her triumph with him. "They all seemed really excited."

Pulling back, he smiled. "Of course they were. You acknowledged their problems, and then you made them look
beyond the problems to the possibilities. You have a rare gift
for bringing people together and helping them find a con-
sensus, Maggie."

"More, more, tell me more." Chuckling, she wrinkled her
nose at him. "My ego loves it."

"I'd rather kiss you again."

"Mmm . . . That sounds nice too."

Before she could collect her kiss, however, Frank loudly
cleared his throat and came back out to the reception area.
"Sorry to interrupt, but there was a message for Maggie
from Baldwin's office in Whitehorn. The lady said it was
urgent."

Sighing with resignation, Maggie settled for a quick
smooch, then took the pink message slip from Frank and
went into his office to make the phone call. Her eyes met
Jackson's when she turned to close the door, and something in his gaze made her hesitate. It wasn't anger, exactly.
No, it was either frustration or impatience—perhaps a
combination of the two.

Whatever it was, it clearly said her time for thinking was
running out. Very soon now, he would demand an answer
to his proposal. Unfortunately, she didn't have one to give
him. Not yet, anyway.

As Jackson watched, Maggie's eyes opened wide for a
moment before she quickly closed Frank's office door. Well,
good, he thought. And he didn't feel a damn bit guilty be-

cause of that look of reproach she'd managed to squeeze in the instant before the door had shut completely.

He'd been as patient as any man could hope to be for the past two weeks. In some respects, they'd been the best two weeks of his life. Living with Maggie, making love with her, sleeping and waking up with her in his arms, had been about as close to heaven as he figured mortals were ever allowed to get.

Oh, he knew they'd been on some sort of a pseudo-honeymoon since she'd moved in with him. If they continued to live together, sooner or later they'd get on each other's nerves and have a spat now and then, like any other couple. That was reality, and he could cope with it fine.

What he *couldn't* cope with was the constant worry that if they had a spat now, she wouldn't feel committed enough to stick around and work it out. Every day he loved her more and put a bigger chunk of his heart at risk. He knew damn well she loved him, so why wouldn't she just come right out and *say* so?

He'd been miserable enough when Nancy had left him. If Maggie left him, too... God, he could hardly stand to think about it. But he couldn't *not* think about it, either. In fact, the longer she refused to discuss the future, the less he could think about anything else.

"Well, nephew, what do you think of our Little Fed now?" Frank said. "Looks to me like you two are gettin' mighty close."

"Yeah." Shoving his hands into his pockets, Jackson sat on the edge of the reception desk.

"You're in love with her."

"Yeah."

Rolling his eyes in exasperation, Frank muttered something in Cheyenne. "So? What are you gonna do about it?"

"I've done everything I *can* do about it, uncle. Maggie's the one draggin' her feet."

"You've already asked her to marry you?"

"Sort of."

"What the hell does that mean?"

Jackson briefly explained the situation, then added, "She's really tied to the white world, through Baldwin and her father. I don't know if I've got enough to offer her to convince her to stay."

Frank came over and gave Jackson's shoulder a sympathetic squeeze. "It's a big decision for her. You're wise to give her time to think it over."

"Yeah, well, it's drivin' me nuts," Jackson grumbled.

"Maybe if I offered her a job coordinating our social programs—"

"I already did that," Jackson admitted, with a sheepish grin. "I figured you'd go along with it."

"After today, there's no question the tribal council would agree," Frank said. "Be patient a little longer. I believe this will work out."

"I hope you're right. But something's eatin' at her, you know? I wish I knew what it was."

Frank nudged Jackson with his elbow and waggled his eyebrows. "You take her home and love her up good. She'll forget about it, whatever it is."

Before Jackson could reply, Frank's office door opened and Maggie hurried into the reception area.

"It's a good thing we had the meeting today," she said. "Congressman Baldwin wants the report on his desk by Tuesday morning. I'll have just enough time to revise it and get it there by express mail."

Frank reached out and grasped both of her hands. "Before you go, I want to say thank-you. We all appreciate your work very much."

"You're welcome. It's been a wonderful experience for me," Maggie said.

"We don't want you to leave, Maggie. When you're all done, you come talk to me about a job with the tribe."

Pulling her hands away, she shot Jackson an accusing look. "You promised—"

"I didn't bring it up," Jackson said. "Uncle Frank thought of it himself."

Frank nodded vigorously. "You handled yourself so well today, and the things you wrote were so helpful, I'd have to be crazy not to offer you a job. You think about it, Maggie. The offer stands, whether you marry this guy or not."

"Oh, you talked about that, too?" she asked, shooting another accusing look in Jackson's direction.

"A reservation's like any other small town," Frank said with a chuckle. "Everybody minds everybody else's business, but there's no harm intended. It's easy for those of us who know Jackson to see he's a man in love. You should put him out of his misery."

"Come on, Maggie. Let's go home," Jackson said, silently adding, *Before Mr. Big Mouth gets me in big trouble.*

But it seemed that he already had. Maggie accompanied him out to the pickup without saying another word. Jackson allowed the silence to continue for five long miles. Then he said, "I'm sorry if Uncle Frank made you feel uncomfortable, Maggie. He didn't mean to—"

"Oh, I'm sure he didn't." She scowled at him, then looked straight ahead again. "I just don't appreciate being discussed when my back is turned."

"I understand, but he's right. Now that you're living with me, it's obvious to everyone something's going on. My uncle asked how things stood between us, and I told him."

"You agreed we wouldn't discuss this until I'd finished my report."

"I agreed I wouldn't bring it up with you," he said. "I didn't promise not to talk to anyone else. Uncle Frank cares about both of us, and you're damn near done with the report, so what's the big problem?"

"Oh, never mind," she muttered, folding her arms over her midriff.

"Damn it, Maggie, don't sulk. I've really stuck my neck out here, and you've kept me danglin' for two weeks. Surely by now you've got *some* idea of what you want to do."

"Don't push me, Jackson. When I'm ready to talk about this, you'll be the first to know."

Though her words reeked of defiance, Jackson heard a hint of strain in them, too. Aw, nuts. This was hardly the way to get her to open up to him. He didn't want to fight with her or spoil what should be an occasion to celebrate. Forcing himself to take deep, calming breaths, he turned into his driveway.

"All right," he said. "I won't mention it again."

"I'm not trying to make you miserable, Jackson. Please, believe that."

"Do you love me at all, Maggie?"

"Oh, yes," she said, her voice soft and husky. "Quite a lot, actually."

Though he wanted to whoop with delight, Jackson forced himself to maintain his dignity, for fear of scaring her off completely. He reached across the seat and squeezed her hand. "Then that's all I need to know. For now."

Parking next to the house, he jumped out and ran around the front of the pickup. She had her door open by the time he reached the passenger side, making it easy to scoop her off the seat and kiss the daylights out of her. Using his foot to shut the door, he carried her into the house.

"Jackson, I should work," she said when he headed up the stairs to his bedroom.

"Later." He paused and gave her another soul-melting kiss. "I can wait to talk, but I can't wait for this."

He climbed the rest of the stairs and set her on her feet beside the bed. She looked up at him with such aching tenderness in her eyes, it was tempting to crush her against him and beg her to stay. He couldn't do that, of course, but there were ways to communicate without words.

Sliding his fingers into her hair, above her ears, he kissed her eyelids, her cheeks, the tip of her nose, her stubborn little chin. She sighed and let her head fall back, raising her lips in a silent demand for attention there. He kissed the underside of her chin instead, then followed the graceful curve of her neck until he reached the top button of her blouse.

Freeing the buttons one by one, he kissed his way down to the waistband of her skirt. Since he was already in the neighborhood, he undid that button, too, and slowly lowered the zipper while he kissed his way back up to her mouth. Her lips parted eagerly for his tongue, and while he dipped inside for a taste, he stripped away her blouse and dispensed with her bra.

Oh, this was what he loved, filling his hands with her soft, warm skin, drinking in her sweet moans with kiss after kiss, inhaling her light, floral scent until he made himself dizzy with it. She reached for the pearl snaps on his white Western shirt, but he captured her hands and pushed them down to her sides.

He wasn't gonna let her get all impatient and distract him into losing his head this time. Since she wouldn't give him a commitment, there might well come a day when memories would be all he had left of her. So this time, he was gonna store up as many memories as he could, like a squirrel getting ready for a long, cold winter.

It only took a little push to make her skirt slide over her hips, but the panty hose she wore underneath called for more aggressive tactics. Sneaking his thumbs under the elastic, he leisurely kissed his way down her neck again and across the swell of her breasts while he peeled the panty hose down her legs, managing to snag her lacy little scrap of panties along with them. He went down on one knee, lifting her left foot, then her right, leaving her as naked as *Maheo* had made her.

She was exquisite.

He sat back on his heel and let his eyes feast on her beauty. And when his eyes were finally satisfied, he raised his hands to fondle and caress and memorize the curves and indentations that so delighted him. Then his lips demanded their turn. Holding her hips, he rubbed his face over her skin, letting her gasps and moans guide him.

Her breasts were luscious, her nipples like sweet berries that begged for his tongue. Her belly was shy and ticklish, but he wouldn't allow it to shrink from his touch. No, he nuzzled it and kissed it all over, following it down and down, to the soft folds where her legs came together.

She grasped the sides of his head, holding it tightly, as if she didn't know whether to pull him to her or push him away. He warmed her with his breath. Smoothed his hands over her hips and down her thighs, stroking them, gently coaxing them to part.

As if of their own accord, her hips tilted forward to meet his eager mouth. He loved and nibbled and drank in her sweetness until her knees quivered uncontrollably and her ragged breaths and cries filled the room. Lifting her onto the bed, he kissed her mouth, letting her taste herself on his lips and tongue. When he tried to pull back, she grabbed his braids and refused to let go.

He kissed her again, slowly, hungrily. Stroked his hands over her breasts and sides. Fondled the plump, moist flesh between her thighs.

She yanked the ties off the ends of his braids and unwound them, burying her fingers in the wild mass of his hair. Ah, yes. The lady had a thing about his long hair. He found her arms with his hands and followed them to her wrists, which he anchored on either side of her head. She huffed in indignation and, he thought, frustration.

Smiling to himself, he knelt beside her and shook his hair down over the top of his head. Then he swept it back and forth, swirling it across her breasts and waist, changed direction, catching her hips and thighs with the next flick of his neck. He rolled her onto her stomach and brushed it over her back and bottom and legs.

She rolled away from him, sat up and, with a mock-ferocious glare, shook her finger at him. "Enough already. Stop it."

He flipped his hair back out of his eyes and gave her a wicked grin. "Come on, you don't really mean that."

"Well, no," she admitted, her tone tinged with exasperation. "But I'm sick and tired of being the only naked person in this room. Now, either you strip, or it's all over."

Sensing there was more behind her request than a desire for shared nudity, he sat back on his heels and studied her for a moment. "I was only trying to give you pleasure."

"You did. You're a wonderful lover."

"Then I don't understand what's wrong."

"Nothing's wrong. It's just that I like to give pleasure, as well as receive it. You've hardly let me touch you. For heaven's sake, you've still got your boots on."

"I was plannin' to take 'em off before—"

She cut him off with one word. "Now."

"But—"

"Now. I mean it. Strip, or I'm outta here."

He scrambled backward off the bed. In an attempt to lighten the atmosphere, he held his hands out at his sides and said, "What? Don't I even get any music?"

Her lips twitched, but she yanked a pillow in front of her breasts, quickly repressing the smile. "Now."

Gripping the front plackets of his shirt, he popped open the snaps with one quick yank and tossed the shirt onto the floor. Then he unbuckled his belt, unzipped his jeans, sat on the edge of the bed and yanked off his boots and socks. Standing again, he shucked off his jeans and shorts and kicked them aside.

Approaching the bed again, he said, "Okay, I'm naked. Are you happy now?"

"I would be, if you weren't glaring at me like that. This isn't like you at all, Jackson. What's going on?"

"I thought I was doing something really special for you." He sat down beside her and tugged the other pillow over his lap. "But somehow, the mood seems to have gone somewhere else."

"Jackson." She took his hand and folded her palms around it. "I'm sorry if I spoiled your fun, but what was happening didn't feel right to me. It felt like you were... I don't know, using sex as a weapon. Like you were punishing me for not wanting to talk before."

"Aw, Maggie, that's not what I was tryin' to do at all."

"Well, what *were* you trying to do?"

There was no other human being on the planet who could have dragged this admission out of him, but for Maggie, he would try to explain. "When you get your hot little hands all over me, sometimes I forget I'm supposed to hold back, and... well, hell, I just plain go nuts. So I thought if I left my clothes on, maybe I could make it last longer, and really satisfy you." He looked down at the pillow on his lap. "And... I wanted to give myself a special memory of you. In case you decide to go back to Washington."

He felt her fingers under his chin, but he didn't want to look at her if she was mad at him again. Or, worse yet, if she felt sorry for him because of what he'd admitted. Her fingers tugged harder. When he finally raised his head, she got right in his face, and her eyes were all misty, as if she might burst into tears.

"That's the sweetest thing anyone has ever said to me, Jackson. But, as for satisfying me, believe me when I tell you I have no complaints whatsoever. Haven't you noticed when you get your hot little hands on me, I just plain go nuts, too?"

"Well, yeah, but I don't ever want to disappoint you."

"Disappoint me? You crazy man! Half of my pleasure is seeing your pleasure. When you go nuts like that, I feel like the sexiest woman alive."

"You are the sexiest woman alive."

She tossed her pillow aside and looped her arms around his neck. "Is that so?"

He tossed his pillow aside and leaned forward, gently tipping her onto her back. "Damn straight it is."

Ah, God, there was that gorgeous smile of hers, the one that never failed to make his heart beat a little faster. He dipped his head and kissed her inviting lips.

She nibbled down the side of his neck, raising goose bumps with each soft nip of her teeth. "Do you think the mood might come back anytime soon?"

"I think it's back already. How 'bout you?"

She narrowed her eyes in a thoughtful pose. "I think it might be possible."

"What do you s'pose it would take to be sure, honey?"

Her eyes glinting with mischief, she spread-eagled herself on the bed. "That thing you did with your hair was quite a turn-on. Why don't you start there, and we'll see what happens?"

Jackson threw back his head and laughed. Then he swirled his hair over her again and did everything else he'd done before. But this time she was with him, matching touch for touch, kiss for kiss, stroke for stroke. It was better than ever before, and they both went totally, joyously nuts at the same moment.

Holding her in his arms when the storm had ended, he realized it wasn't the particular sexual acts or how long they lasted that made a memory special. It was this feeling of oneness, of wholeness and complete acceptance, that came afterward. He kissed her brow and caressed her back, and silently promised her they would always have this together.

If only she would stay.

But she was like a wild bird. The harder he tried to cage her, the harder she would struggle to fly away from him. Which left him with nothing to do but hope, and pray, and wait.

God, how he hated waiting.

Thirteen

On Monday morning, Maggie entered the final revisions on her laptop, copied the report onto a diskette, then drove to the Indian school and printed a copy on the laser printer her father had donated. She proofread it one last time. Confident she had caught as many typos as possible, she made another copy for her own files and one for Frank's, tossed them in the back seat of her car and headed for Whitehorn.

Traffic was light, allowing her to relax and enjoy the sunshine and Montana's big blue sky overhead. She'd been so wrapped up in her work and Jackson lately, she'd barely noticed the passage of time. But it was already the twenty-fifth of April. The calves in the pastures were much larger than when she had arrived.

Thank heaven the report was finally finished. She could have mailed it from the reservation's post office, but she needed some time alone to take stock of her feelings for Jackson. And since she hadn't left the res for several weeks, she also felt a need to reconnect with the outside world.

As Sara had pointed out, she had agreed to give up her Indian heritage without understanding the extent of the sacrifice her mother had asked her to make. She didn't intend to make that mistake a second time. For Jackson's sake, as well as her own, she had to be absolutely certain of the decision now facing her.

The usual assortment of cars and trucks lined the streets of Whitehorn's business district when Maggie arrived. She stopped at a traffic light, thinking the little town looked familiar and oddly strange at the same time, almost like alien territory. Goodness, had she been out on the res that long?

An ambulance roared by, lights flashing and siren blaring. She watched it pass, feeling a moment's sympathy for whoever needed emergency medical aid on such a beautiful day. Then she drove on to the post office and mailed her report, enjoying a deep sense of accomplishment.

If Mr. Baldwin used half of the information she had provided, and Congress enacted half of the recommendations she had drafted, life at the Laughing Horse Reservation, and perhaps on other reservations, as well, would change for the better. Her people would have better medical facilities, better educational and job-training opportunities, and a solid foot up on the ladder of economic independence. And she, little Maggie Schaeffer, would have been instrumental in laying the foundation for all of it.

The thought brought with it a heady sense of power and pride. This was legislation with implications for the entire nation, and only a job such as the one she had in Washington could put her in a position to wield the behind-the-scenes influence she now enjoyed. If she gave it all up in order to be with Jackson and work for the tribe, she would still have opportunities for achievement, but on a much smaller scale.

Would she be satisfied with that? Or would she eventually resent both Jackson and the tribe for her loss of power and prestige? Could she willingly subordinate her own, perhaps selfish, interests for the good of the tribe, as so many others had done on Saturday afternoon?

On the other hand, the power and influence her present job afforded her was secondhand at best. All she really did was provide information in a concise, coherent manner. The elected officials were the ones who actually voted on the issues, and she had virtually no control over their final decisions.

Seen in that light, the alleged glamour of her career faded abruptly. Was she willing to give up the only man she had ever loved for it? Or the dreams she had started to have of the children they would raise together? The new friends and relatives she had also come to love? Give up all of that for a job of questionable influence and a lonely apartment in a crime-ridden city?

With those questions echoing in her mind, Maggie went back to her car and slowly cruised the streets. The contrast between these smug, well-kept homes and prosperous businesses and the unrelenting poverty at the reservation offended her. Compared to Whitehorn, the res looked like a Third World country. Granted, many of her people would never choose to live as the white society did, but the differences didn't have to be so vast.

Driving past the high school, she remembered the day Wanda and Nina had told her they weren't allowed to check out library books. She passed the school district's administration building, and felt a fierce surge of satisfaction at the memory of her confrontation with Edward Reese.

She thought of the many pitiful stories she had heard of people who had surrendered to despair, but she also recalled the ones who had not—the ones who fought in the trenches for social change every single day.

Jackson and Frank, who worked side by side, up to their ears in legal documents and law books, demanding the return of the tribe's land.

Sweet old Earnest Running Bull, who had lost a wife and three children to the ravages of alcohol and drug abuse, and ran the rehab center so that others wouldn't lose their loved ones.

Sara Lewis, who was the artifacts curater at the Native American Museum in Whitehorn and then helped out at the school with the younger children and even at the clinic at the reservation.

Dr. Kane Hunter, who devoted a large share of his time and energy and passed up untold extra income he could have earned in Whitehorn, while he treated sick and hurt tribal members with modern medicine and still managed to respect his patients' traditional beliefs.

The elders, including her own grandmother, who drove over ungodly roads in rattletrap vehicles to pass on beautiful Cheyenne stories and songs to the tykes at the day-care center, maintaining an oral tradition centuries old. The ones who taught the traditional dances to the children.

These people were heroes. All of them. Without their efforts, Laughing Horse would be a miserable, hellish place, with no hope at all.

Maggie pulled into the parking lot of a fast-food restaurant, shut off the car's engine and remembered the traditional Cheyenne saying Sara had stitched in needlepoint and framed on her living room wall. It said:

A Nation is not conquered
Until the hearts of its women
Are on the ground.
Then it is done, no matter
How brave its warriors
Nor how strong its weapons.

Those few short lines had embedded themselves in her memory at first reading. Maggie had thought of them often, but they had never struck her more powerfully than they did at this moment.

Her mother had left Laughing Horse with her heart on the ground. She had run away from the hurt and shame inflicted on her because she belonged to a conquered nation. She had sacrificed everything and fought with all her determination to shield her only child from ever knowing that hurt and shame.

Maggie was grateful for the opportunities she had been given as a result of her mother's sacrifice. She admired her mother for having had such strength and courage.

But she also admired the strength and courage of the unsung heroes and heroines who had stayed on the res, struggled for justice and insisted the Northern Cheyenne could rise above their status as a conquered nation. Despite incredible odds, their hearts were not on the ground, and they never would be.

Margaret Speaks Softly Schaeffer could make a significant contribution to their struggle. These people were her people, their fight was her fight. Her background and education gave her a unique perspective and unique skills to build bridges between the res and the white world, instead of walls. She desperately wanted to do so.

The question was, could she do it without feeling she had betrayed her mother's dying request?

Maggie was ninety-nine-percent certain she'd already made her decision, but there was one person she wanted to talk to before sharing it with Jackson. Spotting a phone booth on the other side of the parking lot, she got out of her car and hurried across the pavement. Using her credit card, she placed the call, smiling when she heard her father's voice.

"Maggie, I was just thinking about you," he said.

"That's probably because I've been thinking about you," she replied. "I need some advice, Daddy."

"Uh-oh, there's that *daddy* word again. What's up?"

And there, in a grungy phone booth in the middle of a funky little Montana cow town, Maggie poured out her heart. Her father was silent for a moment after she'd finished.

Then he said, "What happened to your mother happened a long time ago, honey. Nothing you do or don't do can change it. If I were you, I think I'd try to respect the intent behind the promise Bev demanded of you, and not worry so much about the actual words."

"I'm not sure I understand what you mean," she said.

"All she ever really wanted was for you to be safe and happy. If you feel safe and happy with this Jackson Hawk fellow, well, I don't see why your mother would object. Even if she would, it's *your* life, Maggie."

"Thanks, Daddy. That's what I needed to hear."

"When do I get to meet this guy? Maybe I should fly up there tomorrow and check him out."

Maggie laughed. "Give me a little more time than that. We still have some things to work out."

"You really love him, huh?"

"Oh, yes, Daddy. Almost as much as I love you."

"Aw, you're just saying that to protect my ego."

"Nope. It's a different kind of love, that's all. I'll always be your little girl."

"Good. Now, you'd better find Jackson and start working out those things you mentioned. And don't forget to keep me informed of your progress."

Feeling as if an elephant had been lifted from her shoulders, Maggie bought a burger and a soda in the restaurant, then stopped at the congressman's office to use the WATS line to call Washington. The second she stepped through the door, Bonnie Jenkins, the executive secretary who ran the operation, heaved a melodramatic sigh of relief.

Bonnie was a heavyset woman in her mid-forties. She wore her fading red hair in a curly do that always looked a little frazzled. She had run the congressman's Whitehorn office for fifteen years. Though extremely efficient, she was a friendly soul, and Maggie had enjoyed getting acquainted with her.

"Oh, thank goodness you're here. I've been trying to reach you all morning," Bonnie said.

"Why? Is something wrong?" Maggie asked.

"Haven't you heard the news?" Bonnie rushed on before Maggie could even shake her head. "Jeremiah Kincaid died today. Mr. Baldwin can't get away from Washington for the funeral, and he wants you to act as his personal representative."

"I was planning to ask for two weeks of vacation," Maggie said, grimacing at the thought of doing funeral duty instead of being with Jackson.

"You can probably take it after the funeral," Bonnie said. "Oh, please do this, Maggie. There's a family visitation thing tomorrow at the mortuary, and you already know Mary Jo Kincaid better than I do. Mr. Baldwin asked for you specifically. You're supposed to call him right away."

"I will, but what happened to Mr. Kincaid?"

Bonnie's voice dropped to a confidential murmur, as if she feared being overheard. Maggie glanced toward the inner office the congressman used when he was in town, but didn't see anyone.

"Well, they say he fell in the shower, hit his head, and then drowned in the bathwater," Bonnie said.

"But you don't believe that?" Maggie asked.

"Oh, I suppose I do. He was getting on in years, and sometimes, he was a little absentminded. But you know, it just doesn't seem like Jeremiah to be so careless. He was always such a powerful man around these parts, it's not going to be the same without him."

"What about his son?" Maggie said. "Won't he take over?"

"Dugin?" Bonnie rolled her eyes, then let out a derisive laugh. "He's not half the man Jeremiah was. Back when we were in high school, he was nothing but a spoiled-rotten rich kid, and he hasn't improved one bit with age. Please, say you'll do it, Maggie. You don't know Dugin well enough to hate him, but I'd have to bite my tongue bloody to be nice to him for five seconds."

"I'll call Mr. Baldwin," Maggie said.

"You go right on back and use his office. I'll even bring you a fresh cup of coffee."

"Bribery, Bonnie?" Maggie asked with a grin.

Bonnie winked at her. "Whatever works, hon. Don't you know that's the first rule of politics?"

Five minutes later, Maggie found herself ensconced behind Baldwin's big desk, a steaming cup of coffee at hand and the phone's receiver clamped to her ear.

"Maggie, it's good to hear from you," her boss said, using the hearty politician's voice he usually reserved for constituents. "How are you?"

"Fine, Mr. Baldwin. I sent my report by express mail this morning. You should receive it tomorrow."

"Excellent. We'll be glad to have you back in the office. Do you mind staying on for Jeremiah Kincaid's funeral? Bonnie filled you in, didn't she?"

"Yes, sir. Actually, I was hoping to take my vacation now," Maggie said.

"I thought you'd requested time in August."

Maggie considered telling him of her intention to resign, but an odd flash of intuition made her opt for caution. "That's right, but I've gotten involved with some things at the reservation I'd like to finish before I leave."

"Couldn't you represent me at the funeral and still do those things at the reservation? You can take your vacation then, and I'll throw in an extra three days off. I really would appreciate this, Maggie."

"All right, sir," Maggie said.

"Great. Stay in touch these next few days. The new president of the Whitehorn Ranchers' Association will probably want to talk to you at the funeral."

"About the Northern Cheyennes' grazing leases?"

"What do you know about that?" Baldwin asked, his tone suddenly sharp.

Maggie raised her eyebrows at the receiver, then said, "Only that the tribe doesn't intend to renew them. Is there something else I should know, sir?"

"No, no. Nothing important." His voice was hearty again. A shade too hearty. "If anyone says anything to you, just tell them everything's under control."

"Mr. Baldwin, I hope you'll read my report before you take any action on that issue," Maggie said. "I've discussed it at length with the tribal leaders, and I think you'll see they've developed some impressive plans."

"I'll read it as soon as it hits my desk. I've got to run now. Give Jeremiah's family my condolences, and why don't you send a bouquet of flowers to the funeral home? Bonnie can take care of the bill for you."

Maggie hung up the phone and sat at the desk for another moment, feeling uneasy about the conversation with her boss, but unable to pinpoint the exact cause. Then she shook her head, told herself Jackson's paranoia had probably started to rub off on her, and went out to tell Bonnie she wouldn't have to bite her tongue bloody. Leaving the smiling secretary typing at top speed, she got into her car and headed for the res.

It was time to talk to Jackson.

Jackson paced from the kitchen into the living room, glared out the window for a moment, then paced back to the kitchen again. Damn it, where *was* she? He looked at the kitchen clock, swore under his breath and made another trip to the living room window.

He should be at the office, but Uncle Frank had thrown him out two hours ago, telling him not to come back until he stopped feeling so damn irritable and distracted. He'd come home and started pacing, and he'd been pacing ever since. He knew he was acting like an idiot. He also knew he wouldn't be able to stop until Maggie came home from Whitehorn.

Damn it, where *was* she?

And why was he so afraid she wasn't coming back? Her laptop was still on the kitchen table. Her clothes were still in his bedroom. Her makeup was still in his bathroom. She wouldn't just go off and leave all that stuff behind. Irrational though it was, however, his fear persisted.

It was all because of that damn report, of course. Knowing she'd gone to Whitehorn to mail it, that she would no longer be able to use it as an excuse to avoid discussing the future, had his gut tied in knots and a battalion of ants crawling around under his skin. She'd told him she loved him—''quite a lot, actually''—and he'd tried to content himself with those words. But he had too much lawyer in his soul to settle for anything less than a legal commitment.

Just as he reached the kitchen again, a car door slammed out front. His heart lurched, then started to race as he rushed to the window. Oh, God, she'd come back. And she was smiling. That was a good sign, wasn't it? Of course it was.

He ran to the front door, threw it open and charged down the steps. He didn't stop until he had her in his arms, whirled her around in a giddy circle and planted a kiss on her lips that stole his breath and hers. When he finally let her up for air, she looked up at him with a startled laugh.

''What was that all about?'' she asked.

''Nothin' special.'' He grabbed her hand and practically dragged her into the house. ''I'm just damn glad to see you. Maggie, we've really gotta talk.''

She turned to him with a smile that made his poor heart hammer even faster. ''I know, Jackson, it's time. But there's some news you should hear first.''

He opened his mouth to tell her he didn't give a damn about any kind of news, but she didn't give him a chance.

"Jeremiah Kincaid is dead," she said, looking at him expectantly.

"What? Are you sure?"

She nodded. "Evidently he had an accident in the shower this morning. Will this affect your case for the leases?"

Jackson thought about it, then shook his head. "Not really. The suit was filed by the Whitehorn Ranchers' Association, not Jeremiah personally. A guy named Bob Myers will probably take over. He's damn near as rotten as Jeremiah."

"Jackson, the man is dead."

"Doesn't change what he was, Maggie. I'm glad the old coot's dead. In fact, I hope he's already startin' to sizzle."

"That's a terrible thing to say." She shot him an appalled look, then walked into the kitchen and started a pot of coffee.

"It's the truth." Jackson followed her into the kitchen, put his arms around her waist from behind and pulled her back against him. "Jeremiah Kincaid doesn't matter anymore. You mailed the report, didn't you?"

"Uh-huh." She tipped her head back and grinned up at him. "It's gone."

"Good." He leaned forward and gave her an upside-down kiss that made her laugh. "So, Ms. Schaeffer, what are your plans?"

She turned to face him, laying her palms flat on his chest. "Well, I have a few things to do for Mr. Baldwin in Whitehorn for the next three days, and then I'm going to take my vacation. I know you're going to be busy in court, but I'd like to spend whatever time you can spare with you. Preferably alone."

Oh, the smile she was giving him now made him think of hot sex and rumpled sheets. "What about after your vacation?"

"What do you want me to do after that, Jackson?"

"As if you didn't know," he said reproachfully.

"Well, a woman can't be too careful these days, and you're one of those tricky lawyers." She wrinkled her nose at him. "Maybe I'd like to hear you spell it out."

He put his hands on her waist, picked her up and plunked her little tush down on the work island, which put her at eye level with him. Then he said, "I want you to stay here, Maggie. For good."

"Here, as in Laughing Horse? Or here, in your house?"

"Both. If I had my way, I'd never let you out of my bed."

"And why should I agree to this proposition, Mr. Hawk?"

"Oh, honey, it's not a proposition. It's a proposal."

"Of marriage?"

"Sure is. I'll even give your grandmother both of my horses. I love you, Maggie."

"I love you, too, Jackson."

"So, is that a yes?"

"It's a definite maybe." Looping her arms around his neck, she rested her forehead against his. "It's an awfully big step. Maybe you should carry me upstairs and show me why I should put up with you for the next forty or fifty years."

He looked deeply into her teasing eyes. So, she wanted to play, did she? No problem. Crouching down, he grasped her right wrist and gave it a good yank, pulling her over his shoulder in a fireman's carry. Then he put his left hand on her bottom to hold her steady and headed for the stairs.

Shrieking with laughter, she pounded on his back, complaining that this wasn't what she'd had in mind at all. Jackson dumped her unceremoniously in the middle of his bed, and followed her down, kissing her whole face while he stripped her of her clothes. She giggled and wiggled and attacked his clothing with equal fervor.

When the loving was done, he held her in his arms, content at last. She still hadn't given him a straight answer to his proposal, but she had given herself to him freely and completely, and he hadn't seen that worried, haunted look in her eyes even once. Sooner or later, he was confident, she would accept him. If he had anything to say about it, it would be sooner.

Fourteen

After a long, delicious night of lovemaking, Maggie groaned when the sun rose the next morning, assaulting her with bright, obnoxious rays at what had to be an ungodly hour. Raising her head, she squinted at the clock, then groaned again and yanked the covers over her head. When she went into Whitehorn today, she was going to buy blackout shades for the bedroom windows.

She heard Jackson chuckle and felt a hand give her fanny an affectionate pat through the sheet and blanket. Then the mattress dipped, she heard his big bare feet hit the floor, and a second later the mattress shifted again. Smiling to herself, she imagined his every move from the sounds he made.

Now he was at the window, no doubt stretching his magnificent body while he made a visual check on the world outside. A zipper rasped. Okay, he had his jeans on. And he was whistling. Before coffee, no less! Did she really want to marry one of those disgusting morning people?

Several silent minutes passed. Then she heard water running downstairs and the lovely grating whir of an electric coffee grinder. The nice thing about those disgusting morning people was that they sometimes got up and made coffee for nonmorning folks. Chuckling, she rolled onto her back and pulled the covers off her face.

On second look, the sunbeams were actually rather pretty. If she got up right away, they could share a shower and breakfast before Jackson had to leave for the office. She'd go into Whitehorn after that, order the flowers and, if she was lucky, finish her duty call on the Kincaids by noon. Then she could buy the shades, hit the grocery store on the way home, take a nap and still have time to cook a romantic dinner.

"Sounds like a plan," she said, forcing herself to crawl out of bed.

The first part of her plan worked well enough. Jackson was standing near the bottom of the stairs when she streaked from the bedroom to the bathroom. Never one to pass up an opportunity for fun in the shower, he was hot on her heels, and as naked as she was before she could turn the water on. The trouble didn't start until they returned to the bedroom and he saw her take one of her business suits from the closet.

His eyebrows swooped into a scowl, and he crossed the room, zipping up a fresh pair of jeans on the way. "Why so formal today?" he asked, eyeing her intended outfit with distaste.

Maggie sat on the bed and gathered up one leg of her panty hose. "I told you yesterday, Jackson. I have some things to do for Mr. Baldwin in Whitehorn, and I need to dress for the office."

"What things?"

She poked her toe into the toe of the hose, pulled the stocking to her thigh and gathered up the second leg. "He can't come out here for Mr. Kincaid's funeral. I'm going to act as his official representative."

"No."

Maggie glanced up and felt her heart sink. Jackson had folded his arms across his bare chest. His feet were spread apart in a classic fighting stance. The expression on his face could only be called implacable. She didn't like it one bit.

"I beg your pardon?" she said, pulling up the other leg of her hose.

"No. You're not gonna have anything to do with Kincaid's funeral."

She stood and pulled the waistband up where it belonged. Then she calmly walked over to the dresser, took out a bra and put it on. She reached for the pink silk blouse next.

"Did you hear what I said?" he demanded.

"Yes, I did." She whipped the blouse around her shoulders and poked her arms into the sleeves, ignoring his ominous glare as best she could while she buttoned herself up.

"I'm hoping you'll realize how absurd you sound before I have to point it out to you."

"Maggie, you can't do this."

"It's just a courtesy thing, Jackson." She took her skirt off the hanger and stepped into it. "Don't make a big deal out of it. All right?"

"No, it's not all right." He put his hands on his hips, making his chest look even broader, his frown more intimidating. "Jeremiah Kincaid was an enemy of this tribe."

"Well, he may have been, but this is part of my job." She dragged her pumps out of the closet and slid her feet into them. "I'm still on Mr. Baldwin's payroll, and I don't think this is an unreasonable request. Therefore, I'm going to do it, and you can't stop me."

Stepping around him, she opened her jewelry pouch and dug out a pair of gold earrings. Leaning toward the mirror, she inserted the posts into the holes in her earlobes.

Jackson grasped her shoulder with one hand and turned her around to face him again. "You don't understand what you're doing here. If you go to that funeral, the people on this reservation will see it as a betrayal."

"That's ridiculous."

"No, it's not," he insisted. "Sometimes you can't straddle the fence between the white world and ours. If you want to maintain your credibility, you're gonna have to choose a side, and it had damn well better be the tribe's."

"Has it ever occurred to you that if you did less choosing sides around here, you wouldn't have so many problems with the white community?"

"I'm sure there are some occasions when that's absolutely true. But, honey, trust me, this isn't one of 'em. Go call Baldwin and tell him you can't have anything to do with this."

"What about Mary Jo?" Maggie asked, putting on her watch. "She's been coming out here every day for weeks to tutor the kids. Don't you think it's appropriate for someone from the tribe to show her an act of friendship when there's been a death in her family?"

"Send her a card. Hell, send her flowers." He rolled his eyes and snorted, as if the thought of doing even that much

disgusted him. "But don't go there. Jeremiah Kincaid was
a symbol of the white oppression these people have suffered. They won't understand why you're doing this. Much
as they've come to respect you, you've got so many ties to
the white world, they're gonna think you're sleepin' with the
enemy."

Maggie stepped back, as hurt as if he'd slapped her. "I
see. If I want to be accepted, I have to turn my back on my
boss, and on a woman who has befriended this tribe because she picked the wrong father-in-law. I suppose I should
turn my back on my father, too, while I'm at it."

Jackson didn't seem to notice the sarcasm dripping from
her last remark. "Until this case with the grazing leases is
resolved, it might be a good idea not to draw any extra attention to him."

Unable to believe he could be serious, Maggie gaped at
him. "Do you honestly mean that?"

"It's just for a few weeks. Maggie, I don't think you understand how ugly this thing with the leases is liable to get.
Even if the court rules in our favor, we may have to call in
federal officers or even troops to enforce the decision."

"I don't care how ugly it gets or what anyone has to do, I
won't treat my father like some dirty little secret."

"That's not what I meant," Jackson protested.

"That's exactly what you meant. We're in a war with the
whites. They're all our enemies, even the ones who've never
done anything mean to an Indian. If they're white, they're
bad. Isn't that what you're trying to tell me?"

"You're exaggerating what I said, and you're overreacting," Jackson said. "I don't think all white people are bad,
Maggie. All I'm saying is, this is going to be a very emotional time for the tribe. When emotions run that high,
people don't always think straight, and appearances become very important. For a while, you'll have to be careful
to make it absolutely clear your loyalty rests with us."

"What if I think the tribe is wrong, Jackson? Am I supposed to just swallow it down and blindly follow along?"

"For a few weeks—"

"I can't do that." She fiercely shook her head. "This tribe
needs *more* communication with the white community, not

less. I can facilitate that. But if I stay here, the people are going to have to accept me the way I am."

"Maggie, be reasonable."

"No, *you* be reasonable. I don't turn my back on people because it happens to be convenient. If I have too many ties to the white world, that's tough. Nobody chooses who I will or will not associate with but *me.* And nobody owns me or controls me."

"I'm not trying to control you."

"Baloney!" She grabbed her jacket off its hanger, draped it over her arm and picked up her purse from the dresser. "I was planning to accept your proposal this morning, but perhaps we'd better rethink this whole relationship. When you come right down to it, I still may not be Indian enough to suit you."

"You're overreacting again."

She walked to the doorway, then looked back over her shoulder at him. "I think not. And I also think the real question isn't whether the people will trust in my loyalty as much as it is whether *you* will trust in it."

"Honey, if I didn't trust you one hell of a lot, we wouldn't be here right now."

"Try to remember that today, while I'm at work. I'll see you tonight. Unless, of course, you want me to move out."

His answer was gruff, but reassuringly automatic. "No, damn it. I just wish you'd think about what you're doing. Jeremiah Kincaid isn't worth the grief this will cause you, and neither is Baldwin."

"That's for me to decide, Jackson."

With that, she left, feeling as if her heart were hovering perilously close to the ground. This must be love, or arguing with him wouldn't hurt so darn much. She climbed into her car and looked up at the bedroom window. Jackson waved and blew her a kiss. She blew one back and, feeling a little better, drove away from the house.

To be honest, she had no real desire to attend any of the functions connected to the burial of Jeremiah Kincaid. She really hadn't liked the man the one time she met him. And, while she appreciated Mary Jo's efforts with the kids, she had to admit it was pretty difficult to warm up to the woman. Bonnie's remarks about Dugin didn't sound very encouraging, either. So why the heck was she willing to fight Jackson so hard in order to do any of this?

It was the principle of the thing.

The issue really had nothing to do with any of the Kincaids. If she let Jackson tell her what to do before they were married, he would expect to go on doing so. That wasn't the kind of marriage she intended to have. Her mother had drilled the importance of maintaining her independence so thoroughly into her head, Maggie felt uneasy enough about committing herself to a man for a lifetime.

She might have viewed the situation differently if he had asked her not to go. But he hadn't asked. He'd *ordered*, and she couldn't tolerate that. She would never be able to go through with a wedding unless he understood and accepted her need to be treated as an equal, as well as her need to live by her own set of principles.

Keeping that thought firmly in mind, Maggie drove on into Whitehorn and went about her business. After checking in with Bonnie, she ordered flowers for the funeral, drove out to the Kincaid ranch and made a brief sympathy call on Mary Jo, who appeared to be grieving, but holding up well under the circumstances. She also met Dugin Kincaid, who appeared to have every intention of staying drunk for the foreseeable future.

Needless to say, Maggie was not impressed with the man. Nor was she impressed with the gorgeous Kincaid house. It was actually a mansion, by Whitehorn standards, with expensive furnishings and meticulously landscaped grounds. But the whole place had a cold, dismal atmosphere that Maggie was more than happy to escape.

The atmosphere back at Jackson's house was better than she had expected it to be. To his credit, he'd adopted a let's-agree-to-disagree attitude, which Maggie found encouraging. She had made no effort to hide her visit to the Kincaids or her attendance at Jeremiah's wake on Tuesday. When the word got out on the res, she began to receive angry phone calls. While Jackson wasn't exactly sympathetic whenever he had to handle one, he refrained from saying, "I told you so.'' He also remained affectionate with her, which Maggie also found encouraging.

By Thursday, the day of the funeral, she was eager to be finished with the entire mess. Just one more day, and they would have weathered the worst of this particular storm. Perhaps they could even go away for a romantic weekend together.

Maggie felt painfully out of place at the funeral service. She had often been the only nonwhite person attending an event, but she'd never before experienced the subtle waves of hostility she sensed coming from some of the members of the congregation. She didn't understand it until the pallbearers wheeled the casket down the center aisle of the church and cowboy hats started blooming in every pew.

Of course, she thought, calmly returning the cold glances she received from the men who wore those hats. It only made sense that the members of the Whitehorn Ranchers' Association would be among Jeremiah's closest friends. With the grazing leases set to expire in a month, they were bound to see any Indian they encountered as ''the enemy.'' So why had Mr. Baldwin asked her to represent him?

That question plagued her during the graveside ceremony, but she couldn't come up with a satisfactory answer. When the mourners dispersed, Mary Jo approached her with an obviously inebriated Dugin in tow.

''Thank you for coming, Maggie,'' she said, daintily dabbing at her eyes with a lacy handkerchief. ''You're coming to the reception, aren't you?''

''Oh, I wouldn't want to intrude, Mary Jo,'' Maggie said.

''Nonsense, ya gotta be there,'' Dugin said, his voice loud, his words slurred. ''We're gonna have us a party to send the old man off in style. If you don' show, I'll have to call that bastard Baldwin and tell him you were a bad girl.''

Mary Jo elbowed him in the ribs, then gave Maggie a pleading look. ''Please come. Most of these people are Jeremiah's friends. I'd like to have some of my own there this afternoon.''

Unable to help feeling sorry for the poor woman, Maggie agreed. ''All right. But just for a little while.''

Dabbing at her eyes again, Mary Jo nodded and dragged Dugin off to the funeral home's limousine. Maggie returned to her rental car and drove to the Kincaid house again. A uniformed maid answered the door and directed her to the dining room, where a lavish buffet had been set out.

Maggie served herself a cup of coffee, then carried it into the adjoining living room, hoping to find an out-of-the-way place to sit. The sofa and matching love seats grouped in front of the massive stone fireplace were occupied, but she spotted an empty pair of wing chairs tucked into a corner. Carefully making her way through the clusters of chatting guests, Maggie claimed one of the chairs with a quiet sigh of relief.

Trying to be as unobtrusive as possible, she sipped her coffee and listened to the general buzz of conversation, mentally planning the romantic weekend with Jackson that she'd been considering all day. Then a tall, gray-haired man wearing a Western-cut suit broke away from a group standing near the grand piano and headed straight toward her. Half expecting a verbal assault, Maggie braced herself while she plastered on a polite smile.

Without waiting for an invitation, the man sat in the other wing chair and looked her over with an expression that was barely short of insulting. "You work for Baldwin?"

"That's right. I'm Maggie Schaeffer. And your name is?" she asked, declining to offer her hand.

"Robert Myers. I'm the new president of the Whitehorn Ranchers' Association."

Maggie studied him for a moment. Myers wasn't nearly as handsome as Jeremiah had been, but he had the same arrogant bearing she remembered. "Is there something you need from Mr. Baldwin?"

"Yeah. You tell him he's not off the hook, just because Jeremiah's dead. We still expect results, and he'd better produce 'em, if he knows what's good for him."

"Results in regard to what?" Maggie asked, struggling to maintain a neutral tone of voice.

Myers looked her over again, and this time he made no bones about being insulting. Then he leaned closer, giving her a predatory smile that chilled her blood. "I don't think I have to spell it out to you, honey. Just tell him what I said. And you can also tell him he's got one hell of a warped sense of humor to use you as his messenger."

Then Myers walked back to his companions. Her stomach knotted with fear that Jackson had been right about her boss all along, Maggie got up and left the room. She had to find Mary Jo and say goodbye as quickly as possible. And then she had to talk to Jackson.

Mary Jo Kincaid stood in the entryway, warmly greeting guests as they entered and left, silently cursing her idiot husband. Dugin should be the one listening to all this phony sympathy. But no, he was too busy celebrating the death of the old son of a bitch who'd sired him. Still, she had to admit it *was* fun to flaunt her wealth in front of all these self-righteous prigs.

Dugin was a wimp, but as Jeremiah's sole surviving heir, he was now a filthy-stinking-rich one. God, it was wonderfully ironic. Here she was, wearing designer clothes, playing lady of the manor, with the town's leading citizens sucking up to her like she'd always been one of them. Hah!

If only they could have seen her the day she was standing on a street corner with her boobs practically falling out of a tank top and a short, tight skirt barely covering her ass, trying to pick up her first trick. It seemed like it was only yesterday, but it wasn't. She was a different person now. Completely different.

"Mary Jo?"

The sound of her name startled Mary Jo out of her memories. Turning, she saw Maggie Schaeffer staring at her with concern and sympathy. Dear, sweet Maggie. If it wasn't for her, those other damn Indians wouldn't have allowed a Kincaid onto the reservation at all.

"Hello, dear." Mary Jo clasped Maggie's outstretched hand between both of hers. "I'm so glad you could come. Do you really have to leave so soon?"

"I'm afraid so," Maggie said with a smile.

"Well, then, I'll walk you out to your car. I could use a breath of fresh air."

Mary Jo brushed past the maid and opened the door herself. An old lady dressed in a ratty-looking black polyester pantsuit stood on the porch, her hand raised, as if she'd been about to ring the bell.

"I'm Winona Cobb," she said. "I've come to pay my respects to Jeremiah's kin."

Mary Jo shook Winona's hand. She'd much rather chat with Maggie, but she could hardly neglect her duties as a hostess. The old woman's eyes widened, then rolled back in their sockets. A second later, she slumped to the floor in a dead faint. Maggie dropped to her knees beside Winona.

"She's breathing, but you'd better call an ambulance, Mary Jo," she said.

"When there's three doctors in my living room?" Mary Jo ordered the maid to fetch one, then knelt down on the other side of Winona. "Winona. Yoo-hoo. Winona, can you hear me?"

The old woman frowned, but didn't open her eyes. "No need to shout," she muttered. "I'm psychic, not hard of hearing."

Mary Jo barely repressed a snort of laughter. "Are you having a vision, Winona?"

Winona opened her eyes, but only to scowl fiercely at Mary Jo. Before she could say anything, however, Dr. Wilson arrived. Mary Jo and Maggie stepped out of the way while he examined the old woman. Five minutes later, he came over to talk to them.

"I think she'll be fine, but I'd better get her over to the hospital for tests. Would you mind calling an ambulance, Mrs. Kincaid?"

"Not at all," Mary Jo said, giving him her sweetest smile.

Maggie reached over and squeezed Mary Jo's hand. "I really do need to leave now. Thanks for inviting me."

"You're welcome. I'll be back out to the reservation next week," Mary Jo said. "I'll probably see you then."

She watched Maggie walk out to the long, curved drive, and, for a moment, wished she could go with her. Even the reservation was a happier place than this big old house, with only Dugin for company. Shaking her head at her own foolishness, she went inside to call an ambulance for that weird old bat on her front porch. A psychic. Hah!

Maggie took one last glance at the Kincaid house, then heaved a sigh of relief and drove away. She ought to demand combat pay for this day's work. Thank heaven it was finally over. It would feel wonderful to get back to the res.

When she passed the city limits, she reviewed her conversation with Robert Myers. The longer she thought about it, the more worried she became. If Myers felt confident enough to pass on such a direct threat to a U.S. congressman, something was definitely going on, and it had to involve the grazing leases.

She wanted to call Mr. Baldwin and demand an explanation, but she no longer trusted him enough to do so. No matter how hard she tried to rationalize the message from Myers, it smacked of dirty political deals between Baldwin and the ranchers.

Damn it, much as she would love a romantic weekend with Jackson, her instincts said she should head back to D.C. and see what she could learn from other sources. Gripping the steering wheel more tightly, she mashed the accelerator to the floorboards. She had to talk to Jackson and Frank.

Jackson shook his head, unwilling to believe what his old friend Bennie Gonzales had just told him. "Say that again, Bennie."

"I wouldn't kid about something like this, Jackson. I know it's a disaster for your people. Do you have any idea what Schaeffer put in that report?"

"Yeah. She read it in front of the whole tribe, and spent two full days revising it. It was great."

"Did you read the final version?"

"Well, no, but—"

"It's too damn big to fax, but I'll send out a copy by express mail tonight. This thing is so damning of the tribal leadership, she must have pulled a switch on you. I'll get off the phone now, so you can start calling around for support. You're gonna need a lot of it, pal."

Feeling as if he'd been kicked in the face, Jackson hung up the phone and stared into space. God, no. Maggie wouldn't have betrayed him like that. She wouldn't have betrayed the tribe. She wouldn't—

His throat slammed shut. A burning ache pierced his chest. A bitter taste filled his mouth. He was a lawyer. He believed in facts and evidence. And the evidence in this case pointed toward Maggie.

She had never promised to marry him. She hadn't said she would accept a job with the tribe. She'd insisted on representing Baldwin at Kincaid's funeral. She hadn't shown him or Frank the final report.

Hearing a car door slam outside, he turned to the window and gripped the padded arms of his chair so hard, it was a wonder they didn't crumple. The Little Fed had arrived. Well, wasn't this just as convenient as hell? Taking deep breaths, he forced himself to release the chair arms, sat back and waited. He didn't have to wait long.

"Jackson? Frank?" she called from the reception area. "I need to talk to both of you."

"Frank's gone home for the day," Jackson answered. "Come on in my office."

She rushed into the room a second later and perched on the chair she always used, her forehead wrinkled with worry. "I had a strange conversation with Robert Myers after the funeral today, Jackson. I think I'd better go back to Washington right away, so I can find out what's going on."

Jackson shook his head in feigned admiration. "You're good, Ms. Schaeffer. Damn good. But you can save the theatrics. I already know what's going on."

"What are you talking about?" she asked, staring at him as if he'd suddenly started to speak in Chinese.

"You're not the only one with contacts in Washington. I went to law school there, and some of my old classmates work on the Hill. One of them called me a few minutes ago and spilled the beans."

"What beans?" she demanded. "Jackson, start at the beginning."

"Now, why should I do that? You probably know more about what's going on than I do. I've gotta hand it to you, Maggie. You fooled me, and everybody else on this reservation. I never dreamed you could be involved in something so vicious."

"For God's sake, what are you accusing me of?"

Damn it she really was good, he thought. In fact, she probably had Academy Award potential, if she ever took her act to Hollywood. Well, enough of this bull.

"Your beloved boss introduced some legislation today. According to Bennie, he quoted extensively from your report."

"So?" she asked. "What parts did he quote?"

"The parts where you recommended the termination of this reservation. And the parts where you recommended that all of the people here be relocated to the Northern Cheyenne reservation at Lame Deer, because our tribal leadership is too weak to adequately serve them. Besides, that way we won't clutter up so much of Montana's valuable land."

"What?" She came off the chair as if a nail had suddenly poked through the seat and into her rump. "I didn't recommend anything of the sort. There's got to be some mistake."

"Yeah, and I'm the one who made it. At the very least, the court will extend those damned leases until Baldwin's legislation is passed or defeated. It could take months to settle this mess. Maybe even years. I can't believe how easily you suckered me in."

"I didn't sucker you, or anyone else! I read that report in front of the entire tribe. The only changes I made were the ones everyone agreed to."

"Then why haven't I seen the final copy? Why hasn't Frank? We've both asked you about it."

She rolled her eyes as if she were exasperated beyond endurance. "It's in the back seat of the car, where I tossed it when I was on my way to the post office to mail Mr. Baldwin's copy. I just forgot to bring it in."

"Yeah, that's what you said before."

"Well, I'll go get it, then." She pivoted on one heel and stomped toward the doorway. Jackson called her back.

"Don't bother. It's easy to fake a document with all the computer equipment your daddy donated. How would I know if what you show me now was what you actually sent to Baldwin?"

She turned back to face him again, her shoulders rigid, her chin lifted, her eyes flashing with fury. "You could trust me."

"You don't know how much I wish I could, Maggie. But I'm afraid it's too late."

"I see. Then I'll, uh..." She paused and cleared her throat before continuing. "I'll go pack my things and get out of your house. Goodbye, Jackson."

He sat there, rigid as a chunk of petrified wood, until he heard her car door slam and the sound of the engine faded into silence. Then he rubbed his burning eyes and reached for the phone. He couldn't allow his emotions to get the better of him. He had to call Uncle Frank and tell him the bad news. Maggie wasn't the only one who'd been sleepin' with the enemy. Jackson Hawk had, too.

Fifteen

"Then is it your testimony, Ms. Schaeffer, that Congressman Baldwin has grossly misrepresented the facts cited in your report, in order to pay off illegal campaign contributions from the Whitehorn Ranchers' Association?"

"That is correct, Mr. Chairman. The proof of my charges is contained in these documents."

Sitting off to the left, where he could see the side of Maggie's face, Jackson watched her pass a thick stack of papers to a congressional page, who then delivered them to Congressman Ralph McPhearson of Minnesota, chairman of the House Subcommittee on Native American Affairs. She looked so small, sitting there by herself in this big, ornate hearing room, but she faced the fifteen members of the subcommittee with a quiet dignity that lent credence to her every word.

Three weeks had passed since he'd last seen her. Twenty-one endless days and nights to miss her and regret his hasty accusations. In those same twenty-one days, she had been fighting for the tribe with astonishing ferocity. The woman obviously had plenty of her own connections in Washington, particularly with the press corps; from the size of the stink she'd raised, Jackson figured she'd used them all.

Baldwin had pulled every trick in the book to discredit her, claiming her membership in the tribe created a conflict of interest, hinting she was only acting out of vengeance because he'd spurned her sexual advances, suggesting he'd been about to fire her for shoddy work. Too many of his fellow committee members had seen Maggie's previous work to believe that last charge, however. As a result, they hadn't believed his other charges, either.

Maggie had been interviewed on the morning news programs of all three major networks, as well as the prime-time magazine programs. In fact, the press had been having such a field day with the scandal, the Whitehorn Ranchers' Association had dropped their lawsuit over the grazing leases, and several embarrassed members had agreed to testify against Baldwin. Baldwin, who hadn't had the nerve to show up for this hearing, had already announced he would not seek reelection.

The publicity had brought about some other positive changes for the tribe. A group of Hollywood stars who owned homes in Montana had hosted a benefit for the tribe to pay the expenses of fighting the legislation and buy stock for the land that had been returned to the tribe's control.

Outraged at being portrayed as a bunch of rednecked racists, white citizens from every part of the state were contacting all of Montana's Indian tribes, opening up the kind of communication Maggie had hoped to facilitate.

They still had a long way to go, but the people of the Laughing Horse Reservation were slowly starting to find hope again. Forty percent of the tribe's high school seniors had graduated in caps and gowns. Ten new people had enrolled themselves at the alcohol and drug rehab center. Participation in all the programs at the Indian school had increased.

All because of one stubborn, feisty, compassionate little woman who wasn't afraid to stand up for her principles. A woman he had woefully misjudged. Thank God she didn't believe in "blaming a whole group of innocent people because of the actions of one rude jerk," as she had put it the first day he met her.

The committee members finished flipping through the papers the chairman had passed on to them. Congressman McPhearson gaveled the room back to order and invited the other committee members to question the witness.

Frank nudged Jackson in the ribs, then leaned over and whispered, "You watch. The Little Fed's gonna take care of everything. We won't even have to testify."

Jackson nodded in agreement. After watching Maggie's performances on television, he would be amazed if she didn't have the entire committee eating out of her dainty little hand in damn short order. Sure enough, though the members fired question after question at her, she answered them clearly and directly, without resorting to rhetoric or defensiveness.

By the time the chairman invited her to make a closing statement, Jackson felt like he'd been dragged through ten miles of brush by a runaway horse. Maggie looked as chipper as if she'd simply had a friendly chat with a group of close friends. She sipped from her water glass, set aside the stack of papers in front of her, then began to speak.

"Thank you, Mr. Chairman. I would also like to thank the other members of the committee for your time and attention this afternoon. And, lastly, I would like to thank Congressman Baldwin."

She smiled at the surprised looks she received from the committee members.

"Whatever his motives for giving me this assignment, my life has been tremendously enriched by the opportunity to become acquainted with the people of the Laughing Horse Reservation."

Maggie talked from her heart then, telling the committee, and the rest of the nation through the television cameras broadcasting the hearing live, about her background. She spoke of her feelings of alienation from her own people and the difficulties she'd encountered on the res because she was an apple. She told of her initial reactions to the poverty and despair she had witnessed. She informed them about the discrimination the high school kids had faced, and the involuntary sterilization of Indian women.

Then she really cut loose. "Ladies and gentleman, since the arrival of the Pilgrims at Plymouth Rock, our two cultures have shared this continent. Our history together has often been marred by hatred and violence. We all need to know the truth of our mutual history and understand it. However, I would submit to you, to the Northern Cheyenne, and to all the other citizens of this country, that it is time to look to the future.

"Yes, I found terrible problems at Laughing Horse. But I also found an incredible amount of untapped potential.

Instead of deploring the plight of these poor, conquered people, I suggest it's time for both sides to get to work.

"Let's stop blaming and finger-pointing and fearing each other. Native Americans have much to learn from the white society. They also have much to teach.

"Honor the treaties this government has made with them. As conquered nations, grant them as much compassion and economic development assistance as this government gave to the Germans and the Japanese after World War II. Give them a fighting chance to achieve their potential and contribute their unique talents and perspectives to this society, as the Irish, the Poles, the Italians and every other ethnic group has done.

"Passing the legislation I drafted in my original report is only the first step in this process. But, ladies and gentleman, the time to take that first step is now, and only you can take it. Please, give it your consideration and support. Thank you."

Applause thundered through the chamber. Congressman McPhearson banged his gavel again, repeatedly calling for order.

"Thank you, Ms. Schaeffer." He leaned forward, bracing one elbow on the desk in front of him. After glancing at his colleagues, he directed a charming smile at Maggie. "By the way, if you're ever interested in a position on my staff, I'd be delighted to hear from you."

Two other committee members grabbed their microphones.

"Same goes for me, Ms. Schaeffer."

"Talk to me before you make any decisions."

Maggie chuckled and shook her head. "Thank you. I'll keep that in mind."

McPhearson's gaze searched the room until he located Frank. "Mr. Many Horses, are you prepared to testify now?"

Frank stood and waited for quiet. Then he spoke in a loud voice that needed no help from a microphone. "I would be happy to do that, Congressman, but I think Maggie's already said it all, except for one thing."

"What's that, Mr. Many Horses?"

"Maggie doesn't need a job on any of your staffs. She belongs with her people, and we want her to come home very much. If you folks need help here, though, we can find you plenty of other talented Northern Cheyenne young people who do need jobs."

Maggie looked over at him with a warm smile that never reached as far as the chair Jackson occupied. He stared at her, willing her to look at him, but the effort proved futile. His heart sank. A jagged lump formed in his throat, but he told himself her refusal to acknowledge him was only what he deserved.

Frank sat down. McPhearson adjourned the hearing, and journalists swarmed around Maggie.

"Are you going back to the reservation, Maggie?"

"Is it true you've been offered a million-dollar advance to write a book about your experiences on the reservation?"

"Will you run for Baldwin's seat in the House, Ms. Schaeffer?"

Smiling, Maggie shook her head. "I haven't made any decisions about the future. Thank you all so much for the help you've given us. We really appreciate it."

Frank elbowed Jackson in the ribs again. "See? It's not hopeless. If you'll make peace with her, she'll come home."

"She hates me, Uncle Frank," Jackson replied. "And I don't blame her."

"Nonsense. She's a forgiving soul, but you must ask for that forgiveness. What have you got to lose by trying?"

What indeed? Jackson wondered. His uncle was right, of course. Without Maggie, the rest of his life stretched before him like a thousand miles of bad road.

Fear clawing at his vitals, he left the hearing room. He felt like an idiot, waiting in the hallway in the three-piece suit and wing tips he'd dug from the back of his closet for the occasion. He'd even thought about cutting his hair, but had decided the suit was enough of a gesture to gain acceptance.

Suddenly, she was there in the doorway, reporters still swarming, shouting questions at her like a pack of yapping dogs. Her eyes widened when she spotted him, and she came to an abrupt halt, forcing the journalists to crash into each other or run her down. Luckily, they chose the former option.

Jackson's voice deserted him. His muscles locked up. All it seemed he could do was stand there and gaze into her big, dark eyes—and hurt. A wary expression passed over her face, followed a second later by one that was utterly blank.

Then she turned, and would have walked off without so much as a greeting. Seeing what was probably his last chance to make amends slipping away spurred him to action.

"Maggie, wait. Please."

She froze. Looked over her shoulder at him. Raised her eyebrows at him as if to say, "What could you possibly want from me now, you slimeball?"

"I, uh, really need to talk to you, if you can spare a minute," he said, hating the desperation he could hear in his voice, but feeling helpless to erase it.

The reporters pivoted toward him as a group, their noses practically twitching with the scent of a new story. Jackson ignored them.

"Please, Maggie. It's important."

"Hey, Chief," one of the reporters called. "What's your name, and whaddaya want with Maggie?"

"No comment." Jackson shot the man a mind-your-own-damn-business glance, then returned his attention to Maggie. "You want me to beg in front of these people?"

Shaking her head, she stepped away from the crowd. When she reached Jackson's side, she turned to the journalists. "Come on, folks, I've been answering your questions for weeks. Give me a little break, okay? If there's any real news, I'll be sure to let you all know."

They grumbled a little, but gradually moved off down the hallway. She waited until the last straggler rounded the corner, then turned back to Jackson. Standing this close, he could see exhaustion in her face and feel tension quivering inside her like a guitar string pulled so tight it would snap at the slightest touch. He desperately wanted to pull her into his arms and offer her his strength and comfort. She'd probably kick him in the nuts. Just to play it safe, he shoved his hands into his trouser pockets.

"All right, Jackson," she said. "What is it?"

"You did a magnificent job for the tribe, Maggie. Thank you."

"I don't want thanks, from you or anyone else. They're my people, too."

"I know. And I'm sorry for what I said. I should have trusted you."

He saw her work down a hard swallow, and felt the lump in her throat as if it were his own.

"Yes, you should have," she said.

"Will you forgive me?"

"I did that a long time ago." She smiled at him, but it was a smile tinged with sadness and resignation. "Hating you was taking more energy than I could spare."

"God, if you only knew how much I've regretted losing my temper like that. It was a stupid, knee-jerk reaction. When Bennie used the word, *termination,* I went nuts. I knew I was wrong an hour later, but when I got to the house, you were already gone."

"It doesn't matter anymore, Jackson."

How could four little words, so quietly spoken, strike such terror into a grown man's heart? Jackson wondered, staring at her in dismay.

"Doesn't matter?" He yanked his hands out of his pockets and reached for her shoulders, ignoring the inner voice that warned him to stop and think. He was long past the ability to think rationally, anyhow. "Of course it matters."

When she tried to pull out of his grasp, he gave her a little shake. "No. I love you, Maggie. You've got to believe me."

"I believe you loved me as much as you could," she said slowly. "And I honestly don't blame you for the way you reacted."

"Then come back. If you'll give me another chance, I promise I'll never doubt you again."

She glared at him until he let go of her. "Don't make promises you can't keep."

"But I *can* keep it," he insisted. "I've learned so much in the last month . . . Hell, Maggie, you'd be amazed."

She shook her head and stepped back, holding up one hand as if she feared she would have to fend him off. "No. Jackson, I'm really sorry. I wish I could believe you, but I couldn't handle it if you ever turned on me like that again. It's too late."

Though he'd expected as much, hearing her say those words with such finality hit him like a kidney punch. He inhaled a deep, shuddering breath, let it out, then shoved his hands back into his pockets. "All right. But what about the tribe? They still need you."

"No, they don't. According to what I've heard, the prospects at Laughing Horse look much better now. You and Frank will lead the people just fine."

"You're wrong. If it's too uncomfortable for you to come back with me there, I'll leave Laughing Horse."

She gaped at him as if he'd just offered to commit suicide in front of her. "That's ridiculous, Jackson. You're their lawyer. You're a vital part of the leadership there. You can't just leave."

"The people see you as their champion, and it's been too many years since they've had one. There are other Indian lawyers around. There's only one Maggie Schaeffer."

"Well, it's out of the question, so don't even think about it."

"What are you gonna do?"

"I'll have to stay here until the legislation passes. After that, I don't know. I need some time to rest and figure it out."

"You'll let us know if there's anything we can do to help? With the legislation, I mean."

"Of course. By the way, I hope you've noticed how many white people have stepped forward to help our cause. I never would have gotten this far without them."

Jackson grinned slightly. "Yeah, I've noticed. And it's already different when we go into Whitehorn now. I figure, if some of those knotheads can change their attitudes, so can I."

"Good. Take care of yourself, Jackson."

"You too, Maggie. If you ever change your mind about trying again, you know where to find me."

A stiff nod was her only response before she turned and left. Letting her walk away was the hardest thing he'd ever had to do. Frozen in torment, he stood there long after she disappeared around the corner. He started when a big hand descended onto his shoulder.

Looking up, he found himself gazing into his uncle's sympathetic eyes. "It was a good effort, nephew," Frank said.

Jackson laughed, without much humor. "I suppose you listened to the whole thing."

Frank nodded. "I'm sorry it didn't work out. C'mon, I'm tired of this big-city stuff. Let's go home."

Grateful for his uncle's understanding, Jackson accompanied him out of the building. By the time they boarded their flight at National Airport, dusk had fallen. Jackson took the window seat, strapped himself in, then sat back and closed his eyes.

He didn't open them again until the plane took off. Hunching forward, he looked out the small window at the lights flashing on all over the city. Maggie was down there somewhere. He didn't want to believe she really intended to end their relationship for good. He couldn't approach her again himself, but he'd be damned if he'd give her up, either. Not just yet.

So what the hell was he gonna do? Wait and pray for Maggie to change her mind? Hah! Well, he wouldn't count that out entirely, but as stubborn as she was, a man could get too old to enjoy sex before she budged a centimeter. Talk about a criminal waste of resources.

Tapping his fingers on the armrest, he struggled to come up with some other options. If he could just find a way to get her back out on the res, so that she could see all the things that were happening... Yeah, that was what he needed to do, all right.

But how? She wouldn't come to see him. Hell, she probably wouldn't want to get within a hundred miles of him. But what about her grandmother? Would Annie Little Deer help him? Well, there was only one way to find out.

* * *

Four weeks later, Maggie sat at the dinette table in her apartment, flipping through the stack of job offers she had received. Though some of them were extremely interesting, she was tired of looking at them, and even more tired of being holed up in her apartment. But for the life of her, she couldn't bring herself to make a decision.

She'd managed just fine while the legislation she had proposed was working its way through Congress. Congressman McPhearson and his subcommittee had really gotten behind it. One of Montana's senators had sponsored identical bills in the Senate at the same time, and since no politician wanted to risk being labeled anti-Indian after all the recent publicity, the legislation had been enacted with record speed. The president of the United States had signed the bills last week, and had personally thanked her for her efforts at the ceremony.

The excitement had died down quickly after that. When she first returned to Washington, the danger to the tribe's survival had been too immediate for her to be able to afford the luxury of tears over Jackson's betrayal. The minute she returned from the White House, however, all the pain and rage she'd been forced to repress had hit her like the proverbial ton of bricks.

She'd wept off and on for the better part of three days. Then she'd pulled herself together and spent the next three days going through the mountain of mail she'd received from all over the country. Now it was time to get on with her life.

There would be no melodramatic depression over her failed romance with Jackson Hawk. She refused to sit around whining and feeling sorry for herself. She'd gambled and lost, and she'd acknowledged the hurt. As far as she was concerned, that should be the end of it.

The only problem was, she couldn't stop thinking about Jackson. Couldn't stop dreaming about him at night. Couldn't stop missing the wretched man, though why she would miss someone who had believed such vile things about her, she hadn't a clue. Perhaps she should see a shrink about these masochistic tendencies.

Sighing in disgust, she flipped through the job offers again, setting the most appealing ones to the right. Now wasn't that interesting? All the congressional offers had landed on the left, as had the ones from other government agencies and national Native American organizations that wanted her to become a lobbyist. It must be time to get out of Washington.

Shoving that stack to the edge of the table, she went through the remaining letters more slowly, again setting the most appealing offers to the right. Now she could count out the universities that wanted her to teach Native American studies or public administration courses. Great. She was finally making progress.

Piling the newest rejects on top of the others, she repeated the process. This time it bogged down completely. She hadn't been offered a million-dollar advance for a book about her experiences at Laughing Horse, but the offer she *had* received was certainly respectable. The idea of writing such a book intrigued her more than the money involved, anyway. Okay, so she wanted to write the book.

But what would she do after that? It wasn't as if she anticipated a long career as a writer. She could do a credible job with this one project, but she didn't have any other stories screaming to be put on paper.

The other offers were from Indian tribes all over the country. Some wanted her to coordinate social programs. Others wanted her to conduct a needs assessment similar to the one she had done at Laughing Horse. She couldn't even decide what kind of work she wanted to do, much less which tribe she wanted to work for.

The Seminoles in Florida? The Lakota in South Dakota? The Blackfeet in Montana? The Oneida in New York? The Apache in Arizona? The Choctaw in Oklahoma? Perhaps she should hire herself out as a roving consultant and travel from tribe to tribe. Did she want anything to do with Native Americans at all?

Yes. Nothing had ever given her as much personal satisfaction as helping the Northern Cheyenne had. Would she feel the same way about another tribe? Or had knowing she was working for her mother's people, her *own* people, added a special dimension?

Flipping through the stack one last time, she pulled out the letter from Frank Many Horses. Her throat constricted, and a film of tears blurred her vision. Damn it, she wanted to go home. Not to Denver, although she would love to visit her father soon. But somehow, home had come to mean Laughing Horse.

She couldn't go there, of course, because she wasn't ready, might never be ready, to see Jackson. The temptation to try again would be too strong. God, it had been so hard to walk away from him that day after the hearing. So hard not to fling herself into his arms, when he'd apologized so sincerely. Even after all this time, it hurt to remember that conversation. Had she made a mistake?

"No," she said aloud, pushing herself away from the table. "You did what any self-respecting woman would do, so don't start second-guessing yourself. You're lonely and confused, but you'll get over it."

The phone rang. Grateful for any form of distraction, Maggie lunged for it.

"*Pave-voona o!* Maggie. This is Rose."

"Good morning to you, too, Aunt Rose," Maggie said with a smile. "*Ne-toneto-mohta-he?*"

"I'm fine," Rose replied. "Your Cheyenne is improvin'."

"Thanks, but you've now heard most of my working vocabulary, so you'd probably better stick with English."

Rose chuckled. "Well, hey, you should come home and get to work on it. That's why I'm callin', Maggie."

"Oh, Aunt Rose," Maggie said, "I haven't decided what I'm going to do yet."

"I didn't mean forever. I'll nag you about that some other time. This time, I just want to make sure you're comin' to Mama's birthday party on Saturday. You got a plane reservation, don't cha?"

"Yes, but—"

"Don't give me no buts," Rose said. "She's gonna be eighty years old, and she wants to hold a giveaway in your honor. Everyone in the family has contributed. You must be there, or you will shame her.''

Maggie gulped. Holy smokes, there was no graceful way to get out of this one. According to Northern Cheyenne tradition, you simply did not shame your elders, intentionally or otherwise. Not unless you never intended to see any of your relatives again.

''Well, um,'' Maggie stammered, ''I, uh, I really don't know what to say.''

''Say yes,'' Rose demanded. She was silent for a moment, but when she spoke again, her voice was soft with sympathy. ''Maggie, we know you and Jackson broke up. He won't be at the party. You won't have to see him. Losin' Bevy hurt Mama enough. Don't you hurt her, too.''

''All right. I'll be there.''

''Good. We'll hold a sweat tomorrow night. Someone will meet you at the airport in Billings.''

''Fine, but I'd rather rent my own car, Aunt Rose.''

''Whatever you want. We'll see you soon.''

Maggie hung up the phone, then stood there and stared at it for a moment, trying to convince herself there hadn't been a sneaky undertone to her aunt's voice. Aunt Rose wouldn't lie to her, would she? No, that was silly and paranoid. If Rose said Jackson wouldn't be there, then he wouldn't.

So why did she feel so... alive, all of a sudden? Granted, she was pleased to be wanted at her grandmother's birthday party. And having a traditional giveaway ceremony, a public expression of love and respect from one's family, held in her honor was certainly a thrill.

Deep down inside, however, she knew her excitement had nothing to do with her relatives. No, it had everything to do with the possibility that while she was at Laughing Horse she would somehow manage to run into Jackson.

Cursing under her breath, Maggie whacked her forehead with the heel of her palm, as if she could knock some sense into her own head. Unfortunately, it didn't help. Not even a little.

Sixteen

Maggie was welcomed back to the res like a long-lost daughter. Tipped off by a child posted to watch for her, the aunts, uncles and cousins rushed out of Annie's house as she parked her car. Unbearably touched by all the talking, laughing and hugging, she wiped away happy tears and went inside to greet her grandmother.

Annie wept for joy at the sight of her, kissed her cheeks and demanded to hear all about meeting the president and what it was like to be on TV. When Maggie had finished, her uncle, William Little Deer, told everyone to get ready for the sweat. The experience was similar to the sweat she had shared with Jackson, with a few notable exceptions.

The lodge was large enough to accommodate fifteen people; the number of family members present required three separate ceremonies, two of which had already taken place. Uncle William conducted the ceremony Maggie attended. Her cousin, Mike Weasel Tail, served as the fire keeper, and Uncle Henry Little Deer was the drummer.

The heat and darkness didn't frighten her this time. All of the prayers were offered in Cheyenne, but the spirit of closeness and safety and belonging with these people was the same. It was as if the sacred steam had cleansed them of all harsh thoughts and feelings.

Because the night was warm and Annie's little house had only one bathroom, everyone plunged into a nearby creek to bathe when the sweat was over. Then they all trooped back to the house, changed into dry clothes and gathered in the kitchen for a feast. Listening to the affectionate teasing and bickering, Maggie told herself she owed Jackson a huge debt for helping her reconnect with this family.

Even in the midst of forty-some loving relatives, she found herself missing him. Wanting him. Loving him. And hating herself for it. For God's sake, she was twenty-seven years old, and she'd never been one of those women who desperately needed a man to make her happy. She should be getting over him by now. Why didn't the nagging ache of longing for him just go away?

She found no answers that night, or the next morning. At noon, the family piled into their vehicles and drove to the Indian school in Laughing Horse for the party. The dining hall quickly filled with people. At first, Maggie flinched inwardly every time a new group arrived. As time passed and Jackson never appeared, however, she began to relax.

Annie received a lovely assortment of gifts from her many friends and relatives. Then, with Uncle Henry announcing an embarrassingly long list of Maggie's accomplishments, Annie gave away an even larger assortment of gifts. It was a lovely ceremony, a way of expressing gratitude to the community for the love and support that had made it possible for her granddaughter to succeed.

Since Maggie and Annie were not allowed to help serve the huge meal the women in the family had prepared, they ate together, chatting and enjoying each other's company. If Maggie had seen Frank Many Horses approaching, she would have made an excuse to leave the room. She was so involved with her grandmother, however, that she didn't notice him until he was only two steps away.

To her dismay, her grandmother invited him to join them, and after a few minutes of polite conversation, Annie excused herself from the table. While Maggie smelled a rat the size of a buffalo in this whole setup, she didn't see any polite way to avoid hearing what he had to say.

"It's good to have you back here again, Maggie," Frank said, giving her a charming smile that reminded her painfully of Jackson.

"Thank you. It's nice to be back."

"Have you considered our job offer?" he asked.

She nodded. "Of course. It's tempting, Frank, but I'm afraid I can't accept it."

"You're refusing because of Jackson."

She started to shake her head, then changed her mind and nodded again. Frank had never been less than honest with her. She believed he deserved the same courtesy. "I think it would be too... uncomfortable for both of us."

"You have accepted another job, then?"

"No. I'm having a hard time deciding."

"I see." Frank clasped his hands together on the table in front of him and gazed down at them for a long moment. "My nephew is sometimes a pigheaded turnip-brain, Maggie."

"Oh, Frank..." Maggie sputtered with laughter and shook her head. "He's not that bad."

Frank smiled, but didn't look up at her. "Yes, sometimes he is. But he has a good heart. He is deeply sorry for the things he said to you, and I know he would tell you so again if you would listen to him. He loves you very much."

"Loving someone means trusting them," Maggie said. "Jackson has never really been able to trust me."

"Trust does not come easy for many of us. It takes a long time to grow, especially if a person's trust has been betrayed before, as Jackson's was. Is it possible you expected too much, too soon?"

"I suppose. I was only here for two months."

"That is not very long. Did you ever really trust him?"

"I moved in with him, Frank."

He shrugged one shoulder in a near-perfect imitation of Jackson. "So, you trusted him with your body. Did you ever trust him with your heart?"

"For a woman, one usually goes along with the other," Maggie said.

"That is not always the case for a man, Maggie. My nephew needed a solid commitment from you. Perhaps if you had given him one, it would have been easier for him to give you his trust."

Maggie thought back to the day Jackson had proposed to her. She had never agreed to marry him, not in so many words. When they argued about Jeremiah Kincaid's funeral, she had suggested rethinking their whole relationship. After the way he'd opened himself up to her, that must have hurt him. And when he'd accused her of betraying the tribe, she'd run away instead of fighting to convince him he was wrong about her.

"Maybe some of what happened was my fault, Frank. But I still have a problem with his attitude toward whites. Every time we disagreed over something, my background became an issue. He always said or implied I didn't understand because I'm just an apple. I can't live with him if he's going to continually point out I'm not Indian enough."

Chuckling, Frank finally looked up at her, his eyes glinting with deviltry. "And here I thought you were supposed to be such a smart gal."

Maggie raised an eyebrow at him. "You mean I'm not?"

"Sometimes I think you kids with your big college degrees don't know anything about livin'."

"Okay. Explain it to me, then."

"Jackson lived with divided loyalties for years, Maggie. He knows how difficult it can be to make choices when a conflict of cultures occurs. He also knows how seductive the white world can be. If he knew in his heart that your first loyalty was to *him,* I don't think he'd be so afraid that other influences would take you away from him."

"That's where all of these apple remarks come from? He's afraid I'll leave him?"

"Your guess is as good as mine," Frank said, "but if you're as smart as I think you are, you'll ask Jackson that yourself."

Maggie studied him for a moment before giving him a rueful smile. "You sly devil. You set me up like a pro."

"Yeah. But you know I'm right."

"So tell me something. How do you know so much?"

His eyes dancing with glee, he shrugged again. "Aw, it's nothing. I'm just a wise old Indian. Like in the movies."

For the first time in weeks, Maggie threw back her head and laughed, laughed until her sides ached. Frank laughed right along with her. By the time they'd both regained control, she felt as if the black cloud that had been her constant companion for weeks had finally given way to sunshine.

"Do you think my grandmother would be offended if I left for a few hours?" she asked.

"I think she'll be more offended if you don't," he answered. "She went to a lot of trouble to get you out here for this."

"I wondered about that." Maggie dug the keys to her rental car out of her purse, then stood and kissed Frank's cheek. "Where is Jackson today?"

"At his house."

"I'll go see him, but I can't make any promises, Frank."

"Just hear him out, Maggie. That's all any of us will ask of you. I'll tell Annie where you went."

Maggie slipped from the room and hurried out of the building. Her stomach suddenly felt as queasy and nervous as it had the day of the hearing, but she squared her shoulders, climbed into her car and drove toward Jackson's house. At some level, she'd known all along that any visit to Laughing Horse would eventually come to this.

She had to face Jackson one more time, and, hopefully, find a way to resolve their differences. Though she had always seen herself as an independent woman, the truth was, her life wouldn't be any fun at all without him.

Rip, plunk. Rip, rip, plunk. Rip, rip, rip, rip, plunk. Wiping his sweaty forehead with the back of his hand, Jackson glanced at the sun, figured it must be about three o'clock, and went back to pulling weeds. The June heat was bringing his garden to full production. He'd planted so much this year, it wouldn't be easy to keep up with the harvesting.

He usually enjoyed being out in the sunshine and working without a shirt. But today, despite the radio he had blaring on the patio, he couldn't find the right rhythm for pulling these damn weeds. Rip, plunk. Rip, rip, rip, plunk. *Rip.* Aw, hell.

Throwing down the bean plant he'd accidentally yanked out by the roots, he straightened up and brushed the dirt off the scars on his chest from last year's Sun Dance, sucking in deep breaths to calm himself. It didn't help, of course. Knowing Maggie was back on the res made it impossible to feel anything close to calm.

Damn it, he shouldn't have let his hopes get so high. She wasn't gonna come to see him today. By tomorrow she'd be gone again. There wasn't a blessed thing he could do about it, so he might as well get back to work. The women in charge of the canning project for the reservation's food bank would be glad to get his produce.

Rip, plunk. Rip, rip, plunk. Rip, rip, rip, rip, rip, plunk. Next year, he'd expand his garden to a half acre. It might not be as exciting a way to provide food for the tribe as it had been in the old days, when Cheyenne men hunted buffalo, deer and elk, but it worked. In fact, he was amazed at how much food a person could get out of a little plot of land.

If Maggie was here to coordinate this thing, she'd probably be running the county extension agent ragged, testing everybody's soil and giving classes on how to improve yields. And she'd be infecting everyone with enthusiasm to get involved. But Maggie wasn't here. She wasn't ever gonna be here to do things like that again. He had to find a way to accept it.

"Jackson?"

He paused for an instant, then shook his head and went back to work. Great. It wasn't bad enough he had to see visions of her everywhere? Evidently not. Now he was imagining the sound of her voice, too. Before long, he'd be having full-fledged hallucinations. Rip, rip, plunk. Rip, rip, rip—

"Jackson."

Still bent over the plants, he froze. Oh, God, it had sounded so real that time, he was afraid to look. Forcing his fingers to release the weeds, he listened to them plunk into the bushel basket at his feet. Then he slowly turned his head.

Twenty feet away, two sleek, nylon-covered legs came into view, followed by a full, bright red skirt. Lifting his gaze, he saw a narrow waist cinched by a belt of silver and turquoise conchos. The fitted bodice of a sundress covering full breasts came next. And finally, a graceful neck and Maggie's face. If this was a hallucination, it was so beautiful, he hoped it would stick around a while.

Maintaining eye contact, he straightened to his full height. "Are you real?"

"Of course I'm real." She squinted at him, then raised one hand to shade her eyes. "Jackson, are you all right?"

"If you're really here, I'm fine. If you're not, it's time to call the guys in the white coats to come and get me."

Maggie walked over to the patio and shut off the radio. Then she came back to the garden and carefully made her way between the rows of plants, stopping two feet away from him. "I'm real, and I'm here, Jackson. I need to talk to you."

Turning to face her directly, he slowly raised one hand to touch her, halting in midair when he heard her gasp.

"Good Lord, haven't you been eating anything?" she demanded. "You must have lost twenty pounds!"

Jackson shrugged. "I haven't been very hungry."

Lifting her right hand, she traced his Sun Dance scars with a butterfly-soft touch. Every nerve ending in his body jumped to full alert. God, she *was* real.

"You're not going to have your chest pierced again this year, are you?"

"Yes, I am. It's an act of gratitude and sacrifice for the tribe's continued survival."

"Wasn't it awfully painful?" she asked.

"That's what a sacrifice is all about. It's an old, old tradition for our people and the other Plains tribes. The scars are considered marks of honor."

She gulped, then raised her gaze to meet his. "The tribe means everything to you, doesn't it?"

"The tribe and my family," he agreed. "Since I killed any hope of a future with you, they're all I have left."

"Could we talk for a little while?" she asked.

He studied her, desperately wanting to believe she'd come for a reconciliation, but fearing another failure with equal desperation. "What do you want to talk about?"

Clasping her hands in front of her waist, she looked down at them. "I saw your Uncle Frank at the party. He, um, helped me to see you weren't the only one who made mistakes. I'd like to try to work things out if we can."

"Why, Maggie?"

"Because I miss you." She looked up at him again, hesitating for what seemed like an excruciatingly long time before adding, "And, because I can't seem to stop loving you."

Jackson exhaled his pent-up breath, feeling the same wonderful sense of release he'd felt at the Sun Dance, when the leather thongs, threaded under his skin by the holy man's skilled hands finally tore loose. That moment had held a promise of freedom from agony, as did this one. Please, *Maheo,* give me the right words this time, he thought. Don't let me screw up again.

He cupped the side of her face with his hand, smiled at the grubby swath his dirty thumb left on her soft cheek, then motioned for her to precede him from the garden. Her skirt swirled around her knees as she turned away from him and hurried toward the grass. His gut knotting with a combination of anxiety and hope, he followed her to a shady patch of grass under the old cottonwood tree.

She sat cross-legged, skirt spread around her, elbows propped on her thighs, fingers tangled in a nervous little ball that dangled between her knees. He sat facing her, with his legs stretched out in front of him and his hands braced on the grass behind him. He wanted to erase the worried wrinkles from her forehead, but he had no idea where to start. So he waited in silence and enjoyed the simple pleasure of looking at her.

Finally, she said, "I lied about something, Jackson."

"What was it?"

"I said I'd already forgiven you, but I really hadn't."

"I don't blame you, Maggie. The things I said were pretty unforgivable."

She nodded. "They hurt me a lot. But your uncle seems to think you might not have said them if I had agreed to marry you. That, um, maybe if I'd given you the commitment you needed, it would have been easier for you to trust me. Is that true?"

"Aw, Maggie..." Jackson sighed. "You're not responsible for my lousy temper. I am."

"I agree. But if you were always afraid I would leave, I can see how my refusal to give you a commitment might have helped confirm your worst fears about trusting me."

"Yeah, it did that, all right," he admitted. "I didn't want to believe you would betray me or the tribe, but when I got that call, I panicked. I could have handled it for myself, but the thought of all those other people paying such a high price for my bad judgment was almost more than I could take."

"I understand that now."

Leaning forward, he raised his knees and propped his elbows on them. "You know, one thing you said has haunted me. It was something about your not being Indian enough to suit me."

"I remember," she said. "It frustrated me half to death. You didn't trust me because I grew up off the reservation. Since I couldn't change that, I couldn't figure out what it would take to win your trust."

"You want to hear something funny? One of my big worries about getting involved with you was the fear that I might be *too* Indian to suit you."

She rolled her eyes in exasperation. "Oh, Jackson..."

"I'm serious. You grew up in the same society my ex-wife did. Nancy liked me just fine, as long as I was a yuppie Indian. But when she saw how my family lived and I stopped pretending I was as white as the next guy, she didn't want me anymore."

"But I'm not like that," Maggie protested. "I may not always understand your traditions and beliefs, but I respect them. Your willingness to share them with me was one of the things I loved most about you."

He smiled at that.

"Hey, intellectually, I know you're nothing like Nancy. Emotionally, it was a whole different story. When someone you love sees who you really are inside, and decides she can't love you anymore because of that..."

"It's pretty hard to trust anyone else," Maggie said. "I didn't trust you, either. And my reasons weren't any more rational than yours."

"Yeah? What were they?"

"If you think you denied you were Indian, you should have seen my mother. The only way I could win her approval was to be what you'd call an apple, but I always knew I really wasn't white. I guess, like you, I never believed the real me was very lovable. And then there was all that stuff with my biological father."

"What did that have to do with not trusting me?" Jackson asked.

She smiled. "He was a man. You're a man. My mother's attitude about men was, don't count on them, you can never trust them to be there when you need them the most."

"I thought she had a happy marriage with Cal Schaeffer."

"She did. But she always insisted I should never forget Cal was the exception to the rule. It's made it difficult for me to go beyond casual friendships with men."

"That's understandable."

"I suppose it is. Daniel Speaks Softly let her down when she was as vulnerable as any woman can get. That hurt never healed for her, and I accepted her ideas without questioning them."

"You were just a kid, Maggie. That's what kids do."

"Unfortunately, that's also how nasty things like racism and sexism get carried on from one generation to the next."

She shook her head and laughed without humor. "While I was accusing you of bigotry for lumping all white people together, I was equally guilty of lumping you with every man in the world who ever let a woman down. I'm sorry, Jackson. I should have known better, and I've hurt you because of it."

"It's not your fault."

He took one of her hands in his so that she'd stop torturing her poor fingers. They sat there, enjoying a peaceful moment of silence. She turned her hand over and clasped his, palm to palm. A deep sense of contentment bloomed in his chest. With it came a feeling of confidence that, at long last, they finally understood and accepted each other.

"Well, we've got some learning to do," he said, smiling because he simply couldn't help it. "But it sounds to me like we've been carryin' around a lot of baggage that belongs to other people, and it's been gettin' in our way. What do you think we should do with it?"

Maggie's eyes glinted with the playfulness he loved as much as he loved her tender heart. She tipped her head to one side and scrunched her face up, as if she were taking his question quite seriously. "We could bury it in the garden."

Jackson shook his head. "It'd kill off all the plants. We're dealin' with poisonous stuff here."

"Yeah, it's like toxic waste," she said. "We can't hurt Mother Earth. How the heck do we get rid of it, then?"

"It's not easy. But this wise old Indian I know told me that if you love somebody enough, just the way they are, and you keep on tryin' to work problems out, even when it's really tough, sometimes this kind of toxic waste will evaporate."

He noticed a subtle quivering around her chin, and her voice dropped to a whisper. "How much love is enough, Jackson?"

"I don't know." He squeezed her hand. "It's one of those spiritual things, you know? Where you just have to close your eyes and take what they call a leap of faith."

A fat tear rolled down her cheek, and her smile looked pretty crooked, but there was suddenly a light in her eyes he'd never seen before. She cleared her throat, as if it felt as tight and scratchy as his own did.

Then she said, "You know, I've always wanted to take one of those leaps, but I always needed a best friend to jump with me."

"I'll jump with you, Maggie. Anytime. Anyplace. You just tell me, and I'll be there."

One second she was sitting in front of him. The next she was a red blur. And, finally, she was in his arms, laughing and crying, kissing him with so much enthusiasm, she literally bowled him over. Flat on his back, he pulled her on top of him and held her sweet face between his palms.

"I love you, Maggie. Don't ever doubt that."

"I won't. Not even when you're being a pigheaded turnip-brain."

Jackson groaned, then had to laugh with her. "You and Uncle Frank must have had one hell of a talk."

She wrinkled her nose at him. "Oh, we did. I guess I'd better do what he told me to, or he'll call me something even worse."

"What did he tell you to do?"

"Give you a commitment, of course." She leaned down and kissed him. When she pulled away, the expression in her eyes was warm, but serious. "I love you, Jackson Hawk. Don't ever doubt that. Will you please marry me?"

"Anytime. Anyplace, honey."

"A week from today, at my grandmother's house. I want my father to be here."

"June 25 it is. And you won't ever have to worry about choosing your father or me. I'll get along with him if it kills me."

"You'll do much better than that," she scolded, poking his chest with her index finger. "Dad's going to love you, and you're going to love him."

"We'll see. But I guess any guy who had a hand in raising you can't be all bad."

"Thank you." She gave him a playful smooch. Then her eyes took on a dreamy, wistful expression that somehow managed to be sexy as hell. "Will you give me those pretty babies my grandmother said you would?"

"We've gotta do our part to keep the tribe alive, don't we? In fact, why don't we get started on those babies right now?"

Wrapping one arm around her waist, he rolled over, reversing their positions. She linked her hands behind his neck and pulled him down for a kiss that was hotter than the sun overhead.

Her eyes held a lusty gleam, her voice was a sultry purr, and her hips moved under his with an unmistakable promise. "You should know I'll expect you to share the child-rearing, Mr. Hawk. I'm going to be very busy with my new job."

"You're gonna work for the tribe?"

"Uh-huh. It's what I've wanted all along. Do you know, this is the first place I've ever really felt that I belonged?"

"At Laughing Horse?"

Her eyes misted over. "At Laughing Horse, and with you. I feel incredibly...safe here. As if I've finally come home."

"You have, Maggie. No matter where we go or what we do, if we're together, we'll always be home."

He kissed her. Gently. Tenderly. Reverently. And then there were no more words. Because, as a wise old Indian had once told him, there was a time for talk and a time for action. Jackson Hawk, tribal attorney, was smart enough to know the difference.

*   *   *   *   *

Montana Mavericks

continues with

THE ONCE AND FUTURE WIFE

by Laurie Paige

Available in November

Here's an exciting preview....

One

Tracy Roper parked across the street from the courthouse. She sat in the car, her hands locked on the steering wheel as she let her gaze drift along the busy avenue, past the mayor's house on the corner, past the Roxy theater where she'd gone to summer movies with friends.

A tremor ran through her as she realized where her thoughts were taking her. Once she'd lived in this town, in a house on Stoney Ridge Road...once...so long ago, it sometimes seemed like a dream.

Sighing, she admitted she was putting off the moment she would have to face Judd Hensley...the county sheriff...the man who'd been her husband...the father of her child...a long time ago.

She picked up her purse, opened the car door and climbed into the hot August sunshine. The breeze was crisp, blowing off mountains where clouds were gathering for an afternoon rain. Before she could cross the street, a couple came out of the courthouse and stood on the steps. She stopped as if struck by lightning.

Judd.

The sun sparkles glanced off his shining black hair with its smooth wave brushed back from his forehead. His skin was evenly, darkly tanned. The first time she'd seen him she'd thought he was an Indian. So long ago...that magical summer when she'd been nineteen and thought all the world was in love.

He'd been kneeling by the creek when she'd rounded the bend on the trail and spotted him. She'd stopped, surprised, alarmed and fascinated as he scooped up water and drank it from his hand. It had dribbled over his chest and belly.

He'd been buck naked.

She'd thought he was a savage or a character from an ancient fable somehow transported through aeons to this moment. She'd known in an instant that she'd never forget him.

He'd whipped his head around, sensing her presence. His eyes, as dark and alluring as forbidden knowledge, had taken in all aspects of her, including her soul, in one glance. He'd stood and turned in one smooth, sinuous movement.

His body had been fully erect, a symbol of the power and creative force contained within him.

Pagan, she'd thought, spellbound by his magic.

She'd stood very still, as if in the presence of a mythical creature, not wanting to startle him into disappearing. They'd stared into each other's eyes for an eternity.

Then he'd spoken, his voice a deep rumble of concern and assurance. "Don't be afraid," he'd murmured.

He'd said the same thing two weeks later when they'd made love for the first time . . .

Laughter broke into her memories.

Judd's teeth gleamed strong and white against his tan while he laughed at something his companion said. The woman reached up and caressed his cheek before running lightly down the steps and climbing into a truck at the curb.

Tracy watched his gaze follow the truck. He turned his head in her direction and suddenly the smile that had lingered on his mouth disappeared. A tight-lipped expression took its place.

Judd had thought he was prepared to meet Tracy again. It had been years since he'd seen her. The pain had long since subsided into the empty place inside him where nothing could hurt.

But he hadn't counted on this. The impact of seeing her was like getting hit with a slug from a buffalo gun. He tightened one hand into a fist, angered by the reaction that raged through his body. He watched as she left her car and approached the crosswalk.

Her hair was still light auburn. It gleamed like copper wire in the sun, but he knew its real texture. It was the same shade, the same downy softness, wherever he'd touched it on her body.

A harsh pang of need drove through him like a heat-tempered spear. He knew exactly what she looked like without the city clothes and the makeup that highlighted her green eyes.

The mountain wind made wanton love to her as she paused, her gaze going in one direction, then the other, as she waited for a break in the bustling Monday morning traffic. Her skirt, coaxed by the wind, pressed between her thighs, outlining the long slender grace of her legs... legs that had once wrapped sensuously around him, demanding he give himself to her completely, holding nothing back. And he had. God, he had!

She'd taken possession of his heart and soul. She'd wound herself around him until no moment was complete without her. Then she'd rejected him, scorning him as if their marriage had become an abomination, his touch so distasteful she couldn't bear it.

He'd waited, making no demands, ignoring his own pain, knowing they both needed time to heal after the death of their son, but their time had never come again. It had been the final grief.

By the time of the divorce, it had been a relief to move out. By then, he'd felt like a dry husk of a man, empty, drained, with nothing left inside to give, even if she had wanted him again.

She never had. She'd left, not returning once during the seven years since the divorce. He forced the unwanted feelings into abeyance. It was better to be empty. Life was easier.

Tracy crossed the street, her heels clicking on the pavement. She should have worn flats, but she would have felt short next to Judd's six-feet-plus frame, even though she was a bit over five-seven herself. She needed to feel in control, now more than ever.

The tribal police and the county sheriff's office were in contention over who was in charge of an unusual case—

some bones had been found on the Laughing Horse Reservation. The federal government had been called in and Tracy, a forensic anthropologist for the FBI, had been sent to Whitehorn. She would have full control of the investigation.

The courtroom steps had an iron railing running down the middle of them. She started up the right side, and Judd, on the other side, started down. They met halfway. He stepped down one more step, so that they stood eye to eye. His hand brushed hers on the railing as she paused. A flash of sensation raced across her skin, almost like pain.

"Hello, Tracy," he said, moving his hand farther up the railing. The other settled below where she had gripped the smooth iron like a lifeline. "How are you?"

"Fine," she answered. "And you?"

He shrugged. His shoulders were broad. He wore the uniform of the county sheriff well, at ease with the authority it imparted.

She looked at him, helpless, haunted by a love she hadn't asked for, hadn't known how to handle, by a passion that wouldn't leave her completely.

"I thought I'd check in with you to let you know I was in town," she said, gathering herself.

"What are your plans?"

"I want to go to the site where the bones were found as soon as possible."

"Right." He sounded crisp and official. "You have a meeting with the tribal chairman and attorney in the morning. They want to discuss the situation."

"All right." She could tell Judd didn't like the idea of consulting with the others. If a crime had been committed in the county, he wanted to jump right on the case.

He was a man who took his responsibilities seriously. When they'd suspected she was pregnant that summer many years ago, he'd insisted they marry immediately. "Growing up is hard enough in this day and age without being a bastard in the bargain," he'd said, then grinned. "I don't intend to let you go."

She knew his own youth had been unhappy. His parents, though married and wealthy, had quarreled all the time.

When he'd come out to Montana on a vacation after practicing law with his father for three years, he'd like the wind, open spaces, the peace he'd found there. That was the summer they'd met.

He'd stayed—against his parent's wishes—and started work as a rookie in the sheriff's department when they married. They'd been deliriously happy that year. At least, she had been.

"We'll go to the site after the meeting. You'll need to wear jeans and hiking shoes. It's rough country." He looked at his watch. "Have you had lunch?"

"I'd forgotten about it."

He nodded and looked away. "Yeah."

Tracy knew he was recalling the past. He used to tease her about losing herself in whatever she was doing, whether researching forensic techniques or planting a garden. He'd often arrived home to find her buried in a project, no supper on the table, the bed unmade, in spite of her good intentions. He would always chuckle at her consternation, and they would end up making love. Later, they would prepare the meal together.

Judd had been a patient, forbearing husband. Eight years her senior, he'd been indulgent toward her enthusiastic rush through life. He'd made no demands, except that she welcome his caress....

She turned her back on him and the memories he invoked, and headed for her car.

"We'll go by your...house first. Then we'll pick up something to eat and go to my office. I have the reports you requested and the topography maps," he said, easily keeping up with her, his stride long and surefooted.

She wondered at the hesitation before he mentioned her rental house. Was it because he, too, remembered the house they'd built together? It had been small, but perfect, set on its own ten acres with woods all around it, next to Route 17.

After the divorce, the house had been sold, and the profit split between them. She'd invested her share, unable to bring herself to spend it. It had felt like blood money, spoils from the death of their marriage...and the death of their son.